Daughter of Fire and Ice

MARIE-LOUISE JENSEN

OXFORD
UNIVERSITY PRESS

OXFORD
UNIVERSITY PRESS

Great Clarendon Street, Oxford OX2 6DP

Oxford University Press is a department of the University of Oxford.
It furthers the University's objective of excellence in research, scholarship,
and education by publishing worldwide in

Oxford   New York

Auckland   Cape Town   Dar es Salaam   Hong Kong   Karachi
Kuala Lumpur   Madrid   Melbourne   Mexico City   Nairobi
New Delhi   Shanghai   Taipei   Toronto

With offices in

Argentina   Austria   Brazil   Chile   Czech Republic   France   Greece
Guatemala   Hungary   Italy   Japan   Poland   Portugal   Singapore
South Korea   Switzerland   Thailand   Turkey   Ukraine   Vietnam

Oxford is a registered trade mark of Oxford University Press
in the UK and in certain other countries

British Library Cataloguing in Publication Data

Data available

ISBN: 978-0-19-272881-4

1 3 5 7 9 10 8 6 4 2

Printed in Great Britain by CPI Cox & Wyman, Reading, Berkshire

Paper used in the production of this book is a natural,
recyclable product made from wood grown in sustainable forests.
The manufacturing process conforms to the environmental
regulations of the country of origin.

For Gregory

Thank you to everyone in Iceland who helped me with my research, especially Guðrun Bjarnadottir who gave me so much advice on clothing, dyes and plants and to Jón Pàll at the Settlement Exhibition in Reykjavik, who was a mine of information about the Viking age. And thanks to my friend Þorvaldur Danielson for his support.

HISTORICAL NOTE

I've used the Norse or old Icelandic calendar in *Daughter of Fire and Ice*. This is divided into twelve months just as our Gregorian calendar is today. However, the months do not run parallel to ours. They run mid-month to mid-month. Thus, for example, Harpa month, the first month of the summer half year, runs mid-April to mid-May. Harpa month and Góa month are believed to be named after a forgotten Norse goddess and god respectively.

I have found calendars from two different sources, one of which gives alternative names for a couple of months. Thus the month I've called Ram month also appears as Mörsugur, or 'fat sucking month'. Lamb-fold time is also referred to as Skerpla month, named after another forgotten goddess.

All my characters are fictional in *Daughter of Fire and Ice*. I have taken the names from the old Icelandic sagas. Due to the extensive records that were kept in Iceland, and the strong oral tradition of reciting genealogies, the names of all the original settlers are known.

I wanted to write a new story, not rewrite any of the existing sagas, however, so I have been deliberately vague about where exactly in Iceland the story is set.

Marie-Louise Jensen

CHAPTER ONE

Midsummer

Miðsumar

A sense of menace grew on me all morning. Not a vision. No glimpse of the future disturbed me. It was more a shadow of approaching danger. That was the first warning.

The second warning was the pounding of my younger brother's bare feet on the earth outside the longhouse. I stood frozen, one hand still on the shuttle of the loom where I'd been working. The next moment he staggered through the open door.

'Thora, he's coming!' he gasped. 'Four men with him.'

Sigurd gazed at me, wide eyed with horror. I thought of running away, through the back door and out into the forest. But my parents were away. If we left the house empty, it might be burned to the ground. Just as our crops had been burned, and even our cowshed, after the animals had all been stolen.

We had an enemy. Bjorn Svanson. He was the chieftain of this district of Norway, and the bane of our lives. Ruthless and cruel. And on his way to our farm now.

'He wants father. He wants this year's tribute from him to give to the king.' My brother was pale under his summer tan. He was only ten winters old and very frightened.

1

'No.' I spoke sharply to hide my own fear. 'He knows we don't have it. He's made sure of it. He wants me.'

I was surprised how calm I was. As I put down the shuttle, I found my hands were quite steady. I could face him.

'Stay with me, please,' I said to my brother. 'I'll be safer if you're here.'

Murmuring prayers to Eir, the goddess of healing, with whom I had a special bond, I snatched a scarf up from a hook by the door and wrapped it around my hair to hide the golden shimmer. Then I stooped to the fire and scooped up some ashes from the edges where they had cooled.

'Thora, what are you doing?' asked Sigurd, surprised, as I smeared the ash across my face.

I glanced at him.

'Looking as unattractive as possible.'

'I don't understand.'

'You soon will.'

Under my breath, I added a swift prayer to Freya, the goddess of prophecy. She usually warned me of danger, but she hadn't warned me of this visit. 'Please let that mean I'm in no danger this time,' I whispered to her. 'Protect me and my brother.'

I could hear hoof beats approaching the house now. My heart started to beat more quickly as fear began to pulse through my veins. I had just time enough to fish a filthy apron up from behind the woodpile and tie it over my dress. It was stained with blueberry juice and it had been used for making cheese when we still had cows. I'd spilt whey all over it and it stank.

There was a hammering at the door; it was flung open and the chieftain strode in, flanked by two dogs. I suspected his men were standing guard outside in case anyone tried to slip out the back way.

'My lord,' I nodded to him, hiding my fear. 'It's a great honour that you call in person at our poor farm.'

'Thora, pretty maid. I bid you good morning.' Svanson's eyes gleamed maliciously.

Svanson was a relatively young man who had come to his inheritance early through his father's untimely death. His father had been respected as a brave warrior and a just overlord. No one respected his son, though many feared him. He was a glutton and a heavy drinker, and his face and figure already showed traces of it. His eyes were bloodshot and his lips thick and fleshy. He had a paunch developing and a sword hand that was no longer quite steady. He also had the ugliest aura I'd ever seen. It was distorted with greed and cruelty, all the colours muddied and spoiled. I found him repulsive.

'Your father's not here?' Svanson asked, glancing into the dark corners of the house as though father would be lurking there.

'Out hunting,' Sigurd replied before I could forestall him. It wasn't true. My father and mother had set out early that morning, and hadn't told us where they were going. It was harvest time, and they should have been cutting the barley. But our barley crop lay in ashes upon the ground.

A smile curled Svanson's lips as he realized we were alone.

'He'll be back this evening,' added Sigurd.

'Out, whelp,' ordered Svanson. 'My business is with your sister.'

He took a step closer to me. Sigurd held his ground unhappily, torn between fear of this man and loyalty to me. I wanted to reach out and take my brother's hand. I was afraid for both of us.

Svanson stopped, irritated by Sigurd's disobedience.

'Out, I said.'

'I'll stay with my sister,' replied Sigurd, his chin jutting bravely.

'You'll do as you're told by your elders and betters, sissy girl,' said Svanson roughly. He grasped Sigurd by the scruff of his neck and the seat of his leggings and threw him bodily out of the house.

I winced as I heard the thud of my brother's landing and the laughter of the men outside. I was afraid of what they might do to him out there. He was just a child. But Svanson was walking towards me now. I backed away before him, heart thudding in my chest with fear, until I was up against the rough timber of the house wall. He stopped much too close to me and carelessly twitched off my headscarf. My fair hair cascaded down over my shoulders and I cursed myself for not braiding it this morning.

'That's better,' muttered Svanson. 'I thought for a moment you were letting yourself go. But you're still as pretty as ever. You can't hide it.'

I could smell Svanson's breath in my face and turned my head away. He rubbed at the ash on my face with a thumb and I flinched away from him.

'If you wish to speak to father about the tribute, you'll

4

need to come back another time,' I told him, my voice trembling.

'Let's not pretend,' said Svanson harshly. 'Your father hasn't got any money for the king's tribute.'

'No, you made certain of that,' I retorted swiftly, glaring at him. I thought of the fires, and the missing sheep, cattle, and slaves. He had systematically destroyed our family's livelihood this past year. Our farm had once been prosperous, my father wealthy. Svanson had robbed us and destroyed our crops until we were brought to the edge of destitution. All the families around here had suffered from his greed and brutality, but none like us. He wanted me. The knowledge made me prickle all over with fear and disgust, but it wouldn't do to let him see that.

'I don't know what you're talking about, girl,' Svanson growled. 'But I know it's just as well you've lost none of your beauty. Your father has nothing else to give me in tribute. There's only you.'

'Are you thinking of giving me to the king?' I asked sarcastically.

Svanson grasped my wrist and yanked me towards him. My breath quickened with terror. I was completely at his mercy. If only my parents were here. What had they been thinking of leaving me alone today?

Svanson reached behind me, untied my filthy apron with one deft pull and threw it into the fire. I knew an impulse to tear myself away and rescue it from the flames. We had lost almost everything we had this year. But I forced myself to remain still and passive. I was terrified of angering Svanson. He was bad-tempered and unpredictable.

5

I was afraid that he would take me away today, when there was no one here to protect me. No one would ever know for sure what had become of me. He could do that. There was no longer anyone in the district who dared stand up to him. I looked at his face, and then beyond it at the colours that swirled unpleasantly around his head and shoulders. What I could see reassured me. He was playing with me, like a cat plays with a mouse. He wasn't yet ready for the kill.

Svanson put one hand none too gently on my throat and pushed up my chin.

'Tell your father,' he ordered, breathing in my face, 'he has two days to hand over money or goods. Or I collect you instead.'

So saying, he bent forwards and kissed me swiftly on the mouth. I could smell the mead on his breath and feel the cold wetness of his mouth on mine. Anger gripped me. Without stopping to think, I slapped him. Then I gasped, horrified by what I had done. At once his hand tightened on my throat, squeezing till I could hardly draw breath.

'You'll pay for that,' he snarled. 'When you're mine. And you will be mine, make no mistake.' He gave an ugly laugh and released me.

I fell back against the wall, fighting to breathe through my bruised throat. Svanson walked towards the door, and then paused and turned back.

'But it's good you've got some spirit,' he added. 'You're going to need it where we're going.'

And then he was gone.

CHAPTER TWO

It was evening when my parents returned. The summer sun was in the west, lighting up the landscape with a golden glow. They walked towards the house looking weary and anxious, and we both ran to meet them with relief.

'Mother, father! Where've you been?' cried Sigurd running to hug them. 'Svanson came!'

He'd been frightened and restless all day, terrified Svanson and his men might return before our parents did. I'd found it difficult to reassure him; I was afraid myself. My father turned to me, grasping my shoulder, panic driving the tiredness from his face.

'You're not hurt?' he demanded.

I shook my head. 'No, father,' I said. 'Please, come in and sit down. Warm yourself by the fire.'

We went into the house together and I bent over the fire, stirring the embers and adding fresh wood. My parents both looked chilled. The temperature dropped fast when the sun was no longer high in the sky.

'There's no time,' exclaimed my father, restlessly. 'We need to leave again at once.'

'Leave?' I asked, surprised. 'Why? To go where?'

'To your uncle's,' said my father. His face looked

strained and tired. He was the wreck of a once tall and powerful man, now shrunken and bent with age and trouble. In his young days he had sailed the seas, fought for kings in foreign lands and brought back slaves and wealth to our home. But a wound that had disabled his left arm had put an end to his wanderings and had also injured his spirit.

'My brother has promised us shelter and protection as long as we need it,' explained my mother. No trouble ever daunted my mother. She grew stronger with every reverse of fortune, her aura shining with determination. 'Come, Asgrim,' she chided my father. 'You have to rest at least for a short while.'

'We can speak as we walk,' my father argued, but submitted to my mother pushing him into his seat by the fire.

'Do you need food?' I asked.

My mother shook her head. 'We ate at your uncle's house,' she told me.

I was relieved. There was nothing in the house but a little borrowed skyr, the curds we made to preserve the milk, and a few blueberries.

'Why've you been to my uncle's?' asked Sigurd.

I saw my parents look at each other. It was an intimate glance, betraying the close bond between them.

'Tell me what Svanson said first,' said my father.

'He'll be back in two days,' I told him. 'He expects payment then. One way or another.'

My father nodded. We all knew what Svanson wanted. My father had chosen to refuse his demands for me last year. To my lasting shame, we'd all suffered the consequences.

'If he returns, it will be far sooner than that,' my father told me. 'We've just heard that King Harald himself is marching on him with his whole army. He's discovered that the heavy tribute Svanson collects doesn't all find its way into the royal coffers. The king believes him to be a traitor and an enemy.'

Mother nodded, eager to share telling this momentous news. 'Svanson is afraid for his life,' she said. 'He doesn't have an army that can stand against the king's and he doesn't plan to fight. Instead, he has a huge ship lying at anchor down in the fjord, a league from here. It's being loaded with wealth and provisions.' She clenched her fist suddenly. 'May Thor help us now; we are all in danger because of Svanson,' she added. 'The king's not likely to be merciful.'

'Svanson plans to flee?' I asked, scornfully. 'What a coward the man is. Only fit to bully old people, women, and children.'

'He intends to sail to the new land,' said my father.

I caught my breath. My father was talking about Iceland. I'd always been fascinated by the tales of the new country. I was given to visions, to glimpses of the future. All my life I'd seen pictures of a strange place, a country I didn't recognize. The tales I heard of Iceland matched the pictures in my mind. I was meant to go there one day. I knew it with absolute certainty. It was my destiny. Inescapable and unchangeable.

'At least that's what my brother-in-law thinks,' continued my father. 'It's where all the king's enemies are going, if they have money enough to equip a ship.'

'Fertile land, just for the taking,' sighed my mother. 'An empty country full of promise.'

'Promise of hunger, I should think,' retorted my father. 'You've heard the stories of the huge glaciers that stretch further than the eye can see. And the vast expanses of black sand and rock where nothing can grow.'

'Yes,' admitted my mother. 'I've heard that. But there are also huge green areas, where cattle can graze all summer and not go hungry.'

My father shook his head. 'Settling a new land is a great hardship.'

'And our lives are so full of ease here,' retorted my mother.

'What do we care about Iceland?' my father said abruptly. 'We have no ship and no possessions we could take. We have to prevent Svanson from taking Thora away with him. That's what's important.'

'Take me with him?' I cried, horrified. 'Surely not?'

It was true I dreamt about sailing to the new land. I longed to see it. But not in Svanson's company. Definitely not. I'd never seen so much as a glimpse of him in my visions. Instead there was a different face. A dark-haired, dark-eyed man whom I'd never met. He, I was sure, was part of my future. Not Svanson.

There was a silence as all three of them stared at me.

'He couldn't take Thora away!' exclaimed my brother.

'She'd be extremely useful to him,' my mother told him gently. She turned to me. 'You're the most skilled healer and midwife in the whole district. He won't go without a healer when there's one on his doorstep for the taking.'

'No.' I shook my head, hardly seeing them. 'Sigrun is the most skilled. I still have so much to learn from her.'

'Yes, Thora,' said my father. 'But Svanson wouldn't take an old woman of fifty winters with him when he could have a beautiful one of fifteen.'

I became aware my breathing was harsh and uneven, my fists clenched so that my nails were biting into my palms. The room was going dark around me. I wondered if it was fear, or if the sight was coming to me. A picture began to form in my mind, cloudy and elusive. Then my father spoke again and it was gone. I shook my head to clear it, frustrated at losing the glimpse.

'We won't let him take you. Don't look so frightened, Thora—or you, Sigurd. Do you really think we would condemn you to life with such a man? Have we not stood by you all winter?'

I nodded, still shaken by what I had heard and by what I had almost seen.

'Thank you, father,' I whispered. 'But how will you prevent it?'

My father glanced at my mother again. 'We're going to your uncle's now. He's promised to hide you. Until Svanson has sailed or been defeated and the army has gone. Then, if we've been spared, we'll be able to return. We must hurry.'

He struggled to his feet and we fetched cloaks and shoes for the journey. My father took down his spare sword from the wall and buckled it around his waist. His best sword, his pride and greatest treasure, had been taken by Svanson last summer.

Before I left, I unlocked my wooden chest of medicines

and packed my bag with a few essentials. My runes in their leather bag. Some herbs, pastes, and other articles of my trade. I also packed the iron knife that my father had made for me in better days. It was shiny black, completely free of rust, and I kept it as sharp as the day he had made it.

We all left the house and my father pulled the door shut behind us. I saw him looking anxiously at the building and I knew he was afraid he wouldn't see it again. The king was a fierce warrior and merciless in his quest to bring all of Norway under his control. If he had any reason to suspect we weren't loyal to him, he'd burn our house to the ground. If Svanson didn't do it first.

Together we crossed the ruined barley field behind the house and melted silently into the woods. It was slower than taking the road, but we'd be unobserved. However, as we walked, a feeling of unease began to steal over me. As though someone were watching us.

The light among the pine trees was dim. I told myself the eyes that I felt were hidden people; elves or fairies. They were unlikely to approach or harm us. And there had never been trolls in these parts. But as we walked, the certainty grew in me that we were not alone in the forest. I hurried to walk beside my father, taking his arm and warning him, with the pressure of my hand, that all was not well.

'Are we in danger?' he asked softly. I nodded, listening anxiously. But it wasn't my ears that told me of danger. It was that extra sense the others didn't have.

We walked on a little faster, staring among the trees

around us. My father loosened his sword a little in its scabbard and grasped the hilt in his good hand.

Then, out of the darkness, they came upon us with only a heartbeat of warning. With a cry, my father pushed away from me and drew his sword to defend us.

Two men on horseback loomed over us, weapons raised. They must have been lying in wait. My heart lurched sickeningly and then, an instant later, I felt fear come flooding through me.

Father managed to get between the enemy and my mother and brother.

'Run!' he shouted to my mother. 'Take Sigurd and run!' I couldn't see if they did as he said. I was trapped between my father and the two men. My father pushed me behind him roughly and stood to defend me, sword lifted. I trembled with terror, seeing him standing there, ready to die for me. He was an old man with only one good arm and they were two, mounted and with no pity in them.

'Drop your sword, old man!' said one of the men. His voice was low and menacing. Only Svanson's men would speak so disrespectfully to my father.

'You don't need to die,' said the other man. 'Just hand over the wench. But if you do fight us, don't doubt that we'll kill you.'

'Please, father,' I begged, trying to prevent my voice shaking with fear. 'Let me go.'

He was no match for them. They would defeat him and take me anyway, I was certain of it. I couldn't bear to watch him die.

Ignoring me, my father fell upon the two men with a

13

battle cry that was loud in the silent wood. He wielded his inferior sword with skill and strength, disabling one rider's sword arm with a lethal blow. The man gave a scream of pain and shock. His horse threw up its head and shied violently, unseating him. My father whipped round to face the second man, but he was an instant too slow.

This man carried no sword, but he had a huge wooden club which he was already swinging straight at my father. The force of the blow caught him in the back of the head and he crumpled and dropped without a sound.

My impulse was to rush forward. I wanted to hold him in my arms and tend him if he was still alive. But that was not why he'd fought. He'd tried to give me a chance to be free. So I turned and fled into the darkness, sobs of shock and grief crowding my chest, stealing my breath. I could hear the hoofbeats behind me before I'd gone more than a few paces. I ducked and wove among the trees, hoping the low branches would hinder the pursuit.

The horse fell behind. I was getting away. I speeded up, flying over the silent carpet of pine needles. I would catch up with my mother and brother and escape with them, and my father's sacrifice would not be in vain. But suddenly the horse bore down on me from another angle. The rider had skirted the trees I was running among, and I had no chance of avoiding him. I twisted aside desperately, trying to avoid the horse that was thundering towards me, but as I did so, I lost my balance. With a cry, I fell headlong. The last thing I saw was a rock, rushing up to meet me.

CHAPTER THREE

I came to myself again breathing in the smell of horse. I was lying over its withers, my face pressed into its neck, my hands tied behind my back. Everything spun dizzily around me. I was lurching and jolting. As reason returned to my groggy senses, I realized the horse was moving beneath me. I hurt everywhere. Ropes bit into my wrists and ankles, my head pounded from where it had struck the rock. My face and hair felt wet and sticky. I felt desperately sick and fought the urge to empty my stomach.

I had no idea where I was. And where was my father? Had he been killed back there, among the pine trees? I prayed fervently to Eir to spare his life, but I had little hope.

We were following a track I'd never seen before. Or perhaps I'd just never seen it from this angle before. The effort of trying to look made my senses swim again. Another wave of nausea swept over me. I groaned.

'Lie still and don't make a fuss,' said a rough voice somewhere above me. 'What we've done to you will be nothing compared to what you'll get at Svanson's hands.'

So it *was* on Svanson's orders I had been taken. I filled with despair. What was to become of me now? I was beyond anyone's help. The horse lurched on and on and

I sank into a stupor of pain. I wasn't roused from it until I heard my captor give a sudden shout.

'My lord! We have her! And her chest of medicines.'

I was alert in an instant, my heart pounding, the sickness worse than ever. What was that about my medicine chest? Had they been in our house?

'Show me her face!' Svanson's voice ordered. The very sound of it filled me with terror.

My captor dismounted and undid the rope tying me to the horse. I slid off, feet first, and landed unsteadily, jarring myself and biting my tongue. The man, whoever he was, caught hold of me, preventing me from falling. He grasped a handful of my hair and forced my head up so that the chieftain could see my face.

'It's her. What have you done to her? She's covered in blood.'

'She tried to run away, and fell over,' the man excused himself.

I said nothing, fighting the dizziness as I struggled to stand.

'Here,' said Svanson, and threw a length of rope. 'Bind her hands in front of her so she can run behind my horse.'

I risked opening my eyes for a brief moment and saw a dark-haired, dark-eyed man, probably a slave, judging from his clothing. He was standing quietly, eyes cast down, his chest heaving. He'd been forced to run already, tied by a length of rope to Svanson's saddle. How would I keep up, feeling so weak and sick?

My wrists were untied and the blood rushed painfully back into my stiff, numb hands. But they were bound

16

again, this time in front of me. I didn't try to escape. They were two strong men, and I could barely stand on my feet. Through all my fear and despair, I felt a sense of destiny. If this was meant to happen, there was little I could do. If it wasn't, then the gods would show me a way to escape.

Svanson slid down from his horse and checked the rope was tied tightly enough. I could smell the wine on his breath, and I knew he'd been drinking.

'You fool,' he said, grasping my hair and pulling it, so that I gasped. 'Did you really think you could hide from me?'

At his touch, something charged and vital ran through me. I knew at once it was the power of a vision. And at last the images that had been eluding me came into bright, sharp focus behind my eyes. For a moment everything disappeared.

Svanson lying on a dusty road, with anger in his eyes. His anger changes to fear. Clasped hands reach out and stab him with a small but evil-looking knife. Stab him repeatedly. I can't see who the hands belong to. But I can see the blood. So much blood. Pouring from the wounds in his chest. I hear him screaming, screaming out in pain and fear. And then blood runs from his mouth, and he lies still, eyes staring sightlessly into the distance.

I was back in the present again and I could no longer hold my nausea at bay. Heaving painfully, my stomach turned itself inside out. Svanson flung me from him and I fell to my knees. I vomited again and then coughed weakly.

'You're lying, you evil wench,' I heard Svanson hiss. I

looked up, forcing my eyes to focus on him. He looked terrified. I'd spoken my vision aloud. Svanson was gripping his hands into fists, and I wondered for a moment if he would strike me. But he didn't and I could smell his fear. He was more afraid of me, now, than I was of him.

I was taken aback at the depth of the horror I could feel flooding out of him. It is not the Viking way to fear death greatly. Our lives are predestined from the moment we are born. A man can go into battle armed only with a club, and if it's not his day to die, he won't. Or he can arm himself with plates of iron and take a sword of great name and lineage, and still fall, if the gods will it so. Death in combat is glorious. It's rewarded by a place in Valhalla, as one of Odin's chosen warriors. And yet Svanson stood here shaking with terror at the very thought that his time was near.

He was no warrior, I realized. He'd grown up spoilt and indulged, feasting and drinking in his father's hall. A life of privilege and ease. He had no acts of valour to his name that I knew of. Only bullying those less fortunate than himself. I despised him from the bottom of my heart.

I noticed that the slave was staring at me too, his dark eyes wide. I couldn't read his expression and the sun was behind him, hiding his aura from me. I met his eyes and felt sure he was trying to tell me something. But Svanson drew my attention back.

'I know what you're up to,' Svanson said angrily, his fear fading. 'You are lying, in the hope that I'll take fright at your foolish words and let you go. Well, it won't work. You're coming with me.'

I remained silent, and cast my eyes down. My head was throbbing with pain and the low sun was like a knife in my eyes. Svanson snatched up the rope that bound my wrists and made it fast to his saddle. He took care not to touch me again. He thrust his hand into his pouch, withdrew some coins and let them clink in his hand.

'I don't know whether I should thank you or curse you for bringing her to me,' he said to the man who had captured me. But he tossed the coins to him anyway.

'She had this with her,' the man said, and he held up my bag. 'It's full of seeds and suchlike. Do you want it?'

Svanson nodded. 'Yes, give that to me. But go ahead of me now and take that medicine chest to the ship. Stow it carefully in case she has poisons in there.'

The two men rode off. Svanson put my bag into his saddlebag, mounted his horse and kicked it forward. The ropes on my wrist yanked me after it. I staggered, regained my balance, and began to walk shakily. I was light-headed from the blow to my head. The slave walked beside me. He hadn't spoken. As we fell into step together behind Svanson's horse, I felt his eyes on me again. I looked up and met his gaze. There was neither fear nor servility in it. His look was open and slightly puzzled, yet oddly familiar. I looked again. Did I know him? His face was dirty and badly bruised and it was hard to see his features clearly. What I noticed most, now that it was visible to me, was the glow of the deep blue aura around his head and shoulders. It was a peaceful colour, but shot through with the dark brown of anguish. He was a peaceful man, deeply distressed, I thought.

There was no time to wonder about it. Svanson urged

his horse forwards into a trot and we were forced to run. My legs were shaking and my breath coming in painful gasps, and still the pull of the rope was relentless. Svanson dragged us on beyond endurance, beyond mercy, laughing as he kicked his horse faster and faster. I thought over and over again that I couldn't take another step. But the alternative was to fall in the stones and dirt of the road and be dragged along. So I kept finding more reserves of strength deep within me, to keep putting one foot in front of the other. Once I missed my footing and fell, the hard ground knocking the breath painfully from my body, tearing my tunic, grazing my skin. But the slave beside me managed to grasp my arm and heave me back onto my feet.

'Thank you,' I croaked, my voice hoarse. He had no breath spare to reply.

We kept moving, sometimes at a walk, more often at a run. At last I could smell the sea in the air, and I thought we must be close to our destination. The path reached a cliff top and curved to the left to follow it. Svanson paused. We bent over, gasping, dragging the air noisily down into our overworked lungs. There was a dizzying drop at our feet where the cliffs fell away to the water below. But this wasn't the open sea. There were steep cliffs across the water from us too. This was a fjord that stretched as far as the eye could see in either direction. Though there was a stiff breeze here on the cliff top, there was barely a wave on the water so far below our feet.

'I could throw you both over here and be done with it,' said Svanson. He gave a crack of laughter at the thought.

I felt the hairs rise on the nape of my neck. 'But I need you in the new land,' he continued. 'So I think I'll spare you for now. But any disobedience, any disloyalty, and that will be your fate. Do you understand?'

His voice was a cruel sneer. The slave beside me, who had been so silent and so contained throughout our long journey, suddenly fell to his knees and groaned aloud. I was surprised. From what little I'd seen of him, I hadn't thought he'd show such weakness.

'You're my new master now,' he said hoarsely. 'I beg you to cast me over the cliff if that's your will.'

I saw Svanson look down into the man's face and read the bleak despair that was written there. He smiled unpleasantly. I looked from one to the other of them, aware that there was a tension between them that went far deeper than master and slave.

'Afraid?' Svanson taunted softly. 'You should be. To your sister, I was more merciful than I will be to you. This is nothing to how hard you will be driven when we reach Iceland,' he promised. 'So you'd better accustom yourself.' He looked gloatingly at his slave, enjoying his misery, then he turned and glanced out at the fjord.

In the few seconds that his back was turned, the slave reached a hand down to his ankle and pulled his legging up a little. I wondered what he could be doing; how he had the energy to do anything other than simply breathe. He withdrew his hand, clutching something in it. I couldn't see what, but I was suddenly afraid. Svanson hadn't seen the movement.

Svanson was still smirking to himself, obviously enjoying the memory of whatever had happened earlier. I wondered that he had the leisure to sit around taunting us like this. Didn't he know he had an army marching towards him as he spoke?

Svanson quite suddenly wheeled his horse round, riding it between us, forcing the slave to the other side of his horse, nearest the cliff edge. He doubled back and rode on. Once more I had to force my stiff, weary legs to run. But at least I was on the inside. The slave was running between the horse and the cliff edge. Svanson kept laughing and pushing him right out to the edge as he rode. Any moment, I thought. Any moment now, and he will stumble and fall.

Suddenly the slave gave a cry and leapt from the very brink of the cliff onto the horse. He clung on to Svanson's leg, half on, half off the horse, and in his hand, I could see a wicked-looking iron knife. Suddenly everything became horribly clear. I knew exactly what was going to happen next.

Svanson gave a furious yell and wrestled with the slave, at the same time pushing his horse into a canter along the cliff path, moving away from the edge, trying to shake the man off. I was dragged along at great speed. The slave reached down and cut the girth beneath the saddle. Svanson kicked out at him, catching him in the mouth. The horse shied, jerking me off my feet. I fell, hitting the ground hard with one shoulder. This time, the slave was not beside me to help pull me up. The ground was tearing at me, ripping my clothing and bruising my body. I'd never felt such pain. I tried to cry out, but my voice was only a parched whisper. The grass was whipping my face and I could no longer see what was happening. Then, abruptly, the dragging stopped and I was still.

I looked up and saw that saddle, rider, and slave had all fallen to the ground. Svanson was winded, gulping ineffectually at the air like a fish on land. He had a sword hanging in a scabbard at his side, but before he could recover himself and draw it, the slave was on him. Stabbing at his chest with his knife.

I screamed. As I did so, I understood that the screams in the vision had been mine, not Svanson's. I couldn't stop myself. It was an appalling sight. Blood spurted and flowed over the slave's hands as he knelt astride the chieftain. He lifted the knife once more, and dealt him a death blow. I cried out once more, and then there was silence.

CHAPTER FOUR

Both the slave and I were panting and the sound of it was loud in the still air. Small sounds were magnified in the sudden quiet. In the distance I could hear the sea stirring against the rocks far below and the faint cry of gulls. The horse was standing a few paces away and I could hear him tearing up mouthfuls of grass, apparently undisturbed by the violence. The slave was kneeling on the grass looking at me. There on the ground between us lay Svanson's blood-soaked body.

'You murdered him,' I whispered, shocked. I pushed myself painfully into a sitting position. I was used to the sight of blood, but my business was healing not fighting and I had never seen violent death before.

'He killed my sister,' the slave croaked. His voice was as raw as mine after our forced march. 'He took us both from our master in place of tribute today. And when my sister couldn't run behind the horse, he murdered her.' He shuddered and passed a shaking hand over his face. 'In cold blood. Right in front of me. I was tied by the wrists, there was nothing I could do but watch her die.' His voice broke. 'Her and her unborn child,' he added, shakily. Tears of grief leaked from his eyes, and I looked away while he wiped them.

I sat silent, appalled. 'I'm so sorry,' I tried to say at last, my voice hoarse. 'His men killed my father too, I think. I saw him fall.'

The man gave me a sympathetic look. Then he simply knelt there on the grass staring at the body of Svanson, ghastly in death. I sat frozen, unable to move.

'This was a fair fight,' the slave said at last. 'He was on horseback and armed, and I was bound.' He was speaking more to himself than me. I sensed he was trying to come to terms with what he'd done. The colours of guilt rather than satisfaction were lighting his aura.

He shuffled towards me on his knees, the bloody knife held out in front of him. I flinched away, terrified, suddenly afraid he might attack me too.

'I swear I won't hurt you,' he said. 'I want to cut your bonds.'

My instinct was to thrust him away, but I forced myself to sit still and allowed him to cut the ropes that bound my wrists, his hands slick with Svanson's blood. The knife sawed through the rope, and my hands were free. My torn wrists throbbed painfully. They were smeared with blood, and I had no idea whether it was mine or Svanson's.

'Here,' said the dark-eyed slave, holding out the knife to me. 'Will you free me now?' he asked.

I hesitated only for a moment, then cut at his bonds until they fell away and he too was free. I heard his sharp intake of breath at the mixture of pain and relief the sudden freedom gave. The slave rose unsteadily to his feet and staggered a little. He wiped his brow on his sleeve, inadvertently smearing his face with Svanson's blood.

'I've never killed a man before,' he said. He coughed, and I wondered if he would be sick, as I had been earlier, but he seemed to recover himself. He wiped his hands on the grass and tried to clean his knife. I looked into the slave's bruised and bloody face as he knelt beside me. It still had that edge of familiarity, but the memory eluded me.

'What do we do now?' I asked. I felt quite lost in the enormity of what had happened.

'There's no "we",' he replied, getting to his feet. 'Svanson kidnapped you, but now you are free to return home. I'll have to flee. They would put me to death for far less than this.' He indicated Svanson's body with a sweep of his hand, and then paused and met my eyes again, his own wondering.

'You knew,' he said quietly. 'Didn't you? You knew that I was going to kill him. You described it before it happened.'

I swallowed painfully. My mouth and throat were parched and sore.

'I didn't know it was you,' I whispered. 'But I saw his death, yes.'

'I have heard of such things,' he said. He stood up and went to where the saddle lay upon the ground next to Svanson. He untied the saddlebag that was fastened there and rifled through it. My own bag was in there, and he put it aside for me. He found bread and cheese and a flask of some strong drink. There were also two purses full of heavy coins. He weighed them in his hand, and put one into my bag. I said nothing. I felt nothing. I was numb with exhaustion and shock. I watched him tie the other purse around his neck.

'You take the horse,' he said. 'I must go. Before I'm seen.'

'Wait!' I exclaimed. 'Don't you know that his kin will hunt you down? How will you escape them?'

I didn't want him to go. I didn't want to be left alone with Svanson's body.

'I think they are going to have their hands full with the king's army for some time to come,' replied the slave drily. 'They won't have time to trouble themselves over me.'

'You know the army are coming then?' I asked.

'I heard about it when Svanson did.' The slave hesitated a moment and then he turned back and offered me his hand to pull me to my feet. It was still stained with blood, but I took it. And it happened again. The vision was not so blindingly vivid this time. But there was no mistaking it.

The slave standing in the prow of a magnificent ship, his dark hair streaming back from his sun-weathered face. He's looking eagerly ahead at a wide, empty bay. A place unlike anywhere I've ever seen before. I'm standing beside him.

'Do you do this all the time?' I heard the man ask me. His voice sounded distant. 'It must be very disconcerting for your kin.'

Now I remember your face. I've seen it before, but only in my visions. This is the face that's bound up in my own future.

I released his hand, and reeled back from him, gasping. Sitting down in the grass, I put my head in my hands, sick and dizzy. I was shaking uncontrollably. My fate was tied up with that of a slave? It wasn't what I'd expected, but I didn't doubt it for a second.

The slave was standing watching me. I took a breath and gathered my scattered wits.

'I'm exhausted and fasting,' I told him. 'It makes the future clearer. I saw us sailing together in Svanson's ship. It's our destiny to . . . '

'I don't believe in your Viking destiny,' interrupted the man angrily. 'How can my sister have been destined to die? I was just a child when my family were captured. How can we have been destined for slavery? What would be the point of living?'

I shook my head silently, unable to answer this. 'Perhaps it's all been leading to this moment,' I said at last, my voice barely above a whisper.

'Why do you care?' the man asked, unexpectedly.

I hesitated. How could I speak to him of the many times I had seen his face before? It would be throwing aside every rule of my world. Free women didn't aid and abet slaves to escape, and they certainly didn't accompany them.

'You've spared me from a terrible fate,' I said at last. 'And I saw us. In the prow of Svanson's ship. You were wearing his clothes and sword,' I added.

There was a silence that seemed to stretch on for ever. The man broke it at last.

'You're covered in blood,' he said. 'You have a cut on your forehead and it's bled all over your face and hair.'

He picked up Svanson's flask, shook some liquid onto his hand and knelt down beside me. He rubbed a little of

28

the spirit onto my face. It stung as it reached my cut, but his touch was gentle as he wiped away the worst of the blood.

'That'll do until we find some water,' he said. He smiled at me, and I found myself smiling back. He took a deep draught of the liquor and shuddered, then passed it to me. I took a mouthful, and it burned my dry throat unpleasantly.

The sound of footsteps approaching startled us both. We jumped to our feet, fear quickening our senses. I was painfully aware of Svanson's body just a few feet away. We had lingered far too long. Now we would be caught red-handed. Literally. The slave pulled his knife out and moved in front of me, hiding me from view. It was an instinctive movement; an impulse to protect me.

But the man who ran into view, staggering, and as bruised and blood-stained as we were, was my father, and he was alone. With a cry of joy and relief, I pushed past the slave and ran to him, flinging my arms around him. There were tears pouring down my face as I hugged him, and I could hear him muttering in my ear, 'Oh thank the gods! Thora, you are safe!'

Then his eyes alighted on Svanson's dead body and he released me with a cry of shock. 'What happened?' he demanded, fear in his face.

'Svanson was trying to kill this man,' I said quickly. 'He was defending himself.'

My father was grey with pain and exhaustion and had a huge lump on the back of his head, his hair matted with blood where the club had struck him. I reached for my bag to tend him, but he waved me away.

'For Odin's sake, dispose of this body!' he exclaimed. 'We'll be sentenced to death for murder. The army are approaching; I ran from them all the way here. We're trapped on this path. It only leads down into the fjord.'

'Trapped?' echoed the slave.

'No,' I said. 'Svanson's ship is down there. We can flee by sea. Father, I've had a glimpse of the future. I've seen it.'

'Steal Svanson's ship?' uttered my father, blankly.

'The ship is the only escape.' I spoke decisively, knowing I was right.

Distantly, carried on the wind, the sound of many feet marching reached my ears. The others heard it too. My father wiped his hand down over his face. It was obvious that only his will was keeping him going.

'Thora, I've failed you once already. For Odin's sake, do as the sight told you,' my father urged. 'Your visions always lead you right.' He put his arms around me and hugged me.

'You're not coming with us?' I cried, horrified. I clung to my father's arm and looked up at him imploringly.

'No!' said my father. 'We can't ride three. You'll stand more chance without me.' He saw my distress and clasped my hands. 'Don't fret, Thora,' he begged me. 'I know how to hide in the trees. I'll be safe. Your mother and Sigurd need me.'

My father turned to the slave. 'I know you, don't I?' he asked. 'You're Hoskuld's storyteller. I've heard you speak and recite poetry more than once. Are you man enough to look after my daughter and win your freedom?' he asked him, a trace of his fierce, proud self returning to his voice. 'It's a sacred trust.'

The slave bowed slightly, acknowledging that he knew my father.

'I will protect her with my life,' he said. He turned to me. 'Though I don't even know your name,' he said, the faintest of smiles disturbing the solemnity of his manner.

'I'm Thora Asgrimsdottir,' I told him. 'And you?'

The man looked at us both in silence, and then gave a short, rueful laugh.

'It seems that I am Bjorn Svanson,' he said. 'Now, let's dispose of that dead slave.'

CHAPTER FIVE

My father and I swiftly put Svanson's body into the slave's bloodstained clothes, weighted it with a rock and threw it over the cliff, as he had threatened to do to us. The distant splash as it hit the water far below us made me feel sick.

The new Bjorn pulled fresh clothes from the saddle-bags and dragged them on. The tunic was too long, it looked like a woman's. As I picked up Svanson's sword to pass it to him, I paused, recognizing it. I withdrew it a short way from its scabbard and ran my finger along the engravings on the blade. My father saw and gasped with recognition.

'Foe Biter,' he said, reaching for it.

'That's a fine sword,' said Bjorn, suddenly interested. He leant forward to look more closely. 'That's not home-made iron. That's traded steel. It must be worth a fortune.'

My father took the sword, touched it lovingly and then pushed it back into the scabbard. 'Foe Biter was my sword,' he said. 'My most precious possession. Svanson took it from me.' He held the sword a moment longer and then held it out to Bjorn. 'Take it,' he said. 'I'm an old man and have no more use for such a weapon. I can no longer wield it with honour. Use it well, and defend my daughter. She is more precious to me than life itself.'

Bjorn took the sword almost reverently, buckling it to his waist. Then he clasped my father's hand. 'I swear to you, I will honour your trust,' he said.

We could hear the sound of marching clearly now and my father shifted uneasily.

'You must hurry, my children,' he said. 'May the blessings of Thor and Odin go with you. Thora, send me word if and when you can.'

I embraced my father, and found I couldn't let go. I was clutching at him with all my strength. My healer's training had taught me to conceal emotions, but that was all forgotten now. Tears ran unheeded from my eyes.

'I can't leave you, dear father,' I sobbed. 'Please, don't ask me to.'

'You must, Thora,' said my father sternly. 'You must survive. Go.'

When I still didn't move, he spoke to the slave.

'Take her with you now whether she will or not.'

I felt the man's hand gentle on my shoulder but shrugged him away. 'Leave me alone,' I told him, and I sensed him backing off, giving me the moment alone with my father that I so desperately wanted.

'I'll go,' I wept. 'But father! Tell mother and Sigurd that I love them. And take this purse,' I said, pressing it into his hand. 'We found it in Svanson's saddlebags. It'll help you restore the farm. And one more thing,' I lowered my voice to a shaky whisper, struggling to master my emotions. 'This man, he is the face I have seen in my visions. This is meant to be.'

My father pulled back and looked into my face. A look of relief came over him. 'Thank Thor,' he said. 'I've only ever heard good of him. And we have no choice but to trust him.'

My father led me to the new Bjorn, who'd caught the horse. He swung himself onto it, riding bareback. My father hugged me and kissed me one last time and then lifted me up behind him. Bjorn took my hands and drew my arms around his waist.

'Hold on tight, Thora,' he said, clasping my hands comfortingly with one of his.

'Go swiftly,' my father said and slapped the horse on the hindquarters. It took off along the path, leaving my father standing there alone, looking after us. I prayed he would escape the army safely. I leaned my face against Bjorn's back and wept as we rode away. I felt as though my heart was breaking.

The path wound along the top of the cliff and then descended into the fjord. The horse was swift and sure-footed, but struggled to carry both of us, puffing and blowing as he cantered down the slope. Once, we paused briefly by a stream, to drink and to help one another wash the blood properly from our hands and faces. Bjorn was gentle with me. I could sense his deep sympathy although he said very little. The sun had set now and the long hours of daylight were fading from the night sky.

When we reached the bottom of the cliff, Bjorn reined in again. The shore was narrow and barren, a jumble of huge rocks and pebbles, where rough grass and a few pine trees had a precarious hold. Bjorn looked up and down the fjord.

'This way,' he said, turning left. 'There's a track along the shore, with animal droppings and hoof prints.'

I nodded, and shifted my position on the horse a little. I hurt everywhere and I was exhausted. It had been the hardest day of my life and I knew it wasn't over yet. Around the next corner, we stopped abruptly.

'Voices,' I whispered. 'And the bleating of lambs. They sound close.' Our plan felt real now, and fear came flooding back.

I slid painfully off the horse and crept forward softly. There were two huge ships at anchor in the fjord before us. They were an awe-inspiring sight in the dim light. I'd heard tales of ships, but had never seen one before. They lay low and graceful in the calm, black water, the elegant sweep of their sides rearing into a fearsome figurehead at the prow. They looked like sea monsters. There were animals and people on board, and it was their voices we'd heard.

'One cargo ship, one raiding boat,' Bjorn murmured. 'We'd have to steal both. If we left one, they could use it to pursue us.'

I looked at him, dismayed. 'Steal two?' I whispered. 'But how will we manage that?'

'I hoped you could tell me that,' said Bjorn grimly.

My eyesight wasn't as good as most people's but I could see the glow of the fire further along the shore and the men sleeping around it.

'If those are Svanson's men,' I said, pointing at them, 'they'll be dead drunk. They always are by this time of day.'

'So what do you suggest?' Bjorn asked.

'The small boat there,' I said, pointing to the rowing boat that lay beached on the shingle. 'Can't we just take it and row out to the ships?'

'It couldn't possibly be that simple,' said Bjorn, shaking his head. 'How do we do that without being challenged?'

'I'm not sure they'll even wake up,' I said, looking at the sleeping men. One was snoring, I could hear him from where we stood.

'Can't you seek some more guidance from your gift of sight?' Bjorn asked.

I shook my head. 'It never comes when bidden,' I told him.

He held out his hands to me anyway. I took them in mine, and closed my eyes, trying to reach that state of calm in which visions sometimes came to me. I could feel the roughness of his work-callused palms in my own, and the energy flowing between us, but I could see nothing of the future. I released him, shaking my head. My distress was still strong in me, clouding everything else.

'But earlier, you saw something, you said,' Bjorn asked. 'What did you see?'

'We were on board a ship,' I told him, remembering. I pointed at the larger of the two ships at anchor. 'That one. We were sailing into a wide bay. Mountains on one side, hills on the other. No place I've ever seen with my waking eyes. The sea was a luminous, clear green, and there were seabirds.'

Bjorn sighed. 'This will be dangerous. But if we stay here, we'll certainly be caught. I'm afraid for you, Thora. You're just a child.'

I looked up at him. 'I'm fifteen winters,' I told him. 'Grown up and nearly as old as you, I'd wager.'

'Well, you'd lose. I'm twenty-three winters old.'

Faintly in the distance, I heard the sounds of voices and I thought my ears caught the ring of iron on iron.

'It's got to be now,' I whispered. A feeling of danger, of panic, pressed in on me. 'I can sense the soldiers coming.'

'Very well, then, listen,' said Bjorn, pulling Svanson's cloak from the horse. 'My one skill, and it's a poor one, is voices. As your father said, I'm a storyteller. I can imitate Svanson, as long as they don't see me.'

He flung the cloak around his shoulders. It swept the ground, but the light was poor and no one would notice the ill fit. He pulled the hood up so that his face was entirely in shadow and then held up a piece of rope. 'Do you mind pretending to be bound again?' he asked. 'It would be more realistic if anyone wakes.'

Bjorn tied my hands loosely at the wrists, and looped the rope across the horse's withers. 'Can you free your hands if you need to?' he whispered.

'Yes,' I said, testing it. My wrists were sore and the rope chafed them, but I could slip them out.

'Good. Now promise me something.'

'What?'

'Promise me that if this goes wrong, you'll run for your life. Promise you won't think about me.' Bjorn's voice was earnest and he gripped my hands painfully tight as he spoke. My heart gave a strange lurch.

'There's nowhere to run,' I whispered. 'The soldiers have reached the top of the cliffs.'

Bjorn exclaimed under his breath and then vaulted

onto the horse's back. We moved forward swiftly but quietly towards the shore, the horse's hooves scrunching softly on the stones, while I walked beside it, praying to Eir to watch over us.

The shapes by the fire didn't stir. I could smell the smoke of the campfire and hear the low pop of the burning embers.

I could feel my heart thumping and my mouth was dry. I was afraid now, but I breathed deeply and slowed my heart rate as Sigrun had taught me. It's important to show no fear even when you feel it, I reminded myself. I could sense that Bjorn was jumpy beside me. If this went wrong, we would both be put to the sword.

I swallowed, terrified. I could feel the tension building up in me. Was I mad to be attempting this? I thought longingly of my father. Had he made it past the army, or had he been caught?

We reached the small boat that lay half in, half out of the water.

'So far so good,' murmured Bjorn. With a swift glance at the sleeping men, he slipped down out of the saddle and reached a hand into the boat to feel for the oars. He drew his hand back with a gasp of shock that was loud in the still air and made me jump. I had even more of a fright a moment later as a dark shape rose up out of the boat. I fell back but Bjorn stepped forward and grasped the man, clapping a hand over his mouth.

'Not a sound from you,' he hissed. 'You can take us out to the ships. If you do it quietly, I'll reward you well.'

The man nodded. I could see the whites of his eyes, wide in the darkness.

'What's your name?' asked Bjorn, lifting his hand from his mouth.

'Erik,' gasped the slave hoarsely.

'Then hurry, Erik, for the soldiers are coming,' said Bjorn, and released him. Erik climbed out of the boat and throwing his weight against it, gave it a push towards the water. The boat moved with a dreadful grating, crunching sound against the stones. The noise was like a thunder-clap in the still air. I heard Bjorn catch his breath. One of the men by the fire stirred, mumbling something in his sleep.

'Is that you, Bjorn?' a drowsy voice called.

'Yes, it's me,' called out Bjorn in Svanson's thick voice. I thought it sounded convincing, but my heart was ham-mering with fear now.

'Where in the name of Thor have you been all day? We had to do all your work for you.'

The man threw his furs aside and staggered to his feet while speaking. He started stumbling towards us. Bjorn stayed still as a statue beside the horse. I stood beside him, head downcast, like a properly subdued slave, and tried to master my fear. Erik gave the boat another push, so that it floated. Then he stood there in the shallow water, wait-ing, holding the boat.

Meanwhile the newly-awakened man came up to us and stared at me. 'Where's the other one?' he asked stu-pidly. 'The man you took.'

'Threw him over the cliff,' said Bjorn with relish.

'Ha! But you're not going out to the ship now are you?' asked the man, obviously confused. His voice was slurred with sleep and mead, his footsteps unsteady.

'Come and lie by the fire with the rest of us. It's not too late to drink your health.' The man burped loudly and patted his belly.

'I've got this one to see to first,' said Bjorn. As he spoke, he tugged at the rope that bound me and I staggered against him. He put an arm around my shoulders, steadying me against him, so that I didn't fall. To the other man, it clearly looked like an amorous embrace, because he leered at us.

'Let the slave take her out to the ship,' said the man. 'Why trouble yourself now?'

'She needs taming,' Bjorn said. 'Right now.'

I fell to my knees beside him. 'No, please, my lord Svanson,' I begged. It wasn't difficult to sound afraid.

'Get up, woman,' Bjorn snarled, leaning down and grasping my hair and pulling me to my feet. The pain of it made my eyes water, and I whimpered, hoping I was playing my part as he wanted me to. I wished the other man would go away, but instead he laughed coarsely, stepped closer and grabbed my arm, pulling me against him. He smelt as if he hadn't washed for several weeks.

'Bring her to the fire and we'll all help you,' he suggested, squeezing me. I shrank back against the horse, trying to get away from him. I was no longer feigning fear. It was real now. I could hear the other men waking up. This was all going horribly wrong.

'Leave her alone,' ordered Bjorn angrily and gave the man a shove. My heart jumped into my mouth. He'd forgotten to use Svanson's voice. The man peered curiously up at him.

'What's bitten you?' he asked. 'You don't usually mind sharing your wenches. I'll hold her down for you if you like . . . '

Before he could say any more, Bjorn had pushed him out of the way so hard that he stumbled and fell to one knee. Then Bjorn was dragging me towards the boat, leaving the horse behind. The water was icy cold against my legs as we waded into it and I began shivering with a mixture of cold and terror. Bjorn picked me up and threw me into the boat, jumping in after me. The boat rocked and swayed.

'Row, for Thor's sake,' Bjorn ordered Erik urgently. Erik immediately jumped into the boat, fitted the oars and began to pull on them. I could hear shouts from the shore now and realized the men's suspicions were aroused.

'What are we going to do?' I whispered urgently to Bjorn. 'They suspect us . . . ' I broke off, aware I was betraying my terror.

'Tell them . . . ' whispered Erik, but then paused, looking frightened.

'Tell them what?' hissed Bjorn.

'Tell him he can have her after. It's what Svanson'd say. That man is Thorbjorn.'

I realized with a shock that Erik knew that Bjorn was not who he pretended to be. But he was choosing to help us.

Bjorn stood up in the boat and hailed Thorbjorn who was standing staring after us.

'Hey, Thorbjorn,' he sneered, in Svanson's voice. 'You can have her after me. What's left of her.'

Another of Svanson's companions had woken and joined Thorbjorn on the shore. He chuckled deep in his throat at Bjorn's words.

'And then me next,' he called. But Thorbjorn didn't laugh. He started talking to the other man, gesticulating and pointing. The other two men joined them. They were all staring at us, sinister shadows in the dusky light. I began to whisper prayers to Eir and Freya, my hands tightly clenched in my lap. They would come after us, I was certain of it. I didn't dare think about what they might do if they caught us.

'Trouble,' Bjorn muttered. 'Is there another boat, my friend? Can they follow us?'

'Depends,' puffed Erik. He began to cough, a deep, racking cough that shook him so that he had to pause in his rowing. Bjorn took the oars from him and Erik moved out of his way.

'Depends on what?' Bjorn asked as he pulled the oars in a steady rhythm.

'On where the second boat is,' Erik said, catching his breath. 'It's usually out by the other ship, but I think I saw them haul it onto the beach tonight.'

Bjorn cursed under his breath. 'We should have taken that one, too,' he muttered.

'Have you had that cough a long time?' I asked Erik, unable to prevent myself, even in the midst of a crisis, from noticing the ills of others.

'Since last winter,' he said. 'Why?'

'I can give you something that might clear it,' I told him.

There was no time for him to reply. We reached the

largest of the two ships, just as we heard the tell-tale crunch and splash of the second boat being launched behind us. Svanson's friends were coming after us. We were running out of time.

Bjorn swung himself aboard and then reached down to grasp my wrists, pulling me onto the deck after him. Erik was about to follow when Bjorn stopped him.

'No,' he said. 'Go to the second boat. Tell them to man the oars and make ready to follow us out of the fjord. King Harald's army is on our heels. We're leaving now.'

Without a word, Erik dropped back into the boat and hauled on the oars again. The sound of oars splashing was coming closer behind us. Svanson's friends began to call out:

'Svanson, what are you doing? What's going on?' I heard Thorbjorn shouting.

I looked up at Bjorn, desperate to know what we should do, relying on him to take charge. How could we get away fast enough?

Bjorn was looking around the ship we now stood on. In the semi-darkness, many pairs of eyes were watching us. Most people were bound, one large man wasn't. He stood staring at us from under bushy brows. Svanson's two dogs appeared from behind him and approached us. One lowered his head, flattened its ears and gave a low, rumbling growl. I felt sick with fear. I'd forgotten the dogs.

'Quiet, boy!' ordered Bjorn at once. The first dog seemed to recognize the voice, and abased itself, whining softly. But the other dog came closer, sniffing at Bjorn's hand. It clearly smelt something wrong, despite the fact that Bjorn was wearing Svanson's clothes. It growled and then let out a deep, angry bark. Bjorn kicked out at it and ordered it to lie down. It did so, but continued to growl low in its throat. I could feel myself shaking. What if the dogs attacked us?

'Your own dogs don't know you, Svanson,' remarked the tall man suspiciously.

'Stupid brutes!' Bjorn managed to sound completely indifferent. I wondered how he was staying calm. My own mouth was so dry, I wasn't sure I could speak at all. This must be the captain, but we didn't even know his name.

'Set the slaves to the oars,' Bjorn ordered him. 'We're leaving at once.'

'What?' The captain sounded outraged. 'In this light? Do you want to get us all killed?'

'Are you questioning my orders?' demanded Bjorn angrily.

'We don't even have all the slaves here yet,' argued the captain, sounding stunned. 'They're arriving tomorrow. There aren't enough people on board to row.'

Bjorn and I were both silent, shocked by this news. It was completely unexpected. What should we do now?

'How many are there aboard?' Bjorn demanded.

'Only nine . . . and there are fourteen pairs of oars.'

My heart missed a beat. We were trapped aboard the ship with no escape route while the king's army closed in. We'd be caught. I thought of my father and wished I'd gone with him. I was close to panic now, and forced myself to remember my vision. We were going to escape. I just couldn't see how.

Bjorn drew himself up to his full height.

'Those men on shore are traitors. They've betrayed me to King Harald, told lies about me, and his army is arriving as I speak. We could hear them as we left. They want these ships for themselves. I suggest we man four pairs of oars and go. But if you think it's safer to sit about and wait for them to catch us, by all means do so.'

He paused a moment, staring at the captain. His face was hidden in his hood, but it seemed to me all too obvious he was an impostor. I clenched my fists, willing the captain to do as Bjorn ordered, to obey him. Bjorn spoke again. 'I heard them planning to slit your throat,' he told the captain deliberately. 'Is that what you want?'

This seemed to galvanize the captain into action. Without another word, he began to move along the deck untying the slaves and ordering them to the oars. Feverishly, Bjorn and I began to do the same on our side of the ship. I kept glancing over the side at the small rowing boat.

'It's getting closer,' I whispered to Bjorn as he passed. 'What do we do?'

'Hurry,' he said in an urgent undertone and I could hear that he was not as calm as he pretended. Frantically, I tugged at the knots that bound the slaves. Who had tied them so tightly? We would be lucky if they could use their hands at all. It was almost as though time had been slowed down on board the ship, while it continued at its normal pace on shore. Svanson's men were hurrying towards us and the army was moving ever closer. Whose side were the gods on tonight?

As I freed the last woman on my side of the ship, I

could suddenly clearly hear the sound of men marching. I looked towards the shore and saw a column of flaming torches held aloft. They were approaching fast. The army was pushing on through the night to try and cut off Svanson's escape. I prayed they were too late.

I wasn't the only person to have seen them. There was a flurry of activity on board as the slaves hurried to the oars. The captain called one away to help him weigh the anchor. Bjorn took his place and grasped his oar.

'For Odin's sake, Bjorn,' I hissed in his ear. 'Svanson would never demean himself like that!'

'Thora,' muttered Bjorn, through clenched teeth. 'This is life or death!'

By this time the anchor was up and the oars were out. The captain called the first stroke. The oars pulled out of time, splashing and uncoordinated. I almost screamed with frustration. The crew were inexperienced and now the rowing boat was so close they could almost touch us.

'Svanson, for the love of Thor, wait for us!' one of the men shouted. 'Don't you see there are soldiers coming?'

I reached into my bag and wrapped my hand around my iron knife. I knew if we let these men on board they would discover our deception and kill us. I was prepared to defend myself by any means necessary.

The next pull on the oars was stronger. I felt our ship stir sluggishly. Across the water, I could hear splashes. Someone on the second ship was calling the stroke as well.

The rowing boat crashed into the side of our ship and one man leapt onto the rail. I gripped my knife tighter and fought back the fear that was making me feel sick. We had been so close to escaping.

'What in the name of Odin is happening—?' he began to shout.

Bjorn leapt to his feet and pushed him hard in the chest. He fell backwards into the water with a cry and a splash.

'Traitor!' Bjorn shouted in Svanson's gutteral voice.

We were moving now, but slowly, painfully slowly with so few people to row. Could we get away? I leant over the side to see, and two cold hands grabbed hold of my wrists. I cried out and tried to pull away, desperately fighting not to lose my balance and be pulled overboard. The hands were like steel bands on me. I dropped to my knees and bit one of the fingers as hard as I could. There was a cry of pain from its owner and I managed to twist one arm free. Then I took a firmer grip on my knife, gathered my courage, and stabbed into the hand that still clutched me. Blood spurted dark out of it. There was a scream and abruptly I was released. I staggered back, feeling my hands wet and sticky. I could see the rowing boat falling behind us now. Two men were still in it, one staring at us, the other on his feet, shaking his fists and calling the curses of the gods down on us. Two more thrashed desperately in the water, calling for help. The ship was picking up speed now, and we glided away from them.

The men were looking back over their shoulders. They knew they had lost us, and yet they couldn't return to shore. I watched as they rescued their comrades from the water and began to row out into the fjord away from the king's men on the beach they had just left. They would be hunted men, now. Fugitives. Outlaws. As were we. But we had the ships. We had escaped.

All the exhaustion and pain I'd been holding at bay suddenly overwhelmed me. My knees gave way and I leant heavily on the side of the ship, breathing fast. The relief was almost too much to bear. I realized Bjorn was beside me when I felt his hands on my shoulders.

'Are you all right?' he asked anxiously. He saw the dark smear of blood on my hand and I heard his sharp intake of breath.

'It's not my blood,' I said tremulously. I wondered if I was going to be sick again.

'Brave girl,' Bjorn said softly. 'We're away now, but it's not over. Go to the prow and be lookout, will you? There may be rocks or islands ahead.'

He returned to his oar and I walked to the front of the ship, feeling weak and drained. The shifting dusk around us seemed unreal, as did the cool summer breeze fanning my cheek. It seemed impossible that just this morning I had woken up in my father's house and looked forward to a day of weaving and other household tasks.

Behind me I could hear the captain calling the stroke from where he stood at the tiller. He had a deep, booming voice that carried across the ship. I knew that however exhausted I was, I couldn't rest yet. I needed to be lookout and I also needed to plan for the next step in our escape. Bjorn had to convince the captain that he was Svanson until we were out to sea and it was too late to turn back. It would help if we knew his name. Then Bjorn would have to reveal himself. That would be dangerous too.

I paused to speak to a woman who was straining at the oars, her breath coming in gasps already.

'What's the captain's name?' I asked her.

'Thrang,' she told me breathlessly.

'Thank you,' I whispered, and took up my post at the prow.

CHAPTER SIX

We rowed steadily, the ship gliding through the dark water. The splash of the oars and the creaking of the rowlocks were loud in the still night air. I stared ahead, straining my eyes and ears to catch the least sign or sound of rocks before we ran upon them. I wasn't the best person for this task, but the others were all rowing.

It grew steadily lighter and before long, glancing back behind us, I saw the first flush of dawn in the sky. I also saw Bjorn on his way to join me. There were now only three pairs of oars in action and one woman was resting, leaning against the side of the ship, breathing hard.

'We're almost out of the fjord,' Bjorn said, pointing ahead. 'As soon as we're on the open sea, we'll be able to hoist the sail.'

'And the captain will see you're not Svanson,' I said. 'He's called Thrang, by the way. What are you going to tell him?'

'Whatever I think is most likely to convince him to work for me,' replied Bjorn. 'Do you have any advice for dealing with those dogs? I can't go near them without them growling. I don't fancy getting bitten.'

'Feed them,' I said. 'Let no one else give them food but you. It'll take time, but there's no other way.'

Bjorn nodded and went to look for meat. I heard angry snarls and he returned quickly.

'As you say, it might take some time,' he muttered, nursing a bitten finger.

I took a strip of clean cloth from my bag and wrapped it around the bite. As I tied the knot, Bjorn grasped my hand. 'Thank you,' he whispered.

'It's nothing,' I said, surprised. 'I bind cuts for people all the time.'

'No, I meant thank you for this escape. I'm glad it's you I'm running away with.' Bjorn released my hand, and without giving me a chance to reply, he went to relieve one of the slaves of their oar. I watched him, pleased at his words. He must have felt my eyes on him, because he looked up and straight at me from his seat at the oar. I felt myself blushing slightly, and turned away.

The cliffs began to slowly peel back on either side of us as the fjord widened. The wind freshened and the water grew more choppy, lapping against the sides of the boat.

Now I could see the open sea ahead of us, the low grey sky coming down to meet the water in the far distance. It was an exhilarating sight. It filled me with a sense of adventure. I was setting out to explore the unknown. I would see sights that no one in my family had seen before.

The thought of my family sobered me. I longed to know that my mother and brother had reached my uncle's. But even then, there was no certainty of safety with an army in the district. As for my father, I hardly dared hope he'd made it back to them. I felt tears close to the surface and breathed deeply to dispell them. I needed to be brave. It was what they would want.

When the sun peeped above the horizon in a blaze of pinks and oranges, the slaves were ordered to ship the oars. I helped tie them securely inside the ship, watching and learning from what the others were doing. Thrang and two other men were hoisting the vast woollen sail. I gasped as I saw it lift on the mast and billow, catching the wind. The ship bounded forward and tilted, suddenly revealing its power and speed.

'Beautiful, isn't she?' said Bjorn, coming towards me.

'I'd never imagined anything like it,' I agreed, awestruck.

We swung round and instead of continuing out to sea, we headed north, hugging the shoreline. The other ship was following us, I could see. I could make out the people on board scurrying around the deck, readying the sail as Thrang had done.

'Now,' said Bjorn softly. He walked away from me to where timber was stacked along the length of the ship and swung himself onto it, holding onto the mast with one hand. Then with a dramatic sweep of his other hand, he flung his hood back.

He wasn't a tall man, but he was broad and powerful, and stood proudly with his shoulders thrown back and one hand on his sword hilt. His long black hair blew back in the wind and he had a growth of stubble on his chin. He was very handsome, I noticed for the first time. He had fine features and clear eyes. He looked so confident, that for a moment my fear faded.

At first there was no reaction. Then a few people

noticed him, and stared, confused. There was a sudden silence that spread away from us across the ship. The captain caught sight of him and stood frozen for a long moment.

'What in Thor's name . . . ?' he blustered at last. 'Where is Svanson?'

'I am Svanson,' Bjorn announced brazenly.

'Liar!' shouted Thrang, and so swiftly that I barely had time to blink, he'd drawn his sword with a scrape of iron and thrust it at Bjorn.

Bjorn had been expecting it. My father's sword flashed out, parrying the blow. He swung Thrang's sword up with his own weapon and then threw himself on the captain, bearing him heavily to the deck. Both men dropped their swords. There was a brief, confused scuffle, and then I saw Bjorn had his knife to the captain's neck. The captain roared with rage, but didn't dare move. The dogs danced around them barking frantically.

'I'm Bjorn Svanson,' Bjorn shouted. 'Will you serve me or do you prefer to die?'

There was a silence. I watched, horror-struck, praying I was not about to witness a second killing. The sight of that iron knife pressed against Thrang's throat made me feel sick. Thrang didn't reply. The seconds drew out painfully.

'Yield,' hissed Bjorn. 'Yield and you'll be well paid for your trouble. What were you offered for this voyage?'

'Ten pieces of silver,' uttered Thrang in a strangled voice.

We needed the captain. Without him, we had little chance of reaching Iceland. Our voyage hung in the balance. Thrang was rigid with fury, his muscles braced against Bjorn's hold, the veins standing out in his neck and forehead, his eyes bulging.

'Well, I offer far more,' said Bjorn. 'I offer you the second ship. You'd be a man of means.'

'Madness. How do I know I can trust you?' Thrang panted.

'How do I know you can find the way to Iceland?' said Bjorn. 'We have to trust one another.'

Thrang had no choice. All at once he stopped resisting.

'I yield,' he muttered.

Bjorn released him abruptly, pushing himself to his feet and tucking his knife away. He picked up both swords, climbed back onto the timber and addressed the whole ship.

'My friends!' he cried. 'A word!'

There was a collective intake of breath as everyone on board who hadn't had a clear sight of him before, now saw for certain that he wasn't their chieftain and master.

'Our good captain Thrang recognizes my authority. Does any other man on board wish to challenge me?'

There was a dreadful silence.

'A man chose to cross me yesterday and he ended up dead,' Bjorn spoke into the silence. He had everyone's attention.

'He was a man of immense cruelty and he deserved death. I lay claim to his name, his title, and his goods. But I'm a very different sort of man. I swear to you all, that every person on board will be better off serving me. You'll be well fed. You'll be treated with respect. And you'll be paid for your labour and your loyalty.'

I was astonished at Bjorn's ability to speak. He was addressing the ship with total confidence. It was a rousing speech and everyone was listening intently.

'Why?' asked a black-haired, dark-skinned woman with broad cheekbones. 'Why would you offer us all that?'

'I don't hold with slavery,' answered Bjorn calmly but in a clear voice that carried the length of the ship. The switch from dramatic speech to understated utterance worked more powerfully than any energetic protestation could have done. It sounded sincere.

I could see the slaves exchanging looks of hope but also of scepticism and disbelief. I too was surprised and doubtful. He couldn't let these slaves go. If they were recognized, they'd be considered runaways. Their lives would be forfeit or subject to a new bondage. Besides, we couldn't do without them.

'If you work hard and well for me for one year in the new land,' Bjorn promised, 'I'll give you your freedom and one silver mark each—to every man and woman among you. And child,' he said, acknowledging the presence of a girl of about ten winters who clung to her mother. 'Then if you choose to stay with me,' he paused and glanced across at me, 'to stay with Thora and me,' he amended, 'you stay as paid labourers. Or you will be free to leave and make your own lives. There is land for the taking in Iceland.'

I felt a glow of excitement and pride. Bjorn was acknowledging me as the head of the house, the woman in charge.

'He's mad,' I heard someone by me whisper. 'Who in Odin's name is he?'

'I will await an answer from each of you,' Bjorn announced.

He stepped down from the timber and came to stand beside me.

'Do you think I've persuaded them?' he asked me quietly.

'I don't know. What will you do if they all choose to leave?' I asked uncertainly. 'You can't run a farm with two or three people. I've tried.'

'They won't all leave,' he assured me. 'Because they'll be better off on a bigger farm in a house such as we can build with all this timber.' He pointed to the stacks of posts and planks that dominated the entire centre of the boat.

Bjorn moved away and began walking among the slaves answering their questions.

'How do we know you mean what you say?' demanded an older man, his head bound in a scarf.

'You'll have to trust me,' Bjorn replied simply.

The slaves exchanged looks once more, but it seemed to me there was more hope than doubt in their eyes. No one said anything more.

I glanced back at Thrang. He was at the tiller, his face stormy and dark with suspicion. His aura was full of anger. I felt a chill of fear pass through me like a light shiver. I wasn't sure he could be trusted. I would warn Bjorn to beware of him. He was a free man, not a slave grateful to be untied. And he'd been defeated and humiliated.

CHAPTER SEVEN

We made fair sailing that day. Bjorn moved about the ship and spoke with each slave individually. One by one, they pledged their loyalty to him and the mood on board the ship lightened. Bjorn further improved it by asking me to distribute a meal and a goblet of ale to everyone. He himself took over the tiller from Thrang, leaving the captain to manage the sail.

We'd left the coast behind us now, and the breeze had freshened. The second boat followed us at a distance. As I moved about, handing out food, the deck lurched suddenly under my feet, causing me to grab hold of some timber to prevent myself falling. I grazed my fingers on the wood and stubbed my toes. Annoyed at being so clumsy, I righted myself and walked on, a wary eye out for the next thing to catch hold of if the boat should move again.

'First time on a ship?' asked Bjorn with a grin when I reached his side.

'Yes. But not your first voyage, I believe?' I replied, watching him handle the tiller confidently.

'No. I—' Bjorn stopped suddenly, recollecting himself. 'No, not my first voyage,' he finished simply.

I handed him a goblet, which he held while I filled it. Thrang approached us.

'Are you the healer Svanson spoke of?' he asked gruffly, looking at me from under his brows.

'I am,' I admitted.

'In that case, you should know that the *chieftain*,' he emphasized the word with a dark look at Bjorn, 'had your chest of medicines sent aboard.'

He pointed to the centre of the ship, and I could see, stacked next to the chicken pens, my familiar wooden box. I was glad to see it had reached the ship safely. I pulled my way across to it as the ship plunged in the swell.

I withdrew my key from the pocket of my tunic and fitted it to the lock. It clicked open smoothly, and I ran my fingers lightly over some of the contents. I was very glad to have them, I admitted to myself. Here was elder and willow bark to cure fevers. Cloves, traded from the east, to ease toothache. Selfheal for burns. And many other plants, collected and dried, or traded, that I couldn't find easily again. I locked the chest and returned to Bjorn. His eyes were fixed on the horizon, and he didn't look at me as he spoke.

'You didn't tell me you were a healer, as well as a seer,' he said. 'I suppose I should have guessed.'

I glanced swiftly at him. 'I'm still in training,' I told him.

'You're a useful person to have around,' Bjorn remarked. He smiled at me warmly and I found myself smiling back.

As we left the coast behind us and headed out into the

open sea, the swell increased and the ship dipped and lifted more steeply. I looked out at the heaving, blue-green sea. This ship that had looked so huge in the fjord now felt tiny and insignificant on this vast expanse of water. The other boat was still beside us, but I could only see it in snatches now, as we disappeared down into deep troughs, and waves the size of hills rose up between us.

It was no longer possible to walk without holding onto something. The slaves started to lie down and hold their stomachs. A few vomited violently over the side of the ship, hanging onto the edge for dear life as the ship dipped and reared under them. Looking around me, I saw it wasn't only the people who were suffering. The animals too were lying down as best they could in their confined spaces, and one of the small lambs was bleating piteously. I staggered to its pen, trying in vain to comfort it.

'If you want to help the animals, tend to that foal there,' Thrang called to me roughly. 'It's lying down, and that's sure death to horses. It needs to be on its feet or we'll lose it.'

Here was a task I understood in this unfamiliar environment. I'd never been to sea, but I'd helped on the farm all my life. I went to the foal, and stroked its nose, speaking to it encouragingly. It lay still, sweat drenched and panting.

'Try to get up,' I urged it, pulling on its halter. The foal, a spindly palomino youngster, resisted. I climbed inside its enclosure and pulled harder, but it was a dead weight. I bent and put my arms around its body, bracing myself against the railings. The foal made a valiant effort to lift itself, getting its back legs under it. It swayed and would have buckled, but for the sudden assistance of one of the slave women. She caught at its hindquarters as they swayed and held it steady while I hauled it onto its front legs too. The poor creature stood swaying and trembling, leaning against us for balance.

'Thank you,' I said to her. 'What's your name?'

'Asgerd,' she told me briefly. I recognized her as the woman who had told me Thrang's name in the night and also the mother of the one child on board.

'Well, Asgerd, if you fetch me a rag dipped in water, we can try to give this youngster a drink.'

We did our best to squeeze water into the foal's mouth, but most of it ran back out. We took it in turns to stand with him, keeping him on his feet. Asgerd's daughter Astrid came to help, chatting to the foal and stroking him. After a few hours, I was sure he was a little stronger and his eyes clearer. Asgerd herself leaned heavily against the pen from time to time, eyes closed. She was obviously suffering too, I could see sickness in the colours that pulsed around her head. I was surprised to find myself unaffected.

As night came, the waves seemed to grow rougher. Or perhaps it was just more frightening to be out on the open sea in the dimness of the summer night. It grew colder and colder. I huddled in my cloak, miserable, uncomfortable and unable to sleep with the wind whipping over me. Sometimes when we plummeted down a wave, the next wave struck us, sending sea spray across the deck. I was soon sticky and damp from the salt water. Thrang moved among us, ordering us to tie ourselves to the ship, and handing out ropes.

'We're in for some heavy weather,' he told me.

For a moment, I was afraid again. But Thrang looked so calm, so in control, that I hoped we weren't in any grave danger.

I watched him set to work with Bjorn, bringing down the sail, furling it and lashing it securely to the mast. The two of them went to the tiller and tied themselves to the side of the ship. I could see them speaking to each other. They seemed to be the only people still able to move about. As I watched them, I noticed that Thrang's aura was no longer dominated by the streaks of sulphurous yellow that had suffused it earlier. His suspicion was fading already. Bjorn's aura was now glowing a confident, beautiful turquoise. He was feeling exhilarated by the storm, confident and powerful. Such a change in one day.

It began to rain, and both men were obscured from my view by the lashing drops that splattered onto the deck and soaked us through in no time. I could hear the men and women around us raising their voices in prayer, imploring Thor to spare us from the storm. I joined them, whispering my prayers quietly. I had heard many tales of shipwreck and knew that ships at sea were the playthings of the gods. But I remembered Thrang's glow of confidence and hoped all would be well.

The bad weather lasted all night and far into the next day before it began to ease. At last, the wind lessened and the rain stopped. I was stiff and numb with cold. The clouds hung low, making the day dark. Miraculously, our second ship was still in sight. How she had managed to stay with us through the storm, I couldn't imagine.

I untied myself and got unsteadily to my feet. I found my dry tunic and, shivering, I changed into it. I wrapped my cloak around me, and wandered the sodden ship, avoiding the puddles of water and vomit that slid across the deck in time with the motion of the ship. The slaves were huddled together in groups, overcome with exhaustion and relief.

Thrang appeared beside me.

'We need to get the ship cleaned up before night,' he said roughly. 'Can you help me get everyone up and to work?'

'They're sick and exhausted,' I started to object. He waved my words aside impatiently.

'They'll get ill lying wet in all their dirt,' he said impatiently. I knew he was right. We went from one huddled group to another, shaking everyone awake. Thrang set the men to filling buckets of water from the sea and sloshing them onto the deck, while the women scrubbed at the muck that floated everewhere, sweeping it out through the drainage holes. Bjorn was at the tiller and called me to him.

'Everyone needs to eat again,' he said. 'Can you see to it?'

I looked through the barrels and crates of food that were stored on deck and found some bread and some dried meat to distribute. I poured more ale too, hoping it would make up for the rude awakening we'd put everyone through.

Mealtimes were cold and comfortless affairs on board

ship, I thought. If ever we had needed hot food, it was now, but there was no way of lighting a fire. I went from person to person, handing out food, asking their names. Grim, Karl, Kai, Brian, Jon, Aud, Vigdis, Astrid and Asgerd. We weren't many to be out on such a huge sea.

Once everyone had eaten, Thrang and Bjorn hoisted the sail. It flapped a moment, heavy and dripping, and then the wind caught it, making it billow. The ship leapt forward, speeding purposefully through the waves once more. Seeing us hoist our sail, our sister ship did the same, dropping behind for a while and then catching up with us.

I watched as the day faded. I hadn't slept since before we came on board the ship and my eyes were sore with tiredness. When I looked around me, I saw the slaves who weren't helping Thrang sail the ship had all huddled together once more, wrapping themselves up against the bitter wind that blew across us. I wished I could join them, but I didn't know any of them well enough. Most of them were as wary of me as they were of Bjorn.

I thought of my own family in Norway and I felt so homesick that it hurt. I had no one here. I found a space in the prow and sat down with my back to some crates of food, wrapping my cloak tightly around me. I couldn't imagine being able to fall asleep outdoors in this temperature. I clenched my teeth to stop them chattering. I was more miserable than I would have thought possible.

A dark shape appeared beside me.

'Bjorn?' I asked uncertainly. I couldn't see his face.

'Yes. You aren't sleeping?' he asked.

'It's far too cold,' I admitted.

Bjorn took my hand in his, and it was warm around my numb fingers.

'I brought some furs,' he said, laying two sheepskins beside me. 'And this cloak is big enough to cover both of us.'

I caught my breath. Was he suggesting we lie down together? When we had had slaves in my father's house, the girls had slept apart from the men. It was done like that in all decent households. Moreover, I was freeborn and a healer. However respectfully and equally we treated our slaves, we didn't cuddle up to them.

Bjorn seemed to have no sense of this. Perhaps he had already put aside all thoughts of being a slave. He'd taken his freedom, and had shouldered the role of being our leader. He noticed me hesitating and smiled. 'Don't you trust me?' he asked. 'I only want to keep you warm.'

When he put it like that, I realized I did trust him. I'd put myself entirely in his power and he had done the same with me. He was my friend and my ally, and I was grateful he was here. I could feel tears stinging my sore eyes and I blinked hard to keep them back. *Don't reveal your emotions*, Sigrun had always said. I thought I had learned her lessons better than this. But then I'd never been torn away from my home before, unsure if my family were dead or alive.

I lay down on the soft, thick sheepskin, and allowed Bjorn to put his arm around me and draw me close. A few tears leaked from my eyes. My body shook with a suppressed sob. Bjorn didn't comment on it, but he drew me closer and began to stroke my arm, and then my hair. As my tears continued to flow, he turned me to face him, wrapping his arms tight around me and laying his rough, unshaven cheek against mine.

I felt breathless with my tears and the unexpected closeness. His embrace could have felt frightening, inappropriate, but instead it felt reassuring. Like me, he had just lost his family. Like me, he needed someone to care for him.

'Do you regret this?' he asked softly in my ear. 'Do you wish you hadn't come?'

I didn't answer straight away. I fought my tears and tried to think whether I regretted it. A few moments ago, I had done. But now I felt comforted.

'I miss my parents,' I admitted. 'And my brother. I wish I knew that they were safe.'

'I miss my sister, too,' Bjorn said. 'It's like a pain in my chest that won't go away. I keep seeing her, dying. I could do nothing. Nothing at all. When I think of that, I don't feel sorry I've killed a man and stolen his goods. I'm glad I'm here, and not fleeing alone and on foot somewhere.' He shuddered at the memory. 'As long as I haven't made you unhappy,' he added.

'I regret nothing,' I told him. 'It's my destiny, and you are part of that. I've seen it.'

Bjorn drew back a little and laid his head on his arm close beside me, looking at me. The light was dim, and his face was in shadow, but I could see his eyes gleam. Around his head and shoulders, the beautiful blue colour that was his essence glowed peacefully.

'You're just a little frightening, you know,' he said. But he softened his words by rubbing his thumb gently along my cheekbone. I could feel Bjorn's warmth begin to steal into me, making my eyelids heavy. Sleep was coming and I couldn't fight it.

'Are you warmer now?' Bjorn asked. His voice sounded as though it was coming from a long way away.

'Yes,' I assured him drowsily. It was a huge effort to speak. I felt my limbs turn heavy as rocks and my eyes slowly close, as sleep took me.

I woke up with the sun shining in my face. I was cold again. I knew at once that Bjorn had gone. I sat up and could see him standing nearby at the prow keeping look out, clad in his tunic and leggings. I rubbed the sleep from my eyes and saw I was still covered in his cloak.

I struggled to my feet, stretching my stiff, painful limbs. The cuts and bruises from our forced march behind Svanson's horse were very sore.

'Thora, you're awake,' said Bjorn. As he turned and saw me, his blue aura was suffused with pink. It was the colour I saw around my parents when they told me they loved me. As I saw it, I knew that in following my vision I had made the right choice. I was meant to be here. I went to stand beside Bjorn and he smiled warmly at me. As I gave him his cloak, he caught my hand as he took it, pressing my fingers lightly, and then releasing them. There was a bond between us now, I thought, looking up at him. We'd only just met, but so much had happened. I could read his feelings for me as clearly as if he had spoken them. I felt a rush of affection for him in return. I'd never felt like this before.

'Are we on course for Iceland?' I asked, seeing nothing but sea in every direction. 'How can Thrang tell where we are going?'

'He has methods of navigation. But I don't think he knows with any precision at the moment,' said Bjorn, frowning. 'He says we've almost certainly been blown off course to the south in the storm. We're looking out for the Faeroe Islands. If we sight them, we'll make land there to take on fresh water. If we miss them, we'll sail straight to Iceland.'

'And if we miss Iceland?' I asked.

'We won't miss Iceland,' replied Bjorn. 'We can trust Thrang. I've never seen a more competent captain.'

'Have you often been to sea before?' I asked, curious. It was clear to me Bjorn wasn't a novice aboard a ship. He had even gained Thrang's respect.

'You forget, Thora. I am Bjorn Svanson. I've made many voyages,' said Bjorn, a smile creasing the corners of his eyes. I understood him. He would put his previous identity behind him and play the part of Svanson so thoroughly that even those closest to him would forget he was not born a chieftain. It was my task to support him and I shouldn't ask questions.

CHAPTER EIGHT

We sighted land later that same day. We sailed into a bay between two high headlands at the extreme end of an island. Huge rocky stacks reared up out of the water like guards watching the mouth of the bay. The sea broke against the pillars sending spouts of spray flying into the air. Sea birds wheeled and glided and as we passed them, the black rocks stained white with their droppings.

It wasn't until both the boats were in sheltered water and the anchors were dropped that I noticed how strained both Thrang and Bjorn looked.

'Was it dangerous?' I asked Bjorn as he paused beside me.

'Very,' he replied. 'These ships are swift and sturdy but they are not manoeuvrable in small spaces. And there are always treacherous currents and rocks outside a bay like this.'

'Will it be just as dangerous to leave?' I asked tentatively.

'That should be easier.' Bjorn managed a quick, reassuring smile before moving off to arrange a party of men to go ashore.

I looked at the island. It was an inhospitable place. A cold sea wind blew directly into the bay bringing with it sheets of drizzle. The air was raw and cold. The land rose steeply out of the sea, a uniform vista of misty green hill-sides disappearing up into cloud. I couldn't guess whether they were low hills or high mountains. The place didn't appeal to me in the least.

There was a low dwelling tucked back into the hillside, clinging to the rocks. I wondered if Bjorn had noticed it. He was climbing into the small rowing boat to be taken across to our sister ship. I watched as Bjorn spoke to Stein, Thrang's apprentice, and the rest of the slaves for the first time, though his words were lost in wind and waves and rain.

We began work to clean our ship. Once more, the decks were sluiced clean of all the unpleasant leavings of our voyage. I saw Asgerd shaking out fresh hay for the calves, lambs, and foals and I went to help her.

'What are the chickens to be fed on?' I asked her.

'There's a bag of last year's grain under the seat,' she said, nodding towards a sack. I pulled it out and threw a handful of grain into each crate. The chicks darted here and there, pecking up the food greedily.

I noticed that the foal we'd helped yesterday was lying down again and hadn't touched the hay we had given him. I went to his head, stroking and petting him. He was damp with sweat again.

'This animal is really sick,' I told Asgerd.

'Sea sickness,' she said. 'Horses get it badly because they can't be sick. When I was brought across the sea from my home country, we ran into a storm and half the horses died. I heard the master say he'd brought enough horses on board to allow for some losses.'

'We shan't lose half these horses if I can help it,' I said with determination. 'Come and help me get him on his feet again.'

Between us we coaxed and pulled the foal onto his legs. He stood there trembling and shivering, his eyes dull. He seemed worse, I thought anxiously.

'Would you fetch me some oats?' I asked Asgerd.

'You'd waste oats on keeping a horse alive?' she gasped. 'And what'll we eat once winter sets in? We can't eat hay.'

'I only need a few,' I told her and reluctantly she fetched them. Painstakingly I persuaded the foal to eat a small handful. The other foals butted and nudged me eagerly, trying to get some too. I gently scratched the sick foal's neck, and spoke coaxingly to him.

'I'll call you Aki,' I told him. 'Perhaps having a name will give you the will to live.'

'Is all well on board the other ship?' I asked Bjorn when he returned.

'As well as can be expected,' he said for my ears only. 'Like here, nearly half of them are women and not pleased at having been made to row. I need to take a party ashore and don't for the life of me know how to best split the party. If I leave Thrang here, what is to stop him making off with the ships? But if I stay and send others ashore, I can't be sure they won't desert and spread unwelcome tales about what has been done here. I need time to win them over.'

I thought for a few moments.

'I think you can trust Thrang now,' I said. 'Especially as we are already too few to row the ships. But if you don't want to take any risks, I suggest you send me with only those who won't want to run away. Keep Asgerd and Astrid here and send Erik. Keep Thrang and send his apprentice Stein. Grim won't run away with Asdis still aboard and Kai won't disappear while Vigdis is on the ship.'

Bjorn looked startled.

'You've noticed all these relationships already?' he asked. 'I've barely learned their names as yet.'

I smiled, knowing that men rarely noticed such subtleties. Besides, I had my aura reading to help me, though I never spoke of this to anyone.

'I'd planned to speak to the people in the dwelling house,' Bjorn said, his brow still creased with uncertainty. 'To assure them we mean no harm.'

'I can do that for you,' I offered.

'You'd be unprotected.'

'But at least I'll know that no one will make off with the ships leaving me behind if you are on board. Erik can go with me to the longhouse, and Grim too.' I smiled at Bjorn reassuringly, showing him I was not in the least afraid. At last he nodded.

'Very well. But Erik and Grim will be armed if you are going up there,' he said. He moved away to give the necessary instructions and then we climbed into the small boat with the water barrels and rowed to the beach.

I led Erik and Grim up the steep, well-worn path to the longhouse while the others of our party filled the water barrels from the stream nearest the beach. We knocked at the wooden door but there was no reply.

'Hello!' Erik called. 'We come in friendship.'

His words were met by a silence that was broken only by the trickling of water in the streams on the hills above us.

A sudden squall of wind brought a sheet of heavy rain with it. I shivered. I could see raindrops glistening in Erik's grizzled hair and knew mine must be as wet. Impatiently, I pushed at the door. It yielded under my hand and swung inwards. Glad to escape the drenching rain, I stepped into the gloomy porch.

'Hello?' I called as Erik had done before me. 'Is there no one here?'

I walked forward into the dark house, my eyes adjusting slowly to the gloom. The only light came from a slight glow in the central fireplace and I could make out little. The smoke caught at the back of my throat after days in the open air, making me cough. The house stank of fish, and I could just make out dried fish hanging from the roof. Strange, I thought. I saw no fishing boats in the bay.

Something moved in the darkness behind the loom.

'Who's there?' I asked quickly. 'We mean no harm.'

'I'm not afraid,' came a grating voice, like the sound of iron scraping on iron. A small figure emerged, moving strangely. As it came forward into the light I could see it was a young woman, dragging one leg.

'Are you hurt?' I asked starting forward in sympathy.

'Not I,' said that metallic voice.

As she spoke, I caught sight of her aura and recoiled in horror. She didn't have a single pure colour radiating from her. All was muddied browns and greys, flushed through with sulphur. It would have made Svanson's aura look innocent and playful. I'd never seen anything like it. My first thought was that this could be no human being. This must be some hidden creature, some dwarf or troll or malevolent spirit lurking in this abandoned farmstead to entrap unwary travellers. Then I looked more closely and saw it was just a woman. She was even pretty. One leg was twisted, probably broken and badly set at some time in her past, I guessed. But she was fair of face, slight and elfin-like in her looks. She had small, neat hands and very white teeth. But none of this could distract me from her aura.

'What do you want?' asked the young woman sharply. 'There's nothing here to steal. We're poor people.'

'We stopped only for drinking water,' I said, spreading my hands in a gesture of humility. I had to struggle with myself to hold my ground and speak to her, facing that swirl of vicious and unhappy colours. My impulse was to flee. 'We simply came up here to tell you so. Surely you aren't alone here? Sorry, I don't know your name . . . '

'I am Ragna. I'm alone, but not unprotected,' she said, and there was a hint of a sinister threat in her voice. 'Drinking water?' she continued. 'And what gift have you brought me to compensate?'

'For water?' I asked, bewildered.

'*Our* water,' said the girl.

I tried to see past this poor woman's tortured, terrifying colours to the person that must have feelings of kindness and sympathy, just as I did. But I couldn't find her. I sensed only darkness and evil. I felt fear course through me and began to back towards the door.

'Don't forget that compensation,' she reminded me.

'I'll speak to our chieftain,' I said.

I left, Erik and Grim following me closely.

Once out in the open, I breathed the clean sea air deep into my lungs, trying to clear away the smells and sights of the dreadful house.

'Are we going to pay her?' asked Erik beside me.

I shuddered, trying to collect myself. 'We'll have to ask Bjorn,' I replied, forcing my voice to be steady. 'How does she come to be quite alone in there? She can't live by herself, surely?'

'Not she,' replied Grim in a reassuringly matter-of-fact voice. His eyes roamed the hillside above us. 'The others will be somewhere near. They most likely fled at the sight of two ships entering the bay, in case we meant harm. That poor girl probably can't walk well enough to go with them.'

'They're almost certainly watching us right now,' added Erik.

I tried to summon up pity for the woman left to face danger alone, but I failed. It hadn't seemed to me that she was in the least afraid.

'Let's fill the barrels with water and leave this place,' I said.

We headed down for the shore, avoiding the patches of sheep droppings that were scattered on the grass, stopping only because I spotted a growth of stunted plants beside a stream on the way. Remembering Erik's cough, I stooped to look more closely. They were a plant I knew, but smaller, probably struggling to grow to any size in this raw, wet climate. I carefully picked off a few leaves, leaving the plant to grow. There were more and I lingered, collecting a leaf here and there, until I had a small handful.

By now, Erik and Grim had gone ahead and I was left alone on the hillside above the beach. I could see that our small boat had left without us already, heading out to the two big ships, loaded almost to the waterline with the heavy barrels of water. Kai and Stein were rowing it. Only Erik and Grim were left on the island with me. As I watched the boat pulling out into the bay, I felt a prickle in my fingertips and the hairs rose on the back of my neck. There was danger close by.

I couldn't place it straight away. I was badly shaken by the encounter in the house, and at first I put it down to that. But the feeling strengthened. It crossed my mind that the three of us could be left stranded here, but that wasn't it either. It was more menacing than that. I felt bad intentions thick in the air. I looked back, scanning the hillside behind me.

The pieces suddenly began to slot together in my head. Sheep droppings, but no sheep. A longhouse that was left empty except for one girl. No boats in the bay, though these people must surely live at least partly from fishing. I'd smelt fish in the house.

This was a trap. We'd walked into a trap. The people were, as Erik had said, hiding somewhere, watching us, waiting to attack. It was that decision that I had sensed just now, I was sure of it.

I ran the last stretch down to the beach where powerful waves pounded the lonely shore, drawing back with a rush and a rattle of pebbles and sand. I was breathless

75

with fear and the sense of danger was growing on me fast.

'They'll be back for us in a while,' said Erik, nodding to the boat that had now reached the ships. 'It wouldn't have floated with all of us.'

I could just make out the people, tiny in the distance, passing the barrels up onto the ship and then one man heading back to pick us up.

'Yes, of course,' I agreed anxiously. 'Will they tell Bjorn what the girl said about a gift? He might choose to send something.'

'Yes, I mentioned that,' nodded Grim.

There was nothing to do but wait. I was reluctant to frighten my companions with my fears, so I passed the time by scraping the bark off a flattish stick and cutting runes into it with my knife. It was intended for the girl in the house and invoked the blessings and protection of the goddess Freya. When it was done, I stuck it in the sand. If Bjorn refused to pay, that would be my gift to her.

As I finished, I became aware it had grown darker and darker around us, though it was still hours until night. I looked up, puzzled, and saw heavy clouds rolling down from the hills behind us. With them came once more the heavy lash of rain.

'What a climate,' shivered Erik. He coughed, drawing his cloak more closely around him. I sensed danger again at that moment, strong and vivid, a picture filling my mind.

Men creeping along the ground towards us under the cover of the fog, their intentions dark and dishonourable. Closing in on us.

'What did you say?' asked Erik, grasping my arm. Shocked from my vision, I focused on his face, blinking.

'People are coming,' I whispered fiercely. 'Be ready with your weapons!'

'I can't hear anything,' Grim objected, but Erik reached for his sword, loosening it in its scabbard. The rain was coming down in bucketfuls, so heavily we could no longer see our ships out in the bay.

Our boat was close, almost within reach, when we heard shouts behind us. All three of us began wading out into the freezing water, but we couldn't go far as the beach shelved away sharply and the waves dragged strongly at us. I cast an anxious glance back over my shoulder and thought I could make out men running down the hill towards us, blurry through the heavy sheets of rain that were falling.

'Hurry!' Erik called to Kai who was rowing. He redoubled his efforts; the boat lifted on an incoming wave and shot towards us. Erik and Grim grabbed it as soon as it came close enough and Erik threw himself over the side, and then reached out a hand to pull me in. Grim pushed us hard away from the beach, jumped in and snatched up the second pair of oars. The mist and rain were so dense now, I could barely make out my companions in the boat, let alone anyone on the shore, but they were closing fast, I could sense them.

'Pull!' shouted Grim over the rush of the waves, calling time to Kai, but a wave pushed us sideways, back onto the beach.

I was breathing quickly with anxiety, feeling the presence of strangers close to us, drawing closer with terrifying speed. They'd been watching us all the time. Why had they waited until now? My heart was hammering in my chest in fear of this shadowy, unseen threat. I couldn't help fearing they were part troll or ogre. We were playing hide-and-seek in the mist with evil spirits.

Suddenly, they were no longer spirits, but men around us in the darkness with clubs and swords in their hands. They were wading out into the water, waist deep, weapons raised. I couldn't see how many there were.

'Row!' I yelled at Grim and Kai.

With a cry of shock, both men threw themselves at their oars and began to pull as though Fenris, the great wolf himself, was after us. But the men were closing in around us. We weren't going to make it.

Realizing this, Grim shipped his oars and started to pull his sword from his scabbard.

'Take the oars,' he cried to me.

I flung myself into his seat, grasping the oars. But I couldn't use them. I didn't know how. Only Kai was rowing and he made little headway into the waves.

Grim swung his sword clumsily, nearly taking my head off. I ducked. I could see he knew nothing of sword fighting. One of the men in the water hit him a blow on his shoulder with a club and it knocked him right off his feet into the bottom of the boat. Erik snatched up Grim's long sword and swept it out in a wide arc towards the enemy. The manoeuvre was blessed with beginner's luck. One opponent fell back with a cry of pain and a splash. His companions rushed to drag him above the waves. In those few vital instants, Kai pulled on his oars and with a few strong strokes, he pulled us beyond their reach.

Grim lay unconscious in the bottom of the boat, but Kai stood and gave a yell of triumph. He stood precariously in the boat shaking his fist into the fog.

'Misbegotten sons of trolls!' he shouted.

I handed my oars to Erik who'd sheathed the sword and slid onto the bench beside me. I turned, shifted out of Erik's way and grasped Kai's sleeve, pulling him down into his seat.

'Don't provoke them!' I urged. 'Help Erik row!'

'We've nothing to fear from those cowards,' Kai scoffed vaingloriously. 'They've lost us now, and they know it.'

I wasn't so sure. My sense of danger was not lessening as we drew away from the beach. It was growing.

They were waiting between us and our ships. All at once, I knew it as sure as if I could see them with my eyes. I felt my mouth drying with sudden fear. I stared into the greyness of mist and pouring rain and thought I saw a movement. A shadow. I opened my mouth to shout a warning, but it was already too late. Two boats collided with us simultaneously, one from each side. All four of us were knocked completely off balance by the collision. In the ensuing chaos, Kai dropped his sword into the sea and Erik lost his oars. All was a blur of shouts and confusion.

Desperate, I drew out my knife. Our boat lurched wildly as someone leapt into it and I slashed wildly at him. The man drew back warily. He was watching me. I could see his eyes gleaming in the darkness. But before I could do anything else, strong arms grasped me from behind, pinioning my arms to my side. The man in front wrenched my knife painfully from my hand.

'Bjorn!' I yelled with all my might. 'Bjorn, beware!'

A rough hand was clamped tightly over my mouth. It seemed unlikely anyone from our still-distant ships would have heard my desperate cry above the pounding of the sea on the rocks and cliffs around us.

Still struggling uselessly, I saw Erik knocked senseless by a blow to his head. Kai fared worse. Slashing wildly with a knife, he caught a huge man a blow on his arm, opening up a long deep cut. Before he could do more, he was caught and pinioned as I was, by two men. They had no need to hurt him. But the man he'd injured came at him out of the fog and ran him through brutally with his sword. There was a hideous slicing, gurgling sound, and Kai collapsed and fell forward into the water with a splash.

It was over.

CHAPTER NINE

The earth was cold and hard, my nose pressed into the dirt. Ropes bit into my wrists and ankles, far too tight to struggle against. The gag in my mouth choked me. I'd lost track of how long I'd lain blindfolded in the darkness. They'd carried me up the hill to the house. That much I knew because I'd recognized the smoke and fish stench. What did they want with me? They must want something or they would have killed me at once. I lay trying to sense something, anything, but my mind wasn't calm enough. I felt only my own emptiness and despair. Fear was crawling into every part of me. I was afraid for myself, but also for Bjorn and the others.

I could hear distant, muffled voices, and then after an eternity, I heard the sound of shouting. My heart bounded with a mixture of hope and fright. Some sort of altercation was going on. The sounds drew closer. I recognized Bjorn's voice. My hope seeped away into the cold earth beneath me. What was to become of us if they'd captured him? I lifted my head painfully off the ground, trying to hear what was being said.

'What have you done with Thora?'

That was Bjorn, loud and clear. And so very close.

I tried to shout but all that came out was a strangled

moan that I could hardly hear myself. I fought my bonds, thrashing my whole body from side to side. I strained at the ropes with all my might, but they were strong and I only succeeded in hurting myself. Wherever I was, I was obviously hidden. I couldn't make my presence known.

'The woman stole from us,' I heard a voice answering Bjorn. 'She took water without payment and stole medicinal plants from our land. She's a thief and subject to our laws.'

The voice was rough and hoarse. It spoke authoritatively. As though its owner were used to giving orders and having them obeyed. I guessed he was head of the household.

'I've brought you a gift in exchange for the drinking water we took, as I always intended to do,' Bjorn replied. His voice sounded reasonable. It was clear he hoped to negotiate.

'A gold bracelet?' I heard the leader's voice say scornfully. 'A paltry trinket. You are a wealthy man—a friend of the king of Norway. You can afford better than that.'

'I'll be happy to give you gifts worthy of your generous hospitality . . . when I have experienced some of it,' said Bjorn. 'Instead of welcoming us, you have hidden away like cowards and spied on us. Instead of offering us food and mead, you begrudge us even the water in your streams. You offer us no shelter from wind or rain, but you sneak up on us in the night, kill our men and kidnap one of our womenfolk. Where is the honour in that, that I should reward you with kingly gifts?'

'How dare you question my honour?' shouted the islander. 'We'll have fair terms. And our terms are that you are free to clear off. And I'll keep the bracelet, as it's all you are offering.'

'And Thora?' demanded Bjorn.

My heart thumped painfully in my chest.

'The woman stays,' growled the leader.

'That's out of the question,' said Bjorn angrily. 'We'll not leave her behind. She's under my protection.'

'She was,' sneered the voice. 'Is she your wife?'

'No,' I heard Bjorn answer. 'She's not, but . . . '

'Is she the wife of anyone on board your ships?'

'No, but . . . '

'Then she stays.'

I heard several people jump to their feet and the scraping of steel that told me a sword had been drawn. I held my breath in terror, dreading to hear the noise of battle joined. There was a confused babble of voices and movement nearby. If I could have screamed out in frustration at my blind, mute, and helpless state, I would have done.

Then to my surprise, I heard Thrang's voice.

'Let's all be reasonable. Chieftain, put up your sword. There must be an agreement we can reach.'

'Get your hands off me, man,' I heard Bjorn hiss. I guessed that it must have been Bjorn that had drawn his sword and Thrang was restraining him. It was violence that could only end in a bloodbath. I was glad Thrang had stopped him. I was surprised to hear Thrang calling Bjorn chieftain though. He must have decided to throw his lot in with us in good earnest.

There was a long stretch of silence, broken only by heavy breathing. I waited.

'What do you want?' Bjorn's voice spoke next. He sounded resigned. 'Money? Livestock? Iron? Though we have little to spare if we are to survive in the new country. And it goes against the grain to bargain with kidnappers.'

I thought the Faeroese leader might be angry at being called a kidnapper. But his voice when he replied was a satisfied sneer:

'You don't understand. She's more valuable to us than anything you have aboard that ship.'

I had guessed correctly then. My heart sank as I realized how unlikely it was they would let me go. They wanted me for my skills as a healer.

'I don't understand,' I heard Bjorn say in mock astonishment. 'Thora is valuable?'

'Don't lie,' said a new voice. 'We know she's a healer. We're very isolated here. We have no one to tend the sick, set bones, or help our women birth.'

'Thora will treat anyone that needs her services while we are here,' said Bjorn. 'She would have done so for the asking. There was no need to attack us. But we won't leave her behind.'

'You have no choice.'

'Thora goes with us,' Bjorn insisted. 'We'll give you a short time to consider this.'

He finished on an implacable note and I heard the sound of departure. I was grateful for his loyalty towards me and for his good sense.

As I lay in a whirlpool of hope and despair, I sensed

movement beside me. Fingers tugged at my blindfold, loosening it. I blinked in the sudden light of a small fish-oil lamp. At first it hurt my eyes, but as they adjusted, I could see the face of the girl I'd seen in the house leaning over me, her aura glowing around her. I shivered.

She was loosening my gag now, with difficulty as it was tied cruelly tight. As she removed it, I coughed. I ran my dry, swollen tongue around my bruised mouth. My teeth seemed undamaged, I was relieved to find.

I was lying on bare earth in a passageway. It must be a secret exit from the house, such as many longhouses had. The doorway within the house was no doubt hidden by a hanging or screen.

I turned my attention to the girl who was sitting on the ground beside me. The lamplight flickered, sending shadows across her delicate, pointed face.

'Are you really worth all this fuss?' she muttered. 'I doubt it.' She stroked my hair back from my face in a gentle gesture, but then twined a strand of it around her finger and tugged it painfully, staring at me all the while. I didn't flinch.

'I suppose you're thirsty,' the girl commented.

I didn't reply, wary of provoking her.

The girl dipped a rag into a goblet of water next to her, and squeezed it over my mouth, as I had done for the foal on the ship. The water ran over my sore lips and down my chin. The next time I managed to catch a little in my mouth. It was deliciously cool and soothing, but it ran down my windpipe, making me cough. At once the girl laid the water aside.

'Please,' I begged hoarsely. 'Let me try again.'

85

But instead of giving me water, she tied the gag back into my mouth, as tight as before. I struggled, but I was at her mercy. She pulled herself to her feet, impeded by her leg. Then, before she left, she bent over me and whispered: 'You'd better hope your chieftain is reasonable and agrees to our terms. Else it might be a very long time before you get a drink.' So saying, she dashed the contents of the goblet in my face, took the lamp and left.

'Did she drink, Ragna?' I heard another woman's voice ask, as she passed into the house.

'She's had all of it,' the girl said.

'Good, because we don't want her harmed,' said the voice.

I lay there in the darkness in despair. The water soaked into my hair and tunic, making me wet and cold, while my thirst continued to burn. I feared the islanders would only give me up in exchange for a very heavy ransom indeed. So heavy that we would be unable to make a decent life in Iceland. I should hope for Bjorn's sake that he would leave me here. I would probably be valued and well treated. As long as I could keep away from that girl. But the thought of staying here and never seeing Bjorn again left me prey to the darkest misery.

I remembered last night on board the ship. I had felt completely safe with Bjorn's arms around me, as though we would always be together. I ached for that feeling again. I must be in love with him, I thought wonderingly. In just three days, I'd fallen in love.

I reminded myself of the vision I'd had of Bjorn and me reaching Iceland together. Surely that couldn't be wrong? But prophecy could be misleading, I knew that. It didn't always give the whole picture.

I tried to lay my fears aside and compose myself to be patient. I breathed steadily to endure the pain of the ropes and the floor digging into me. I needed to trust Bjorn to settle this.

CHAPTER TEN

At some point in the night my ankles were untied and I was half dragged, half carried outside and allowed to relieve myself. I groaned with pain as the blood, allowed to circulate freely for the first time in many hours, pulsed painfully into my feet, causing agonizing pins and needles. I was given a little broth and then tied up and left alone again.

The night lasted a lifetime of pain and anxiety. Why had Bjorn not returned to the longhouse? I hoped over and over again that he'd had the good sense to flee, only to feel despair at the thought that he'd left me. As I lay in the dark and the cold, thinking of him, I admitted to myself how much I loved him. It wasn't just that I had seen him in my future. I also wanted him to be there.

Soon after sun up, I heard a bustle in the longhouse. I could smell food being cooked, cheerful voices and women's laughter. I heard Ragna's metallic voice, but I couldn't make out the words. I was exhausted. I hardly cared any more what happened, just so long as I could be untied.

I thought I heard people leaving. There were fewer voices through the wall. Abruptly, there was someone beside me in the dim light. A man. I could smell him rather than see him. He bent over me and I saw the blade of a knife gleam. I was terrified and tried to cry out, but only a strangled whimper came through the tight gag. The effort almost made me choke. To my relief, the man cut my bonds and stripped the rawhide ropes from my wrists and ankles, making my cuts bleed afresh.

'Get up,' he ordered. I tried to do as he said, but my limbs wouldn't obey me. My arms and legs felt weak and limp. They wouldn't bear my weight. I tried again to push myself on all fours, swayed for a moment, and fell flat on my face.

The man bent over me again and fumbled in the gloom to untie my gag. The cloth had become entangled in my hair and as he pulled the knot loose, I felt some of my hair wrenched away with it. I murmured feebly in protest and pulled out the wad of cloth that had been crammed into my mouth. I coughed and retched.

Impatient with this delay, the man picked me up and carried me through the hidden doorway into the main house. The firelight seemed intolerably bright after the darkness of the passageway. I winced and covered my eyes. He dumped me on a low bench beside the fire, where I managed to stay upright, swaying dangerously. I concentrated hard on not falling into the fire. I thought, with a strange detachment, that that wouldn't be a good place to fall. My eyes weren't working properly and everything in the house was a blur, though I could sense other people around me.

I felt a gentle hand on my shoulder and looked round. The hand held me steady as I lurched sideways. A kindly face was looking down at me.

'They've been too rough with you, haven't they?' she said softly. 'I begged to be allowed to tend you. But Thorkel wouldn't allow it. He asked Ragna to see to you and she . . . '

'Ragna?' I whispered through bruised and swollen lips. Even saying that one word made me cough again. The woman brought me a goblet of whey. I sipped a tiny amount, relishing the sharp, sour taste and the cool wetness in my mouth and throat.

The woman continued talking and her voice was soothing. 'Ragna is Thorkel's daughter,' she told me. 'Kindness isn't in her nature. She's the one who . . . well, you'll see soon enough.'

Her words washed over me as I continued to sip the whey. I had to concentrate on lifting the drink to my lips without spilling any. My hands were clumsy and shaking. I concentrated on each small, painful swallow and the coolness of the liquid in my throat. When it was empty, I tried to set down the empty goblet on the floor. To my shame, it slipped from my grasp, clattering on the stones that surrounded the fire. Wordlessly, the woman picked it up, and then started wiping my face and hands with a wet cloth. She shook her head when she saw the deep cuts on my wrists, but she said nothing.

Lying there on the earth, I'd thought I could bear anything if only I could be untied. But now that I was free, I was still in pain. I was also frustrated by my weak helplessness. More than anything else, I longed to know that Bjorn was safe.

The woman took a comb from her apron and stood behind me to comb my hair. It was sticky with salt and the comb snagged on the many tangles, teasing them out. How long was it since I'd washed? I tried to count the days and gave up. I must be dirty and smelly and I felt embarrassed.

'What's . . . your name?' I managed to ask croakily.

'I'm Gudrun, sister-in-law to Thorkel,' she said. 'I live here with my husband.'

There was a silence. I had to ask: 'Bjorn . . . ' I began. 'Has he . . . gone?'

'Gone? Well, not far. He'll be back soon enough. You're free now. At least you will be soon. I should have told you that before.'

I felt my throat closing painfully with terror. Where was Bjorn and what had he agreed to? Please let them have reached some fair compromise, I prayed. I begged each of the gods in turn. I begged the mighty Thor. I supplicated Odin the all-seeing and all-wise. I prayed to the gentle Frigg and to the powerful Freya. To my own goddess, Eir. All the time, the comb went swish, swish through my hair.

'Are you all right, Thora?' asked Gudrun, clearly concerned about my long silence. I nodded weakly.

'You must need food,' Gudrun said. She went to a pot on one end of the longfire and stirred it. Then, fetching a wooden bowl, she ladled some broth into it and put it into my hands with a sea shell for a spoon. 'Eat,' she said. 'It'll give you strength.'

Despite being ravenously hungry, I found it hard to swallow the lamb broth. It seemed wrong to be eating when Bjorn might be in danger. I ought to be able to sense it if he was, but my powers seemed to have left me. I didn't even have the strength to stand up. I was no use to him so weak and helpless, so I forced myself to eat. Mouthful by mouthful. My movements became firmer and my sight clearer. I became more aware of the house around me. There was a young woman nursing a baby on one of the sleeping platforms. A whole lamb was roasting over the fire. The man who had carried me into the house was whittling wood. There was no one else. A large loom stood near to the fire on my left with an unfinished cloth upon it. I noticed the weaving was the most beautiful workmanship I'd ever seen.

As my energy returned I became more optimistic. Bjorn hadn't abandoned me. He must have found some way of appeasing the islanders.

The sound of people approaching the house reached me. There was talking and laughter. I struggled to my feet. My treacherous legs threatened to give way beneath me, but Gudrun hurried to my side and supported me. With her help, I wobbled to the doorway. I needed to see that Bjorn was safe and well.

It was a cheerful group of islanders, with some of our people among them. I saw Grim, his arm bandaged, and Thrang. They were scowling. Where was Bjorn? As the crowd reached the door, it parted, revealing him. He looked grey and strained, deep shadows etched under his eyes. Next to him in a bright red tunic, her hand tucked through his arm, was the girl I had met in the house that first day. The same girl that had refused me water when I was tied up. She had flowers in her hair and a flush of delight on her face.

'Thora,' said Bjorn, his voice as strained as his face. 'Thank the gods you're safe.'

He made to move towards me, but Ragna tightened her grip on his arm, keeping him firmly by her side. I stared at him, and then at the girl. She smiled at me, a look of triumph lighting up her features.

'Introduce me then,' she said sharply, pinching Bjorn's arm.

'Thora . . . This is Ragna. This is . . . my . . . ' He stopped, unable to continue.

'His wife,' Ragna said smugly.

CHAPTER ELEVEN

Sigrun, my teacher, had always trained me to conceal my emotions. If you show fear, shock, or horror at a patient's injury or condition, she had said, you will agitate them. And your job, Thora, is to reassure them. If they are soothed and convinced of your competence, the task of healing them will be easier. And the worse their condition, the more important that is.

I was glad of my long training as I stood trying to take in that Bjorn was married. Inside me there was a mix of fury and despair. I wanted to break down and weep. But Thora the healer merely inclined her head and said:

'I'm pleased to meet you again, Ragna.'

I swayed a little, my legs threatening to give way and leaned heavily on Gudrun's shoulder, but my face was impassive. I met Bjorn's eyes. He was scanning my face for some reaction, some sign. I gave him none. It went not only against my training to betray myself, but against my pride too. I wouldn't show either Bjorn or the islanders how distressed I was.

The islanders provided a wedding feast which they seemed to enjoy greatly, but we had to sit through in silent endurance. The roasted lamb was divided up and passed around, and mead flowed freely. I touched none of it. I noticed that Bjorn barely ate anything either. He raised his glass in a toast whenever invited, but remained quite sober. Ragna sat beside him throughout, watching everyone with suspicious, hostile eyes. She looked like an angry wolf guarding her prey from anyone who might wish to share it. I couldn't see any joy in her aura, only the murky colours of greed and triumph.

Thrang came to sit beside me, a goblet in one hand. He also seemed sober, unlike our hosts.

'They gave him no choice, you know,' he said brusquely, his eyes on the newly-wed couple. 'They drove a hard bargain for your release.'

I felt my stomach turn over at his words with a mixture of guilt and anger.

'Did they hurt you?' he asked gruffly.

'Nothing serious,' I said, tugging my sleeves down to hide my sore wrists, afraid he would be angry if he saw them.

'Bjorn has been worried sick about you. We all have.' Thrang didn't look at me as he spoke, but I could feel his sympathy and I was surprised.

'I wouldn't have thought you'd have cared much what happened to us,' I said. My voice was still rather hoarse, but that went unnoticed in all the noise. 'We're usurpers. You might have felt thieves deserved this fate.'

Thrang didn't answer for a moment. He sat staring into his goblet, swirling the amber liquid around in it. So much of his face was covered with beard that I couldn't read his expression.

'Perhaps you have both earned my respect,' he said at last. Then abruptly he changed the subject. 'We brought your chest of remedies,' he told me. 'You might not know, but part of the bargain for your release was that you treat the people here before we leave. I thought the sooner you do it, the sooner we can get away.'

'Thank you,' I whispered miserably. 'But whenever we go, we'll have to take her with us, won't we?' I looked at Ragna as I spoke, and then my eyes were drawn to Bjorn. He sat staring straight ahead, oblivious to the riotous talk and laughter around him. There was a deep furrow in his brow. As I watched him, he looked across and saw me. There was such an expression of hurt and pain in his eyes that my heart went out to him all over again. I made myself look away. I longed to go to him. To comfort him as I might have done, just yesterday, if I had seen him look so sad. But it was no longer possible. It never would be possible. We were for ever divided. Forced apart, before we had been together. I felt tears gather under my eyelids and forced them back.

I felt Thrang take my hand and squeeze it and jumped with shock. Hurriedly, I drew it away, before realizing that he was only trying to show he was sorry for me. It seemed so unlike the great burly sailor to do such a thing.

'They killed Kai, didn't they?' I said miserably.

'Aye,' growled Thrang. 'I owe them a grudge for that too. They've robbed us and foisted that woman onto us into the bargain.'

'How much have we lost?' I asked. Again, I felt a sick sense of guilt.

Thrang answered in a low voice that was all but drowned out by the talk that surrounded us.

'We had to trade our second ship and some of the food supplies.'

'But that was to be your ship,' I said, shocked.

Thrang shrugged. 'I agreed to it. There are other ways I can be paid. And Bjorn refused to let them have you or any of the slaves or livestock. He said everyone was under his protection, but . . .'

'But what?' I prompted as he fell silent.

'I'm not a judge of such things, but I would say there was not enough food left to see us through the winter.' Thrang's brow creased with worry as he spoke. 'It's late in the season. Nothing can be grown until next year now.'

'Bjorn had promised them freedom. He couldn't go back on his word,' I said loyally, though I guessed what Thrang would say. I wasn't going to admit that Bjorn had been mistaken.

'Better to be a well-fed slave than a dead freed-man,' he growled. 'Starvation isn't pretty.'

'The bargain wasn't worth it,' I said bitterly. 'I'm not worth it. He should have left me. He should have fled with his ships and stores intact.'

'Not so,' said Thrang at once, surprising me again.

'Does she bring no dowry?' I asked, nodding at Ragna. 'Or is the bargain all one sided?'

'She brings her loom and half a dozen lambs,' Thrang replied. 'Apparently she's gifted at weaving.'

'That's something, I suppose.' I attempted to be generous, though it almost choked me. 'But if she is a skilled weaver, why do they want to give her away? Such women are highly valued.' I looked at Ragna, sitting there beside Bjorn. Pure jealousy pierced me so sharply that for a moment I could scarcely breathe. She had taken him from me. I could tell she knew it and it gave her pleasure.

Thrang was watching me and spoke again, lowering his voice further, till he was whispering in my ear, his beard tickling me. 'I have a feeling there is something not right about her,' said Thrang, shaking his head dubiously. I glanced at him, surprised again at his perceptiveness. 'She's a good-looking woman,' Thrang explained. 'But I wouldn't marry her.'

'Then why did Bjorn . . . ?'

Thrang shook his head. A moment later he got up and moved away. I sat still, a sense of loss swirling in me. I took little notice of what was happening around me, until I heard shouts and realized people were getting up and moving about.

'The bridal couple must be bedded!' shouted the chieftain. Someone picked up Ragna, another man took Bjorn by the arm. Before she was carried off, Ragna sought me out with her pale eyes and smiled at me. It was a spiteful look. It proclaimed victory. I turned my face away and didn't watch as the two of them were led off to a private room at one end of the house. I could hear laughter and ribald humour. But it wasn't funny. Not to me. The man I loved was going to his marriage bed with another woman.

My jealousy overcame me, and once more I couldn't breathe. I pushed myself painfully to my feet and stumbled out of the house, desperate to get out of the smoke and the noise. I wanted to get away from the house, but was too weak to walk far. I sought shelter under an overhanging eave and crouched down, wrapping myself up tightly in my cloak, watching the rain beyond the roof pour down in torrents.

I sat and looked out on the night as the house settled down to sleep behind me. It was heavily overcast. The long, light nights of summer were definitely failing now. I could only just make out the outline of the ships in the bay below, and sheep grazing on the hillside. Their teeth made sharp tearing sounds as they pulled up the grass. Dully, I wondered where they had been when we arrived. The fishing boats too, lay upturned on the beach below. Where had they been concealed? I found I didn't care very much. We'd been tricked. Self pity overwhelmed me. Despite my determination not to give way, tears spilled from my eyes, trickling down my face.

I missed my family. I longed for my mother's embrace. If only I could hear my father speak to me. He was always good with words of comfort. I missed my brother too and ached with the longing to hug him, even though he never liked it.

For the first time, I truly wished I'd never left them to follow Bjorn. I wished I'd risked the oncoming army, tried to dodge through their lines in order to stay with those who loved me. As things stood now, I would have to watch Bjorn sharing his life with another woman, while I was shut out, pushed aside.

This thought brought anger and my tears ceased. Anger was easier than grief. It made me strong. I thought of Bjorn and Ragna being together right now. I imagined them happy, loving one another, and my fury burned so hotly that I clenched my fists into my palms, my nails cutting into my skin. I wanted to beat Bjorn for agreeing to this.

It was in this mood, that I was disturbed by a noise nearby. Further along the wall, a small shutter was pushed open. A shadow emerged, climbing out through the opening, and fell onto the wet grass. I could hear a woman's angry voice calling from inside the house. Ragna's voice, surely? It was unpleasant to be disturbed, and I half turned my back on whoever it was. But then a familiar voice spoke to me.

'Thora? Is that you? Are you all right?'

I looked up to see Bjorn crouching beside me.

If he'd come sooner, I'd have flung myself into his arms and wept. I would have turned to him for solace. But now all I could feel was my fury and my disappointment. I needed to vent it on someone.

'What are you doing here?' I demanded angrily. 'Have you tired of your bride so soon?' I could hear the bitterness in my voice. Bjorn could too. He recoiled from me in shock.

'Thora, how can you say such a thing?' he gasped. Then he lowered his voice, no doubt worried that his bride might hear him: 'I did this for you!'

'Well, I wish you hadn't,' I retorted vehemently.

Bjorn flinched as though I had struck him. 'You can't mean that,' he said hoarsely.

I felt a small amount of my anger against him drain away. He sounded hurt and vulnerable. 'I married so that you could be free,' he said, his voice low, but urgent. 'To honour the promise I made to your father. Do you really believe I wanted to marry anyone but . . . that I could . . . ' He stopped, unable to continue.

I saw a glimpse of how Bjorn must feel. He'd had a

bride forced on him against his wishes, and he was bound to her. I felt guilty as I remembered that promise he'd made to my father on the clifftop. He'd sworn to protect me, and now he had done so, at great personal cost. He must feel as bleak as I did. I hid my face in my hands as tears of pain and disappointment forced themselves into my eyes.

'Thora, I'm so sorry,' whispered Bjorn. He drew me into his arms and held me close, and I could feel him trembling. For a moment we crouched together in the wet grass, finding comfort in the closeness. Bjorn pulled me closer, and softly kissed my cheek. I felt a yearning for him that made me forget everything else for a few heady moments. Another kiss, and then, as I didn't object, he touched his lips to mine. I was reaching up to kiss him back when the full force of our situation hit me again and I pulled back. This was wrong. Bjorn had married another woman this afternoon. We couldn't be together. Abruptly I pushed him away. We sat staring at one another in the darkness.

'Thora . . . ' Bjorn began but he didn't seem to know how to continue.

I struggled to regain control over myself, to use my training to appear indifferent. On impulse, I thought it might be easiest for both of us if Bjorn thought I didn't care for him. I had to send him away.

'Don't touch me,' I told him fiercely, searching in my mind for something final or even hurtful that I could say. I found it: 'I don't kiss slaves,' I told him.

I struggled to my feet, pushing him away from me. I didn't look at him as I ran out into the rain. I didn't want to see the hurt in his eyes or his aura. My body was stiff and sore, but I forced it to run on down the steep slope to the beach. I glanced back and saw that Bjorn wasn't following me. He stood where I had left him, close to the house, watching me.

'Go back to your bride!' I shouted at him.

Then I twisted my ankle on a stone and fell. I gasped with pain, unable to move. I just lay there in the cold, feeling the rain drench me, running down my face and plastering my hair to my head.

I don't know how long I lay there. Perhaps only a few moments. Strong arms scooped me up and lifted me. I thought it was Bjorn and clung to him as he carried me back up the steep slope as though I weighed no more than a baby lamb.

'I'm so sorry,' I whispered.

'I know you are,' he replied, and I realized it wasn't Bjorn I had my arms around after all. It was Thrang. The discovery made me weep, my sobs racking my chest and stealing my breath.

CHAPTER TWELVE

Hay Time
Heyannir

I'd hoped to leave the island behind us immediately, but, in the event, it was hay time before we were once more aboard ship and rowing out of the bay.

For my part, the weeks had been spent tending to every old man with arthritis and old woman with the toothache from miles around. Word spread fast that there was a healer at Thorkel's longhouse, and I had to be sparing with my stock of medicines. I also spent long days out hunting for the plants that I needed, scouring the unfamiliar terrain and searching the sparse fauna for something more than grass. The islanders no longer minded me taking their plants.

One of my first patients was Ragna's father, Thorkel, himself. He had an ugly gash on his arm that looked recent, but was already weeping pus from an infection. As soon as I saw it, I knew he was the man who had slain Kai that night out in the bay. I owed him two great grudges. I cured him, but laced the salve I gave him with pepper and told him the stinging he felt was a sign of healing. I didn't feel bad, not after what he'd done. He deserved it.

I saw little of Bjorn. He spent most of his time aboard

the ship, supposedly supervising construction of a shelter on deck for Ragna. Her father insisted she was not exposed to the elements during the voyage.

'The old fool,' Thrang muttered to me on one of his brief spells on land. 'He thinks he's keeping her safe. But while we tarry here, the nights darken and the autumn storms approach.'

I suspected, or perhaps hoped, that Bjorn kept to the ship to escape the company of his bride. And, though I admitted it only reluctantly to myself, I knew he wished to avoid me too. We hadn't spoken to each other since the night of the wedding. I longed to apologize, to explain why I had said what I did, but I knew I must not. It was better like this. In any case, I had no chance to speak to Bjorn at all. If he came to the house, Ragna's watchful eye was always on him.

I had to listen to many conversations among my companions about the bargain Bjorn had made. All were unhappy about the loss of ship and goods, but it seemed only Thrang and I minded the addition of Ragna. I heard her spoken of mostly as a 'pretty little thing' or 'harmless enough'. Only I could see her aura and I feared the worst.

When at last we sailed, the deck was fuller than on the previous leg of the voyage. We now had the people and equipment from both ships loaded onto one, and enough hands to man most of the oars. We were twenty people on board, twelve men and eight women. We'd lost Kai, and gained Ragna. She had her own little cabin, built aft on the deck, taking up valuable space. There was just enough space in there for a bed, so that she could sleep sheltered from the elements.

The wind had an autumnal chill in it as well as misty rain as the sail was hoisted and we sailed out onto the open sea. I was so happy to be afloat again that I went forward to my old post at the prow of the ship. There I slung an arm around the sea-serpent figurehead and gazed out on the swell, swaying with the movement of the ship beneath my feet. Unlike last time, Bjorn never joined me in the prow. He stayed aft at the tiller or helped Thrang and Stein with the sail. He slept aft too.

'He didn't join Ragna in her shelter, you know,' Asgerd told me after the first night at sea, a wicked grin on her face. 'He just wrapped himself in his cloak and slept on the open deck like the rest of us.'

I felt a certain measure of satisfaction, but I knew it was wrong of me.

'He doesn't wish to set himself apart,' I said mildly. Then I changed the subject. 'There are new people from the other ship I don't know. What are the women called?'

'The dark haired woman is Enys. She's Brian's wife. They're originally from Ireland, I believe. The young, pretty girl is Asdis. And the dark-skinned woman is Hild. Not her real name. Svanson renamed her after he bought her. And you know my daughter Astrid, of course. Ten winters and my greatest pride,' smiled Asgerd fondly. She lowered her voice. 'I can't tell you how I feared for her growing up a slave in Svanson's household. I know why he brought her on this voyage, though he brought no other children. She's going to be a beauty in a few years. Her situation is quite different now. Far safer.'

'Yes indeed,' I agreed with a shiver, thinking of Svanson and his cruelty. 'And how's Erik?'

'Come and ask him.' Asgerd led me to her husband, who sat wrapped in furs leaning against the side of the ship.

'How's the cough?' I asked. I had given him the herbs I'd gathered for him days ago.

'Better, I think. It hurts less.'

'It's done you good.' I nodded my satisfaction, checking his brow for fever and his pulse on his wrist. Both seemed normal, Eir be praised. 'I think you'll do well now.'

'Thank you, Thora,' said Erik. 'I'm sorry it all caused so much trouble.'

I laid a comforting hand on his shoulder. 'I expect they were lying in wait for us anyway,' I said.

The swell increased as we left the islands behind us. It stopped raining but the sky was low over our heads, a lowering ceiling of iron grey. Occasionally white birds flew past us, heading back the way we had come.

'What are they called, Thrang?' I asked him as he paused by me.

'Fulmars,' Thrang told me. 'See the way they just skim the surface? That's how you know what they are from a distance. They're flying south. We're late to be going north.' He looked anxiously at the sky as he spoke.

The mild, southerly wind blew more strongly as the day wore on. I resumed my post at the prow, relishing the pitching of the ship. More and more of our people were succumbing to sea sickness behind me. As before, it didn't affect me. The only feeling I experienced was exhilaration. The lift of the ship beneath my feet was pure pleasure to me; as we surged up the side of the wave and then plunged wildly down the far side, I laughed into the wind, urging it to keep blowing. It suited my mood to be pitted against the elements.

I was interrupted by Bjorn, who approached me for the first time.

'Thora,' he called. It was hard to hear him above the wind, the flapping of the sail and the slapping of the swell on the underside of the boat. 'Will you come and see Ragna? She's sick.'

My insides lurched more than with the greatest wave. Was I now to go and nurse Ragna? If I were to show her the same tenderness she showed me, she would be well served.

'I have no cure for sea sickness,' I told him. 'Nothing I've tried works.'

'Come and see her anyway,' Bjorn insisted.

I didn't want to seem resentful, so I went with him to the shelter where Ragna lay wrapped in furs and blankets. I felt her pulse and her brow which was clammy with sweat. She was groaning, clutching her stomach, and looked as white as a newborn lamb.

'I'm dying,' she moaned.

'Unlikely,' I said briefly, glad that Bjorn had left us alone. 'You're seasick. You need to come out into the fresh air and look at the sea. And you need to eat and drink.'

She groaned loudly and then glared at me. 'You're brutal. That would kill me.'

'Nonsense,' I said bracingly. 'I don't get seasick myself, but Thrang told me these things and he's an experienced sailor.'

'You must have medicines,' she pleaded.

'I've tried them. They make no difference. I'd never been to sea before, so I never learned any cures.'

'You're lying,' she hissed. 'Send Bjorn to me.'

I got up without a word and left her. Bjorn was adjusting the sail with Stein, and wasn't pleased to be sent back in to his wife. He re-emerged in a few minutes looking even more annoyed.

'How could you, Thora?' he asked, accusingly.

'What do you mean?' I asked bewildered.

'To tell her it served her right. And that you hoped she died of it!' Bjorn looked at me and the deep disappointment in his eyes hurt me.

'I said no such thing!' I exclaimed.

'At least go and give her something to help her sleep,' Bjorn commanded and turned away from me.

I felt choked up and tricked. How could Ragna tell such lies? And even worse, how could Bjorn believe them? I returned to her cabin and without saying a word, I measured out some valerian to aid sleep.

'That'll teach you to withhold medicines from me,' sneered Ragna.

I didn't reply and left her.

An hour later, I saw Ragna leaning over the side being vilely sick. I loathed her, but my training won and I went to help. I held her fair hair back from her face as she vomited and then passed her a wetted rag to clean her face with once it was over. Instead of thanking me, she pushed me away.

'I should've known you'd give me something to make me worse,' she hissed weakly.

I recoiled and signalled to Grim to carry her back inside. As I returned to the prow, my usually confident sea legs felt shaky and faltering. The force of the wind around me calmed me, but I was deeply disturbed. It was going to be difficult to live with someone who disliked me so much. And who didn't hesitate to misunderstand me and lie. I felt dread sweep over me and hoped I wasn't sensing the future.

Three days into the voyage, I joined Thrang at the tiller. I sat beside him on an upturned barrel and watched him as he steered. His eyes darted out to sea, then ahead of the ship and then at some sea birds that were passing.

'Not fulmars?' I guessed, seeing that they flew high above the water. Thrang shook his head.

'Kittiwakes,' he said. 'Also flying south for the winter.'

I shivered a little. 'How long till we reach Iceland?' I asked him.

He shook his head again. 'Can't say.'

'Will you hazard a guess?'

Thrang eyed the sun, obscured behind thin cloud, and looked around us again, taking his time. He was a silent man, little given to speech. And he liked to think before he replied. 'We're on course,' was all he said.

'I could swear it's getting colder,' I remarked. 'Is that because we're heading further north?'

Thrang shrugged. I thought he wasn't going to say any more and was about to head back to the prow when he spoke again.

'The ice begins just north of Iceland. Miles and miles of it. As far as you can see. Some say that's where the gods live. Fighting giants and stomping about and whatever else they get up to.' It was a long speech for Thrang.

'Is Iceland as cold as its name suggests?'

'No. It's no colder than much of Norway,' he grunted. Looping a line around the tiller, he moved away to coil some rope. I stared out across the ship towards the north, willing land to appear on the horizon. This absorbed me so completely that it was a few moments before I noticed that someone else had taken the tiller. It was Bjorn and he wasn't looking at me. I got up to go, but he stopped me.

'Stay. I need to speak with you.'

I sat back down and waited. Bjorn appeared as intent on the horizon as I had been a few moments before.

'Why did you give Ragna medicine that made her ill? None of this is her fault, Thora. You shouldn't punish her.'

I took a deep breath and let it out very slowly before I replied. 'I gave her valerian, as you requested. I don't think it was that which made her sick.'

'I don't know if I can trust you, Thora. Is it true that you put pepper in her father's wound? Ragna says you did.'

I was lost for words. How could Ragna possibly know that?

'You don't deny it,' said Bjorn sadly.

I realized that this one act made me look untrustworthy in his eyes. It gave Ragna the semblance of truth and made me the devious one. I felt a surge of bitterness.

'I admit it,' I said at last. 'He deserved it. He slew Kai and kidnapped me. And I did heal him at the same time.'

'Surely a healer shouldn't misuse her skills when people trust her?' asked Bjorn.

He didn't sound angry. I almost wished he was. His tone of despondence, of disappointment, was more than I could bear.

'No, of course not,' I agreed at last, close to tears. 'It was an extreme situation.'

'Thora, I hope we won't have any more incidents of the kind,' said Bjorn. He spoke gently but his words cut into me. 'You'll treat Ragna with respect as befits my wife.'

I couldn't believe I was hearing this. My heart twisted inside me. I had to get up and go.

I found Asgerd halfway along the deck, and she made a space for me to sit beside her. She was out of sight of Bjorn, so I sank down gratefully beside her.

'What's wrong?' she asked.

'Ragna is setting Bjorn against me. He thinks me vengeful and vindictive,' I said. 'And there's nothing I can say or do to convince him I'm not.'

Asgerd put her arm around me. 'He'll find out the truth in time,' she whispered comfortingly. 'Just make sure you don't give her any cause to carry tales with any truth in them. If she's lying and she keeps doing it, sooner or later she'll get caught out.'

'That's good advice,' I said, trying to compose myself.

'Yes, but easier said than done,' confessed Asgerd. 'I'm beginning to get the measure of her and she's not the nice, innocent girl we all thought her at first. She flatters the men, so they'll take longer to discover what she's really like. Life is not going to be nearly as much fun with her as mistress of the house. Every person aboard this ship would have preferred you. And that includes Bjorn, so don't be too hard on him. He's as bitter and disappointed as you are, make no doubt about it.'

'Do you think so?' I asked torn between hope and deep sadness. 'I didn't think he seemed to mind.'

'He's hiding it,' said Asgerd.

CHAPTER THIRTEEN

I awoke three mornings later to brilliant sunshine. It bathed me where I lay beside Asgerd and warmed me through after the chill of the night hours. I stretched sleepily, aware I'd slept late if the sun was already so warm. But my sleepiness was quickly dispelled by the sound of excited voices around me. I sat up, eager to know what was going on.

The sky was a clear, glorious blue with not so much as a wisp of cloud in it. I could see Thrang seated at the tiller, and the sail was billowing in a steady breeze. Then I turned my head to the prow and froze, hardly able to believe what I was seeing.

Sand-coloured cliffs reared up out of the blue-green sea ahead of us. Behind them were dark mountains, their tops sparkling with snow. I leapt to my feet so suddenly that I startled the foals in their pen beside me, making them shy with fright.

'Sorry, Aki,' I said, stooping briefly to soothe my favourite foal. He nickered and lipped my hand, but I was gazing at the land again. The morning was clear and devoid of even the faintest trace of fog or haze, so that the landscape looked bold and bright. It was beautiful. I gazed and gazed at it. Then, almost unconsciously, I found myself making my way to the prow to be closer to the view. Several slaves were already standing gazing their first on Iceland, but they made way for me to take a turn. All of them were smiling and joyful. The dangers of the open sea were behind us now. I found myself standing beside Bjorn, and he too was smiling at the sight of the new land.

'We've made it,' he said softly to me. 'It isn't how we hoped it would be, Thora,' he said in a low voice after a few moments' silence. 'But we're here.'

I nodded, silently. For a moment it seemed there was peace between us again. And my mind was full of how it might have been, had we missed the Faeroe Islands. If we'd come straight to Iceland, we would be looking our first on these shores with the hope of love and happiness together. As it was, I feared the future, and that fear dimmed even the thrill of seeing this new land. I wondered if Bjorn was thinking the same.

We sailed closer and closer to the cliffs. Everyone on board the ship was pointing and talking excitedly. Or, like me, they were simply drinking it all in in silence.

'There are fjords here,' said Bjorn at last in a stronger voice. 'Each one a potential home for us.'

Thrang joined us, leaving Stein at the tiller. 'Do you want to make land here?' he asked.

'For water perhaps,' replied Bjorn. 'But I don't wish to settle in the south-east of the island. If it's the first place we come to, it will be the first port of call for others too. Too many settlers from Norway.'

We both knew what he meant. He wasn't concerned about the land becoming crowded. People might come who had known the real Bjorn Svanson. We had to find a more out-of-the-way place.

'Find us a likely stop over, Thrang,' Bjorn requested, and Thrang returned to the tiller, scanning the shore line as he went. It was impossible to tell from here, I thought, which of these openings were safe to sail into and where there would be access to land. Perhaps there would be steep cliffs right the way in.

Thrang selected the fjord with the widest opening and turned the ship into it. As we sailed between the high cliffs, it felt like a gateway to another world. The ship was dwarfed by the scale of the mountains around us.

We lost the wind. Thrang called for the sail to be lowered and the slaves hurried to the oars. We glided through water that was still and clear. At first all was barren and inhospitable, but quickly we could see pockets of fertile land running along the coast. I spotted sheep grazing and caught my breath.

'Settlers,' I said to Bjorn who was still beside me.

He nodded. 'Thrang says we must risk it,' he said. 'This looks the safest way in.'

I shivered at the thought of meeting more strangers. Would they be hostile like Ragna's family? Bjorn seemed to read my thoughts.

'We were unlucky before,' he said.

Nonetheless, I was anxious as we sailed further and further in. The fjord seemed endless. The strip of land that could be farmed between the shore and the cliffs was narrow, but as we rounded a corner, we could see green slopes at the head of the fjord. There was also a longhouse and people standing watching our approach.

They're probably wondering whether we're friendly too, I reassured myself. I tried to sense their feelings towards us, but could feel nothing definite. As we came closer however, I could see children running along the edge of the water, waving excitedly at our ship. I was reassured. We would be safe here.

We sailed the ship close in to the shore, close enough that a gangplank could be laid. Our people were desperate for shore leave. All of us longed to escape the cramped conditions on board and to set foot on solid earth once more. Some had not been ashore since we left Norway.

The inhabitants of the farmhouse came down to greet us. They embraced Bjorn, and Ragna too, who had emerged shakily from her cabin, and was hanging on her husband's arm. They were invited to stay overnight and to bring some of their people. The Icelanders promised a feast. In return, Bjorn made them a gift of a barrel of mead from the ship.

With their permission I ordered the refilling of our water barrels which were low once more. Svanson must have been an inexperienced seafarer, for he hadn't supplied his ship with sufficient barrels for such a long voyage.

It was as I was directing the men where to take the barrels that I realized I'd committed a grave error. Ragna was glaring at me with unconcealed hatred in her eyes. I had unconsciously taken command and it was her place to give orders.

'I'm sorry, Ragna,' I said to her at once. 'I only thought to spare you the task.' I left her to take over, busying myself instead with tying a rein to Aki's halter and leading him on shore. He hadn't suffered so badly from seasickness in the second leg of the voyage, but he was pitifully thin. Aki trembled with excitement to be on land once more, dropping his head to crop the late summer grass, starting at every sound. I took the dogs ashore with us too, so that they could enjoy a good run. Bjorn had followed my advice and we had taken it in turns to feed them between us, winning their loyalty gradually.

My eyes darted here and there as we walked, searching out the different plants. I noted what was present and what was not, though it was hard to tell when sheep and cattle had cropped the pasture short. I picked nothing, feeling it would be prudent, this time, to keep my skills to myself.

When we returned to the ship, it was to hear that Bjorn had gone ahead to the longhouse and Ragna had decided who was to join the feast and who was to remain on board overnight. It was no surprise to me to learn I was to stay behind. I bit my lip and said nothing. I felt bitter. I should have been at Bjorn's side, the guest of honour, and instead I was treated like a lesser slave.

While the favoured group went up to the house, I helped mucking out the animals and sluicing down the ship. It needed it sorely. It was an unpleasant task, but satisfying once it was done. In Ragna's absence I handed out food and a ration of ale to those left on board the ship. The sun disappeared behind the high mountains early and the cold rolled down from the snow-capped peaks. I wrapped myself in my cloak and lay down to sleep, trying not to listen to the sounds of boisterous merriment drifting from the longhouse. It was hard to be displaced. I wondered that Bjorn hadn't noticed my absence and objected. In the short time since he'd been married, we had already moved far apart. I'd hurt him, I knew, so I only had myself to blame. The thought was no comfort at all.

Erik returned to the ship. 'Thora?' he called.

I sat up, reluctantly. 'I'm here,' I told him.

'Bjorn sent me,' he explained. 'He wants you to join us. It was an oversight, leaving you behind.'

As before, Bjorn's kindness made me want to cry. My throat was hot and tight with unshed tears and I had to fight them before I could reply calmly.

'Please thank him from me,' I said. 'But I'm content to remain here.'

Erik opened his mouth to argue with me, but I waved him away. He looked concerned, but didn't press me. Instead, he turned and left, walking slowly back to the longhouse. The sight of him leaving was completely unsettling. I turned to stroke Aki and the other foals in order to hide my emotion from the slaves. A few moments ago I had longed to be in the house. I still wanted to be there. But I didn't want to be invited as an afterthought. As though I were so insignificant that I had been forgotten at first. Besides, to go now would be to admit that I minded being left behind. I stroked Aki's velvety nose and scratched him between his ears. He nudged me happily, lowering his head to encourage me to continue.

'They can keep their stupid feast,' I told the foal. 'You're better company than any of them.' It wasn't true and I knew it really. They would be telling stories around the fire, talking of the land we'd just arrived in. I longed to hear it all. I was miserable and it was a long time before I fell asleep.

Asgerd was reproachful when she returned the next morning.

'Why didn't you come last night when you were asked?' she said.

I didn't meet her eyes. 'I was happy enough here,' I lied. 'And anyway, Ragna told me to stay behind.'

'Bjorn ordered otherwise. Ragna's just jealous,' said Asgerd.

'Jealous?' I asked incredulously. 'Why would she be?'

'Use your sense, Thora. You're young, beautiful, and your friendship with Bjorn is obvious.'

'She has married Bjorn,' I said bitterly.

Asgerd snorted impatiently. 'She has him in name. But she knows he doesn't want her. He hasn't lain with her one single night, and everyone knows it. Think what that must be like for her.'

I thought about it. I knew that Bjorn avoided Ragna when he could. He was courteous to her, but never sought her company. I'd noted that he slept on deck throughout the voyage and never in her cabin. It must be humiliating for her to have everyone watching this. But my happiness wasn't restored by knowing that she was unhappy too.

'Still,' I told Asgerd. 'He is utterly denied to me. For ever.'

Asgerd took my hand in her own work-roughened hand. 'For ever is a very long time,' she said softly.

My eyes strayed to where Bjorn was helping Ragna back on deck. Another barb of jealousy jabbed at my already troubled heart. Asgerd squeezed my hand. 'It's better not to look,' she advised me.

Obediently, I turned my face away. It was good advice, but I doubted I could stick to it.

CHAPTER FOURTEEN

We remained three days in the east fjords. Our animals were picketed to graze and recover from the journey. We all bathed and washed our hair in the freezing water of the streams, drying ourselves afterwards in the warm, late summer sunshine. Our people enjoyed shore leave and feasting with the household. I was excluded by Ragna and Bjorn didn't countermand her again. Neither did he come anywhere near me. He busied himself preparing the ship for the next stage of the voyage and talking with the settlers.

I kept myself to myself, tending the animals, especially Aki, and roaming the area discreetly looking for plants. There were seeds to collect. I couldn't wander far, however, as I soon discovered that this settlement was completely ringed by high mountains. A boy tending the cattle told me there was a high pass behind the fjord but it was only passable in good weather in summer. It was a stiff climb and took a full day to cross, he said. Especially if the snow lingered.

Although the land was fertile here, it wasn't a large area. I wouldn't have chosen to settle somewhere so cut off from the rest of the land. I hoped we could do better.

The day before we were due to leave, I overheard

Bjorn and Thrang discussing our journey the following day. I pretended not to listen while I sat on deck sorting my seeds. I had spread them to dry in the sun and was now pouring them into leather pouches for the journey.

'The wind is favourable,' Thrang was saying, looking up at the sky. 'Let's hope it holds. I think your decision to go south is a good one.'

'By all accounts the east and north coasts offer less,' agreed Bjorn. 'And it makes sense to go that way, as you know the coast.'

Thrang nodded. They moved past me along the deck, checking the sail was secured and the ropes carefully looped and tied. Thrang adjusted a rope every now and then or redid a knot. Bjorn ignored me, but Thrang inclined his head respectfully as he passed.

Their words disturbed me deeply. I wasn't immediately sure why. There had been a time when Bjorn wouldn't have taken such a decision without consulting me, and it was hurtful that he no longer did, but that wasn't all. Bjorn had decided wrongly. I was convinced of it. I sat quite still, allowing the feeling to grow in me. I calmed my mind and took some slow breaths. If the fates wished to tell me something, I was open.

I felt the vision coming before I saw it. My hands tingled and burned and the deck faded from my eyes as they dimmed, my sight turning inwards.

Churning black floodwater sweeping our ship far out to sea. Huge chunks of ice floating in the swirling current. Screams of distress. A great noise, an ear splitting crack. A mountain of ice bearing down upon our stricken vessel. An iceberg the size of two longhouses on their ends. It strikes, and before my horrified eyes, the ship is dashed to pieces. People flung this way and that, help-less in the grip of such huge forces. I can see Bjorn falling into the churning black torrent. In the blink of an eye he's sucked under.

I cried out and the vision faded. The sun was shining on me again and I was sitting on the deck panting, my breath coming short as though I had run a great distance.

Thrang bent over me, taking my arm in a firm grip.

'Thora, are you ill?' he asked. His voice sounded gruff but concerned. Bjorn was standing staring at me.

'What have you seen?' he asked. 'What did you mean, the ship will be dashed to pieces?'

'You must go north,' I said. My voice was hoarse and it hurt to speak. I coughed to clear it.

There was sweat on my brow; I could feel it cooling in the breeze. My hands were shaking and I gripped them together. Bjorn frowned. Thrang crouched down so that he could look me in the eyes.

'The climate is harsh on the north coast, Thora.' He spoke firmly. 'And the winds are against us. There's good land in the south.'

I shook my head. 'To go south is certain death,' I told him.

Thrang looked startled. I saw him glance uncertainly at Bjorn.

'Leave us a moment,' he ordered Thrang curtly.

'What's this, Thora?' he asked. 'Ragna warned me you would play some such trick.'

I took a deep breath, steadying myself.

'Since when did you listen to Ragna's advice before mine?' I asked, keeping my voice low.

'I've discovered a few things about you that I didn't know before.'

I was tired from the vision, too weary to fight. I wanted to curl up in a corner somewhere. But I didn't. I looked at Bjorn.

'I've seen all of our deaths,' I told him steadily. 'Please don't take your people south.'

Bjorn stared at me, troubled. 'How can you be sure?' he asked. His voice was gentler now. 'You heard what Thrang said. Life in the north will be much harder.'

'How could I know you were going to kill Svanson?' I said. 'I see things, you know I do.' I tried to explain the vision I had seen just now. As I spoke of it, I saw it again, and shivered, goosepimples running over my skin.

Bjorn looked closely at me, and then nodded. 'I'll think about it,' he promised. He smiled at me more kindly than he had done for some time. 'Thrang is going to take some convincing. I'm not sure he has much time for goddesses and their messages. It's all wind, waves, and trusting to Thor with him.'

I managed a weak smile in return. Bjorn gripped my shoulder for an instant and then left. I sat still for a few moments, my eyes closed. Then I forced myself to continue sorting my herbs.

The following morning, I asked Thrang which direction we were taking. He told me we were going north. 'Though I don't know how, in this wind direction,' he added, looking uneasy. I felt relief. Bjorn had chosen to trust me.

We said our farewells and then we were away, gliding out of the fjord.

As we emerged onto the open sea, the easterly wind which had been blowing steadily since yesterday faltered and then dropped. Our sail flattened and dropped at the mast. Thrang ordered everyone to the oars. They bent to their work, and slowly, painfully slowly, we began to creep northwards along the coast. It was so slow, I offered to help. I was allocated an oar and Stein showed me how to use it. It was heavy work, and my hands blistered after only a short time.

We passed a fjord and a rocky outcrop at a snail's pace. A breath of mild wind stirred behind us. Over the next hour it strengthened until the sail filled. The oars were shipped and the ship flew over the water once more. Thrang looked at me warily and shook his head.

'Which god did you pray to for that miracle?' he asked.

'None,' I said. 'They helped of their own accord. But I shall thank all of them now.' And I did so. Sitting in the sunshine on the deck, I offered each god and goddess in turn thanks for the favourable wind.

We worked our way north in increasingly choppy seas. Each night we sheltered in one of the many narrow, inhospitable fjords. Thrang muttered about autumn storms. His words made me uneasy. Had my vision guided us away from one danger, only to face a different one? The coastline we passed was deserted, unsettled. But the soil was poor and the cliffs forbidding.

'The summer's almost over,' said Thrang, his voice surly with anxiety. 'The nights are growing dark again. It's unheard of to settle so late in the year. Bjorn should have chosen a spot by now and raised a roof over our heads.'

This was a long speech from the taciturn captain. He seemed to think so too. He turned from me abruptly and shouted at the oarsmen for slacking. They responded by pulling on the oars until the sweat ran down their faces. We slipped out between the narrow cliffs that guarded the entrance to the fjord.

'Do you see all that white on the cliffs?' asked Thrang, making me jump. I hadn't heard him come to stand beside me again.

'Yes,' I said, squinting into the rising sun. 'Black rock, streaked with white.'

Thrang nodded grimly. 'Bird droppings,' he said brusquely. 'In summer, those are bird cliffs. Where are the birds? Gone south with their young. They know autumn is coming.'

I watched Stein and Bjorn set the sail. The wind caught it, making it billow out ahead of us, and the boat leapt over the waves. I was exhilarated to be underway once more, and banished the chill fear that Thrang's words had made me feel.

Now that we had started on this course, Bjorn pushed us on relentlessly. We skirted treacherous rocky cliffs and fought deadly currents. We were up at dawn, having snatched a few short hours sleep and sailed throughout the long daylight hours. Sometimes we passed tempting fjords and bays with fertile land. Many places were not settled. But Bjorn barely spared them a glance. He was deaf to Ragna's pleadings of sea sickness and Thrang's fear of bad weather.

'How far are we going, Bjorn?' I asked him one evening.

'We need to go further from Norway,' he muttered. His eyes looked haunted. 'People might come. People who knew Svanson. You were quite right to choose the north. It will be quieter here.'

'What if we take shelter now, to sit out the winter? Then we can explore the coast in the spring,' I suggested. Bjorn shook his head.

I hesitated. An image was forming in my mind. Every night I dreamt it and it grew clearer and closer. It was the same image I'd seen after Svanson's death. A wide bay with mountains on one side and green hills on the other. At its head was scrub and meadow. I was unsure whether to share this with Bjorn, but he surprised me by mentioning it himself.

'You saw it, didn't you?' he asked, in a softer voice. 'The place where we will make our home. Will you recognize it?'

I bit my lip. 'Your home and Ragna's home, you mean,' I said bitterly.

'It will be your home too,' replied Bjorn. 'Unless you choose to . . . marry into another household.'

I left him standing at the rail. That was not a conversation I could bear to pursue.

CHAPTER FIFTEEN

I crouched down in my usual spot beside the foals. Aki was suffering from this long voyage. His eyes were dull with misery. All the animals were out of condition. Their coats were matted and stiff with salt. The short stop in the south-east of Iceland hadn't been enough. This was the time of year they should be out at pasture, eating themselves fat on sweet summer grass against the long winter ahead. Aki always cheered up when I spent time with him, but left alone, I'm sure he would have given up long ago.

My other patient was more troublesome. Ragna insisted that I tended her at least once a day. I think it was for the pleasure of tormenting me. As I stooped and entered her stuffy cabin, she glared at me, her eyes gleaming malevolently in the half-light.

'I thought you were never coming,' she said fretfully. 'My head aches and my leg is hurting. I feel sick all the time. You must have something to give me. I'm sure you are keeping your best medicines for the others.'

I wedged open the door to the shelter as she spoke, letting in a rush of light and air. Ragna groaned and shut her eyes tight.

'You're trying to kill me,' she said accusingly.

It was best to say as little as possible. Whatever I said antagonized her and was used against me. Repeated to Bjorn in a twisted form to make trouble.

'You need the fresh air,' I said, as I always did. 'You should come out on deck more.'

Ragna was genuinely unwell. Her skin was pale and her hair unkempt. Her frail prettiness had gone and she looked like something that had crawled out from under a stone.

'You'll feel better when we find a place to settle,' I consoled her.

I'd brought a damp cloth with me and with it I began to wipe her face and hands. Usually she tolerated this, but today she pushed my hands away impatiently.

'Well, why don't we stop?' she asked. 'We've passed enough good places, if you ask me.'

'Bjorn thinks we should go further round the island,' I said carelessly, forgetting that Ragna would be angry to hear that Bjorn had consulted me and not her.

At once Ragna grasped my wrist in an iron grip that had little to do with her invalid state.

'Don't think I didn't see you speaking to him just now,' she hissed at me. 'Taking advantage of my illness. Well, you won't get him away from me. If you so much as look at him again, I'll make you sorry you were ever born.'

I kept my eyes lowered, but I knew Ragna was glaring at me. She already *had* nearly made me sorry I was born. I pulled my wrist away and made to leave the cabin.

'Thora!' Ragna called. 'You've forgotten to empty my slop bucket.' She loved ordering me to empty her bucket.

After that, I tried to stay away from Bjorn. I stood in

the prow for hours on end, watching the coast slip past us. We rounded the north-eastern end of the island and started to sail west. The winds were good to us and veered around and blew from the east, helping us on our way. I was sure Thor was watching over us.

The coast changed. The fjords gave way to wide bays. Sometimes there were mountains and high cliffs, and sometimes wide areas of beach, littered with driftwood. I wondered where the huge trees came from, for I had seen nothing higher than my shoulder in Iceland so far. The trees here were small, twisted bushes, clinging desperately to the ground, sculpted by the winds. The sky was iron grey, leaching the colour from the sea and landscape. The wind blew bitterly cold.

'You must speak to Bjorn,' said Thrang in my ear the next day. 'Get him to stop before it's too late.'

I shook my head without looking at him.

'He would listen to you,' urged Thrang.

'We haven't yet reached the place,' I said. I reached out, in my mind, to the bay we were looking for. It shimmered there, almost too beautiful to be true. 'We won't find it today,' I told him. 'But soon. It is not far away.'

Thrang shook his head. 'You've great trust in yourself. I wish I could be as sure.'

'I have faith in what the goddess shows me,' I told him. 'She's never let me down.'

That was no longer quite true. I'd been shown a vision of a life with Bjorn and it had been a mockery. Nothing had come about as I had expected. Perhaps this would be the same, but I kept my doubts to myself.

That night a thick, chill mist rolled over us, and the

wind died away to a whisper. When morning came, we were trapped in a bay, unable to see enough to move on. As the long, cold day wore on, tempers frayed. First Ragna spoke angrily to Bjorn and then Thrang did.

'Will you listen to me now, when I tell you to stop?' Thrang was saying. 'Or do you want to see everyone dead first? This isn't the travelling season!'

I intervened, stepping between them. 'Please,' I said. 'Resolve your differences.'

Thrang looked down at me. 'What should we do, Thora?' he asked.

I saw that he expected me to offer some guidance. Everyone was looking on, expecting me to say something that would offer some certainty. Ragna had been drawn from her cabin by the commotion and was looking resentfully at me. Every person on board the ship wanted to find a place to settle now, and be safely on land again. I took a deep breath.

'We could ask the runes for advice,' I said. I could sense the relief all around me. Here was something everyone understood.

I fetched my pouch of runes from my bag and dipped my hand into them, feeling them glide smoothly between my fingers. It was familiar and comforting. I sat down on the deck cross-legged, placed a sheep skin before me, skin side up. Then I closed my eyes and tried to still my mind. There was a press of people around me and it hindered me, but I knew this must be a public and not a private undertaking if I wanted their support.

My hands moved among the runes, selecting and then dropping each smooth pebble. One tingled in my fingers.

131

I held on to it, searching for another in my bag. Three stones I selected. Then I drew them out and cast them onto the sheepskin. There was an intake of breath around me. The excitement of anticipation.

I opened my eyes. The runes looked up at me and soon my mind was busy looking for their meaning.

'The sun,' I said aloud. 'The sun will come again. It will bring new beginnings.' In my mind, I could see the tantalizing image of the sun-drenched bay. We would find it in good weather, I was sure. The rune had fallen closest to me, it would not be long coming.

The other two runes were less reassuring, but I spoke them aloud anyway. 'There will be strife,' I said. 'We must guard against it, or it will tear us apart. And I see a death.'

I could hear muttering behind me and spoke again. 'I'm not sure . . . ' I said. 'It's faint, I can't see it.' I could feel an image pushing at the back of my mind. I willed it to become clear, but Ragna's sharp voice broke into my mind, shattering the dim picture like a reflection in a pond when a stone is thrown in.

'Thora predicts whatever suits her,' she said from the back of the crowd. 'I wouldn't trust what she says.'

'Quiet, you'll disturb her,' said Asgerd's voice angrily.

Ragna ignored her. She limped forward and kicked the runes aside. 'It's all nonsense,' she said.

There was angry muttering and dark looks all around me. I could sense everyone's disappointment at the interruption of the reading. I ignored it, and swallowed my own anger. Ragna had done herself more harm than she had done me. She had finally shown herself up in front of everyone, even Bjorn. Rather than trying to continue with the runes, I scooped the pebbles up in my hands, and restored them to my pouch, which I tucked it into my tunic.

'So what do we do?' asked Thrang. He sounded bewildered, as if he had expected something more concrete. As though the runes should have told us to sail west for two days and then follow the cliffs to a ready-made homestead.

I smiled at him. 'Wait for the fog to clear. When the sun shines, we'll find our home.'

My casting of the runes had lightened the atmosphere on the ship. Conversations turned on what our stretch of coast might look like and on how much land Bjorn would claim. Our cold food rations tasted better than usual. We had hope of an end to the voyage.

The very next day at dawn, a wind sprang up. The mist was blown away, revealing a landscape full of blues and greens and browns. Everyone set to with a will and we were out to sea long before the sun had risen. The ship creamed through the water, dipping and lifting in the swell, waves slapping at the planking under us. The sunrise was dazzling and filled with promise of a beautiful day.

The sunshine turned the lowering, hostile mountains into picturesque peaks. The water glowed green, so clear we could all see shoals of fish swimming below the surface.

Several huge brown fish with white noses suddenly broke out of the water beside the ship, leaping high into the air and splashing back in again. Several people screamed with fright.

'What are they, Thrang?' I asked. 'Those huge fish?'

Thrang allowed himself a small smile. 'Not fish,' he said. 'They're dolphins. They won't hurt us.'

The dolphins followed us for some time, leaping out of the water, looking at us and splashing back in. I had the impression they were curious and playful. It was a great wonder to me to see such large yet graceful sea creatures. They were as big as sheep or pigs, but smooth-skinned and sleek.

The sun sank lower in the sky, sparkling on the water. The wind lessened.

'I think you were wrong about finding a place to stop today,' Asgerd said to me, leaning on the figurehead beside me. 'It's been high cliffs all afternoon.'

'We're close now,' I told her. 'Very close.'

My whole body felt tense. The power of the vision and the sense of excitement that came with it overcame all my other feelings. I was leaning out over the prow, straining for a first glimpse of the bay as we rounded the headland.

The first thing I could see was mountains in the distance; their tops sparkling white in the evening sun. I could see how they reared sheer out of the sea. There was nowhere to settle on that side. Then a small island came into view and I cried out, because I recognized it. With a powerful rush, the landscape I saw before me merged with the visions I had seen. Bjorn should be beside me, seeing this. What had gone wrong that I had not foreseen the empty space beside me? I was in the grip of two conflicting emotions. A feeling of destiny ran strongly through my veins, thrilling me. It had brought me to my new home. At the same time I felt a paralysing sense of loss. It kept me frozen at the prow, gazing at the open landscape before me.

Thrang was at the tiller, I knew that without looking. I felt him swing the boat around so that we were sailing into the bay, skirting the small rocky island ahead of us. The wind spilled out of the sail and we slowed to a graceful glide. The air was mild and the water smooth and still around us.

To our left was a long stretch of green scrub, a tangle of small trees and bushes. I could see at once how ideal that would be for our goats and pigs. Further up there would be pasture for horses, cattle, and sheep. The trees were backed by green slopes and rolling hills. And at the head of the fjord was low-lying land that could surely be ploughed. We had arrived. And all around us, I could see not one sign of habitation. We might not be the first people ever to sail here, but no one had settled this place yet. It was an empty bay, just waiting for us.

Bjorn appeared beside me. I turned to him, and he read my excitement at once.

'This is it?' he asked me, his whole face lighting up.

When I nodded, he looked about, awed, as though seeing it for the first time.

We sailed into the bay, side by side as I had foreseen. And yet an invisible shadow lay between us.

CHAPTER SIXTEEN

We beached the ship on shingle on the left-hand side of the bay. An excited, jubilant mood seized everyone as they realized we'd reached journey's end. I watched Bjorn carry Ragna off the ship, and it was as though a knife twisted in my heart. I was sick to my stomach at the wrongness of this arrival.

'Can I help you, Thora?' asked Thrang.

I looked round at him, ashamed to have been seen watching Bjorn and Ragna.

'I don't need carrying, Thrang,' I said ungraciously. He fell back a little, looked as though he would have spoken, but didn't. He simply stood and watched me as I jumped down onto the shingle. We all climbed ashore, the dogs too. They chased around madly, noses to the ground, tails wagging frantically with excitement.

The men sang and laughed as they unloaded animals, timber, and provisions from the ship. We women picketed the animals where they could graze. I watched with pleasure as the foals rolled and rolled on the ground, rubbing the salt out of their coats, and then fell to tearing up mouthfuls of grass. Aki more than any of them showed his high spirits at being on land again by kicking up his heels and neighing loudly in his squeaky baby voice.

We collected wood and built a fire on the beach to cook the first hot food we had had in many days. When the ship was empty, Bjorn ordered it hauled right up above the high tide mark. By then the barley broth was hot and bubbling in the iron cooking pots and an early nightmeal was served.

It was late before anyone closed their eyes that night. Excitement kept everyone talking. At last, one by one, we fell silent, wrapping ourselves in cloaks and furs and lying down around the long fire to sleep. I lay on my back between Asdis and Hild and watched the sky. Thousands of sparkling stars winked into existence above us and I realized how I had missed them through the long, light nights of summer. It was strange to watch them now from solid ground and not from the deck of the boat. Every now and then, I could have sworn the ground rocked beneath me, but the sensation faded as quickly as it had come. It was the after-effects of being at sea, Thrang had told me.

My arrival was not what I had expected, but we were here now. I'd reached the place that destiny had mapped out for me. I breathed in the crisp, clear air and prayed to Freya. I prayed to her for the courage to grasp my future, whatever it might hold. Then I prayed to Thor to thank him for bringing us safely across the sea, and to Frigg for strength and patience. And in the dark of the night as I drifted into sleep, I resolved to accept whatever came to me.

Those who lay at any distance from the fire were visited

by the frost giants that night. A layer of white ice had been breathed onto their wrappings. I awoke just before the dawn and saw it. At first I thought I must be mistaken. It was still summer. But then I realized the reason I had woken up was that I was cold to my very bones. I shivered and huddled in my cloak to warm myself. I curled as small as I could, wrapping my arms around myself. It didn't seem to help.

After a while, I couldn't lie still any longer. I sat up, shivering, and crouched by the fire. A few embers were still glowing faintly. I fed them carefully with twigs and sticks that had fallen out of the fire last night. They blackened and steamed and then slowly caught, tiny flames licking across them. I added some larger pieces, warming my chilled hands over them.

The sky was greying in the east, above the hills. The landscape was slowly emerging from the darkness, regaining first its contours, and then gradually its colours too. I hadn't slept many hours, but I was restless. After a while, I got stiffly to my feet and crept through the sleeping men and women. I passed where Aki was picketed and paused to stroke him. He nuzzled my hand sleepily. I walked some distance up the hill behind us, gazing around me at the new morning. The ice had vanished, dissolving into dampness, which would soon sparkle in the sun.

'A vast empty land,' I said aloud to myself. How far away were the nearest people? We'd seen almost no settlements on these northern shores. I heard a step behind me and turned, catching my breath. But it was only Thrang walking towards me.

'Not as empty as you might think,' he grunted.

I was a little embarrassed to have been overheard talking to myself. 'What do you mean?' I asked. 'There's no one here but us.'

'I saw a glow on the far side of the bay last night,' Thrang told me. 'A fire, I'd wager. I'm waiting for the light to look for smoke or a building.'

'I saw nothing yesterday,' I said. Then I thought back to our arrival and remembered my attention had been mainly focused on the fertile parts of the bay, not the mountains.

'There can't be enough grass to graze a goat on over there,' I exclaimed. 'Who would settle on that side of the bay when there is all this over here?'

Thrang looked at me in silence for a moment. 'Easy to hear you're a farmer's daughter,' he said at last.

I felt vaguely annoyed by this. What was wrong with being a farmer's daughter anyway? But Thrang was speaking again, his voice slow and unhurried as usual.

'Did you not see the whales blowing on the far side of the bay?' he asked me.

I shook my head, not wanting to admit I barely knew what he meant.

'The whales go where the fish are,' he said. 'There'll be rich fishing over there.'

'Well, I couldn't live on fish alone,' I remarked.

I thought Thrang was smiling at me, though it was difficult to tell through his bushy beard. 'It's where I would choose,' he said.

I hoped devoutly that Bjorn had no such notion. It wouldn't be any life to be perched on some rocky outcrop living off fish. Then I remembered all our animals, tools, and seed and felt reassured. We were going to be farmers.

'I couldn't survive away from plants and flowers,' I said. 'I would miss being able to watch them grow and gather them when the time is right.'

'And yet you love the sea,' Thrang pointed out.

I was surprised. This was a whole conversation. I'd never heard Thrang speak so long to anyone. Together, we turned and headed back to the camp.

'I did love the sea,' I answered as we walked. 'But I belong on land.'

Perhaps Thrang was disappointed by my reply, because he said nothing more.

One of the first things we did that morning was to bathe and clean the dirt of the long voyage from our grimy bodies. There was a freshwater lake at the head of the bay. I went there with the women. It was crystal clear but unbelievably cold. We all screamed and shrieked as we tried to get into the water. Most of us contented ourselves with crouching at the edge and scrubbing our bodies hurriedly before staggering out again on numb, frozen feet, gasping with the cold. I couldn't imagine coming here to wash on any but the warmest days of summer.

Once we were clean, the men took their turn. Even from the camp we could hear them shouting and laughing as they braved the icy water. It sounded as if some of them were throwing each other in or wrestling in the lake from the amount of splashing we could hear. When they returned they were pink-skinned and invigorated from the water. Asgerd, I, and three other women gathered all the dirty, discarded clothes and returned to the lake to wash them. We scrubbed them and beat them against stones, stopping regularly to thaw our numbed hands in our armpits. Then we carried them back to the camp and spread them all to dry in the sunshine.

I didn't speak to Bjorn that day. After the bathing, he took several men with him and went to explore the shore. I went among the animals, pigs, goats, sheep, calves, and horses, to check they were all well after the voyage. Aki was very high spirited about being on firm land again. He was grazing eagerly and already had a new shine in his eyes. I rubbed him affectionately between the ears.

'You're glad to be here, aren't you?' I asked him. It was lovely to see him so happy. 'I promise you'll never have to go to sea again,' I told him light-heartedly. 'From here on it's all sweet Icelandic grass and pastures to roam.' Aki nickered softly as though he understood.

We had lost neither horses nor cattle, goats nor pigs. Two lambs had died and we had lost nearly half the chickens. But all in all, we'd done well. It was a good omen and suggested to me that our farm would prosper. That reminded me that I should speak to Bjorn about a sacrifice. Thor had watched over our voyage and we should thank him for holding off storms and other dangers. I was surprised Bjorn had not already thought of it. We could spare another chicken or even two for such an important ceremony.

Once I had checked all the animals, I put Aki on a halter rein and took him for a walk to examine the plant life in the area. I could see from the height and sparseness of the vegetation that this must be a harsh climate and a short growing season. No doubt the south coast would have been kinder. But we were here now, and it had been my doing. Aki stopped to snatch mouthfuls of grass every time I paused to look at a plant. Once, when I lingered too long, he butted me impatiently. I tumbled over into the grass. Aki put his face down to mine and snorted, spraying me with foal spit. I rolled away with an indignant cry and then suddenly I laughed. For the first time since my capture in Norway, I roared with laughter. Aki stood over me looking at me curiously. I laughed and laughed, unable to stop, until my laughter turned to tears and then I put my arms around Aki's warm, comforting neck and wept for everything I had lost.

CHAPTER SEVENTEEN

To my surprise, Bjorn refused to make the sacrifice to Thor. There were rumblings of unease among the company. I myself felt doubt even once he had explained his reasons.

'I don't believe in your gods, Thora. I don't believe that sacrifice makes any difference. Why should a valuable and useful animal be killed for such a reason? How does that benefit anyone?'

I stared at him perplexed. How could anyone not believe in the gods? They were indisputable—a part of our world as much as the sea and the sky. Making sacrifices to them wasn't something I'd ever questioned. It was necessary.

'The gods require blood,' I said uncertainly, 'in return for safe passage across the sea. If you withhold your thanks, we could all be punished.'

Bjorn shook his head and resumed eating his night meal. I could hear mutterings around me and wished I hadn't brought the subject up so publicly. I hadn't intended to undermine Bjorn's authority. I'd forgotten that he had been born overseas and might have learned different ways to ours.

Ragna was sitting beside Bjorn. She said nothing, but I

saw her glance at him, just once, and there was an expression I couldn't quite read in her eyes. I let the matter drop.

Bjorn chose a place to build the longhouse where we would all live. It was to lie above the beach facing inland towards the head of the bay. He had picked a spot in the lee of the wind, where the shoulder of the hill would keep the worst of the winter winds off us.

'We can't easily see ships approaching from here,' I mentioned quietly, pausing beside him as he worked on digging holes for the corner posts of the house. Bjorn looked at me, and a rueful grin just touched his face.

'I've thought it through. I'd like a view of the bay, too.' He paused, and I knew he was thinking of the possibility of pursuit from Norway. It would haunt us for a long time. 'But look at the trees,' Bjorn said, straightening his back and throwing down his spade. He waved at the stunted forest that grew around us. 'Which way are they all bent? They show you the direction of the prevailing wind. And we need shelter from it. Otherwise it'll be impossible to keep the house warm in winter.'

I could see the good sense in this. 'But,' I lowered my voice, 'if Svanson's people *should* come after us . . . '

'They won't be able to see us from the open sea, any more than we can see them approaching.'

I was doubtful this was true. There would be other signs of settlement besides the actual buildings. But I decided that in this matter, Bjorn knew better than I.

'Do you propose starting building today?' I asked him.

'I do.'

'It's just that it's almost the end of *Heyannir*. Hay month. If we don't cut our grass at once, there will be nothing for the winter feed.'

Bjorn nodded. 'I know. And yet if I don't build at once, we'll have no roof over our heads if bad weather comes.'

We stared at each other for a few moments, weighing the importance of the two tasks.

'Give me the women and you have the men,' I said at last, suggesting a compromise. I would have preferred it if everyone could have spent a week cutting hay. We couldn't be sure how long the good weather would last. But we were eight women plus Astrid. If we worked hard, we could perhaps manage it. If only the weather would stay as fine as it was today.

Bjorn looked at me a moment, his eyes softening. 'Very well,' he said. 'You have a great deal of wisdom, Thora. Thank you. Harvest well.'

I turned away confused, but pleased. A better understanding was at last being established between us again. Bjorn called after me.

'Thora? The hay making. Not Ragna.'

I nodded curtly and walked away. I knew Ragna wasn't strong enough for haymaking. Her bad leg prevented her from walking far. He didn't need to remind me; to bring her name like a barrier between us again.

I made my way swiftly down the hill to the camp, while Bjorn went back to digging.

All day the women laboured on the sunny slopes of the bay, cutting grass for hay. We scratched ourselves climbing through the trees and scrub to find the best places. I swung the sharp iron blade until my arm ached and throbbed. Then I passed it to another woman and shook out the hay I'd cut and spread it to dry. The grass was coarse and tough, but plentiful. What flowers had grown among them had now withered and spread their seed. Some plants I could identify but I would need to wait for next summer now to get a full picture of what grew here.

After so long aboard the ship, we all found we'd grown weak and flabby. The work taxed our strength. When the pain in my protesting muscles grew intolerable, I pictured Aki eating the hay I was cutting in the long dark of the winter months. I visualized him growing strong and tall on it, and I was able to keep working. By the end of the day, we had cut a large area. I was satisfied with the start we had made.

We congratulated one another, collected up our tools and headed back down to our beach camp. We could see the men walking down from the building site from the other direction. We met and mingled. That was why I didn't see what had been done. Not until I heard gasps of shock from those ahead of me. The crowd parted to give me a view that brought me up short. I stared at it, trying to make sense of what I was seeing.

On a large flat stone a short distance from the camp-fire, a sacrifice had been made. I saw the ritual blood marks first. Blood had also run down the stone, congealing in sticky pools and dripping into the shingle. That didn't shock me; I'd seen such sights often. What made me falter and turn pale was the gleaming golden coat and limp gangly legs that were the source of the blood.

Someone had sacrificed Aki.

After all my work and care to keep him alive. After my promises that his life would be good now. My friend was dead. My stomach churned with distress and shock. I looked around frantically, searching for the person responsible. Who would do such a thing to me?

Ragna stepped forward, blood on her tunic and on her forehead. Aki's blood. She smiled up at Bjorn.

'I knew you would want to give thanks to Thor for our safe arrival, husband,' she said.

I saw the colour drain from Bjorn's face as he stood looking from his wife to the slaughtered foal. Of all the animals she could have chosen, a horse was the most valuable. The hardest to replace. And everyone knew of the bond I had forged with the young colt.

I racked my anguished brain to remember whether Ragna had been present when Bjorn had said he didn't believe in sacrifice. Of course she had been. She'd been sitting beside him. So why had she done it?

Bjorn took a step closer to his wife, his eyes blazing. For a moment it looked as though he would strike her, but then he seemed to restrain himself. Ragna's eyes narrowed as she glared back at him. We all watched the silent battle for mastery rage between them.

'You didn't forbid me,' hissed Ragna at last, in a voice like an adder.

'I forbid you ever to make sacrifices again,' said Bjorn slowly and clearly. His voice vibrated with anger. Then he turned abruptly away and started giving orders to stack the tools under the boat in case of rain. Ragna darted me a triumphant glance. I understood that she had sacrificed

Aki to hurt me. I had had no idea her hatred for me was so strong.

My knees shook. I fought to control myself, keeping my face averted from the mangled, bloody heap that had been Aki. I needed to master my emotions, outwardly at least. Ragna shouldn't have the satisfaction of seeing my distress.

I tried to walk away, but my legs wouldn't carry me. Intead, I sank to the ground and covered my face with my hands. Asgerd sat down beside me and put her arms around me.

'Why?' I whispered. My mind felt numb, unable to work properly. I couldn't think of anything except that Aki was gone.

'I've told you before, she's jealous.' She whispered the words into my ear so no one else could hear.

'But . . . ' Even my mouth wasn't working properly now, unable to shape my words. 'But I've been kind to her,' I faltered.

'She's like woollen cloth soaking up kindness but giving none back,' murmured Asgerd, stroking my hair. 'That's how she is. It'll never make any difference how kind you are to her. She'll never like you for it.'

I knew she was right and it filled me with despair.

'Asgerd,' called Ragna sharply. 'There's work to be done. Come and help.'

Ragna couldn't even bear the sight of me being comforted. Asgerd had no choice but to go. I sat in silence, feeling the shock fade and the pain begin. I felt a heavy hand on my shoulder and looked up.

'Take comfort, Thora,' said Thrang gruffly. 'The sacrifice

was a princely gift. In exchange for a horse, Thor will be good to us all winter.'

Without saying any more, he went and gathered up Aki's limp body and walked away from the camp with it. I followed him with my eyes until he disappeared from sight.

CHAPTER EIGHTEEN

Harvest Month
Haustmánuður

The weather held fine for many days. I continued making hay with the other women, despite the misery that hung over me. It seeped right inside me, making my limbs heavy and every movement an effort. It was much harder to keep working without the thought of feeding my favourite foal.

The day the frame of the house was raised, we all went to help. As the skeleton of each wall was lifted into an upright position, a tremendous cheer went up and everyone who wasn't hauling on a rope applauded. Even I could feel some satisfaction in seeing our house take shape as men swarmed over the structure, pegging it together. Not that I had any expectation that this would be a happy home. Not for me, in any case. But it would be a shelter against the winter that was coming.

It was easy to forget that winter would soon be upon us. The sun was hot and the skies were clear. Only the lengthening nights with their bitter cold were an indication of the change of the season approaching.

As soon as the roof went onto the house, we broke camp and moved from the beach up to our new home.

Now at least we would have some shelter against the rain when it came. We stacked the hay we had made at one end of the house, feeling proud of our achievement, and beside it we put all the supplies we had brought from Norway. The walls were constructed, seaward first, and we had more shelter from the wind. The fire in the centre of the hall warmed us better. The cooking was faster without a constant wind blowing the flames this way and that.

Another fire was lit at some distance from the house and worked as a forge. Grim turned out to be a skilled smith and set to work with the iron we had brought with us making keys for what would be the front door and the food store. My father had been a skilled smith and I took pleasure in watching Grim work. Sometimes I took a turn at working the bellows for him to keep the fire white hot. It was strenuous but satisfying work as I watched the pieces take shape. Once the keys were done, Grim set to repairing tools that had been damaged and making new nails.

'Now the autumn can come!' cried Asgerd cheerfully as she stirred barley porridge in its iron pot. It was early morning and almost time for breakfast.

'It's harvest month, but we have nothing to harvest,' I said. 'It seems strange. And as none of the animals are old enough to slaughter, we'll have no meat for the winter.'

'We have a fair bit of food stored though,' said Asgerd, undaunted. 'We'll survive the dark months. This time next year, we'll be breaking our backs over the harvest.'

'If the gods are willing,' I agreed. 'And there'll be berries to gather soon.'

'My favourite time of year,' said Asgerd with a smile. 'You've already collected some healing plants, I see.'

I nodded and continued sorting the pile in front of me, tying the stems that had dried into neat bundles to hang up. I had gathered a fresh stock of valerian and some selfheal that I had been surprised to find growing next to the spring above the house. It was a useful little plant for treating burns but I hadn't expected to find it in such an exposed spot. Its purple flowers had dried to brown seed heads, but it was recognizable to the trained eye.

There was a banging behind me. I looked around to see what was being built now. Bjorn and Thrang were fitting the door to the food store. It was an important step in the building of the house. The food stores were always kept locked away to prevent pilfering.

When the door was hung to his satisfaction, Bjorn tried the key. It turned easily. Ragna brushed past me when she saw this and held out her hand.

There was a moment's silence.

'The key. If you please, husband.' There was an edge to Ragna's voice.

I saw Bjorn glance uneasily at me and wished he would not. I tried to busy myself with my herbs, but I caught a glimpse of Ragna's angry, narrowed eyes as she followed the direction of his look. She said nothing, however. That wasn't her way. She rarely argued with Bjorn, but if he failed to do as she wished, she found ways to punish both him and me. Bjorn continually betrayed, in his glances towards me, that he wanted to consult me. He betrayed the closeness that had existed between us, however briefly. It was unwise; Ragna was mistress of the house now. Once the house was finished, she would rule it completely. Even Bjorn would have to do as she said indoors.

My heart sank at the thought.

Reluctantly, Bjorn handed over the key. She put it on a strip of leather around her neck, and shuffled away. I looked up to find Bjorn's eyes on me again. I met his look steadily. We both knew that if things had turned out differently, he would have given the key to me. I shrugged very slightly and bent over my plants again. There was nothing either of us could do.

'Thora!' came Ragna's sharp voice. 'What are you doing sitting around so stupidly? It isn't as though there's no work to be done.'

I sighed and laid my plants carefully aside in order to help serve the daymeal. Everyone gathered around the fire to eat.

'Has anyone else noticed the spring above the house?' I asked, once everyone's first hunger was appeased and talk had begun again. 'It runs hot out of the ground and steams.'

There were some surprised looks at my words and Ragna scoffed audibly. I kept my face expressionless. Bjorn paused, his shell full of porridge halfway to his mouth.

'Are you sure?' he asked.

I nodded. 'It's hot to the touch,' I told him. 'And there are plants growing around it that would normally only grow in sheltered, warm places.'

'I've seen such springs on the south coast,' put in Thrang, in his unhurried way.

Bjorn's eyes lit at once with keen interest. He quickly shovelled the last mouthful of food into his mouth. 'Show me,' he asked, getting to his feet.

'What? Now, in the middle of the meal?' cried Ragna affronted.

'I'm finished,' said Bjorn curtly, already striding out of the house. I hurried to keep up with him, aware of many pairs of eyes following us.

Bjorn paused, waiting for me to lead him to the spring. I climbed the steep slope above the house to a hollow, almost a fold in the hillside. The ground was boggy here; wet and soft but very fertile. When we had reached the spot, I stopped, twitched my tunic clear of the mud and crouched down to pull back the lush growth of grass and other greenery that hid the small pool. A cloud of steam rose as I did so. I dipped my hand into the water to reassure myself that I hadn't imagined the whole thing. It was scorching hot.

'See for yourself,' I said to Bjorn.

He crouched down opposite me and dipped his hand into the water, whipping it out again with a muted cry of surprise. I couldn't help smiling at his astonishment.

'How is this possible?' he asked, bemused, testing the water again, more cautiously this time.

I shrugged. 'I've never come across such a thing before,' I admitted. 'But this is a new land with many wonders. Call it a gift from the gods.'

'It doesn't smell good,' said Bjorn sniffing at the pool.

He shook a few drops into his mouth and grimaced. 'Rotten eggs,' he remarked. 'Some gift.'

Thrang and Erik approached us now. Both tested the water and Erik exclaimed in astonishment.

'I've seen bathing pools built,' remarked Thrang. His words hung in the air, full of possibility.

'That would be wonderful for winter,' I said tentatively. 'We won't be able to use the lake in the cold and the dark.'

'We could channel this water closer to the house,' suggested Erik, enthusiastically. 'It drains down this way anyway.' He got up and began to follow the boggy ground as it wound down past the homestead. Thrang followed, listening as Erik explained how it could be done if the water course were to be lined with stone and clay. I crouched quite still by the pool, hearing Erik's voice fade. Bjorn grasped my wrist and held it tight.

'I'm sorry for the way that Ragna treats you,' he said hurriedly. 'And I'm sorry about the foal.'

He looked at me, but his eyes quickly fell. 'I know you're angry with me,' Bjorn continued after a pause. 'And perhaps you're right to be. But I acted as I thought best for you. I tried to honour my promise to your father. If you think you are the only sufferer, you are sorely mistaken.'

I met his eyes at last and saw pain in them. 'I know,' I said. 'And I'm sorry too, for what I said . . . that night on the island. I didn't mean it.'

I knew I was being weak admitting this, that the confession might undo the distance I'd created between us, but I couldn't bear to see him so unhappy.

'I know,' Bjorn said and released my wrist. I could see the marks where his fingers had gripped me. I got up and walked away a few paces. Erik and Thrang were discussing a location for the bathing pool near the house. I wished I could say more to Bjorn, but it was dangerous ground. And what was the use? To speak of my feelings now could only harm us both.

'This is a great find,' said Bjorn, indicating the spring. He had reverted to his practical manner and I was both relieved and sorry.

'Yes. Once the house is finished, it would be a good project to think about,' I said in as cheerful a voice as I could manage.

We walked back down to the unfinished longhouse. Bjorn joined Thrang and Erik in their discussion. I went on into the house and was brought up short by a strong herbal smell. Ragna was alone by the fire in the empty house. It took me only a heartbeat to realize she had thrown my entire gathering of medicinal plants onto the fire. I started forward impulsively, my hands shaking with shock, thinking it might still be possible to rescue some of them. But all that remained was a blackened twist of shrivelled stalks, the flames still licking around them. I watched them burn and fall to ashes, the precious leaves and seeds that had held so much power in them. Now it was all wasted.

'I can't replace this,' I said as calmly as I was able, whilst inside anger almost choked me. I was used to my skills being treated with respect, even with reverence. I could scarcely comprehend this wanton destruction. It was like a violation.

'Oh, were they important? Well, don't leave them lying around for people to fall over next time,' retorted Ragna.

'You must hope not many of us fall ill this winter,' I said looking directly at her. 'I might not have the medicines I need to heal them.'

If I had expected to shame her, I was disappointed. Her face twisted into a satisfied grin.

'Let's hope it's you that gets ill then, shall we?' she said.

CHAPTER NINETEEN

Asgerd, Aud, and I hauled firewood the next morning. The best driftwood logs had been set aside for building, but there were plenty of smaller stumps and branches or even whole tree trunks that for one reason or another had not been considered building material. Some pieces we could carry up alone; for the largest pieces, we worked together in twos or even threes, dragging them up to the house.

It was hard, back-breaking work. When the sun was just past its zenith, we paused on the beach for a drink of water and a brief rest to restore our strength. Despite the pale sunshine, there was a chill wind and the excess heat quickly left our bodies. Thrang came down from the house to stand near us. He always did his share of work like everyone else, but could never keep away from the shore for long. He was gazing out across the bay now, one hand shading his eyes.

'Looks like we're going to meet our neighbours at last,' he said.

We all looked round. My heart jumped into my mouth. I wasn't sure why. Perhaps I thought this would be another Svanson come to steal from us.

I shaded my eyes like Thrang but could see nothing. I

was too short sighted. Aud and Asgerd were already commenting on the boat while it was still a blur to me. Instead I shut my eyes and tried to sense the visitors.

At first there was nothing, but then suddenly they were quite clear to me.

There are two. Father and son, I spoke aloud. *The father has a favour to ask of us. His intentions are friendly, but he's . . . I think he's not safe. And . . .* I was flooding with emotions. I could feel loss and great sadness. And anger. It threatened to overwhelm me. I snapped my eyes open.

The others were staring at me now, rather than at the boat.

'I'll go and tell Bjorn,' said Thrang. He turned from us and climbed the hill to the house in swift, strong strides.

I took a breath to clear the mists of my vision.

'Where does it come from?' said Aud, gazing at me almost fearfully.

'I feel them,' I said, hesitantly. It was hard to explain my visions. It was like trying to describe sight to a blind man.

'What do you mean, he isn't safe?' demanded Asgerd. 'That's the bit that worried me.'

'I don't think he means *us* any harm,' I said. But I wasn't entirely sure what I had sensed. As though the man was two different people. I'd never come across anything like that before.

We stood looking out towards the boat which even I could see now. Before long, Bjorn and Thrang joined us.

'What is it, Thora?' Bjorn asked. I explained again, as best I could, what I had felt. We all stood together and watched apprehensively as the boat approached. We were joined by others from our household. Erik and Grim crunched their way onto the beach, closely followed by Asdis and Jon.

Soon we could hear the splashing of oars. A small boat came closer and closer until at last it struck the shingle with a rattle and the two occupants jumped out. One was huge, like a walking mountain. He dwarfed even Thrang. The other was a small but broad boy of about seven or eight winters. Both had a halo of red hair and were spattered with freckles. The man was bearded and on his nose grew a large, unsightly mole that sprouted black hairs.

Thrang and the others hurried forward to help pull the boat up out of the water. Then, warily, they all greeted one another.

'I'm Olvir,' said the stranger. 'And this is my son, Ulf.'

Bjorn made our introductions. When my turn came to meet Olvir, I found his blistering stare unnerving. I dropped back a pace.

When Bjorn invited the visitors up to the house, Olvir nodded his huge head and then bent into his boat. He hauled out the most enormous portion of butchered carcass I'd ever seen. It was no animal I recognized. Olvir slung it over his shoulder as though it were merely a sheaf of corn. Everyone stared, but Olvir merely stood and waited for Bjorn to lead the way up to the house. He refused all offers of help on the way up and bore it all the way to the house himself. Then, once we had all entered, and before Bjorn could introduce the others, he flung it down at my feet and said:

'A gift for your store cupboard. Whale meat.'

I was acutely aware of his mistake. Of the women in

the household, only Ragna and I wore coloured clothes. These marked us as free women. The slaves wore plain woven cloth. Olvir had assumed I was the head of the household. There was an awful, lingering silence. I didn't know how to explain the mistake without mortifying our guest or offending Ragna.

Ragna came forward and cleared her throat to get attention.

'Thank you for your generous gift,' she said.

Bjorn hurried to introduce her: 'This is my . . . wife, Ragna,' he muttered.

Olvir looked from one to the other of us and then shrugged.

The awkward moment passed, but I knew Ragna wouldn't forgive me in a hurry. For now, though, she said nothing, obviously taking pleasure in ordering us about in front of our very first visitor.

'Jon and Vali, cut off a portion of meat for a meal and carry the rest into the store. I'll unlock it for you. Asgerd and Thora,' she ordered, 'you can roast the meat for nightmeal, at once. Aud, bake some flatbread.'

We hurried to do her bidding, while Ragna ordered Karl to broach a barrel of mead. I watched the men covertly as I sliced the unfamiliar meat and spitted it on sticks ready to roast. They talked in low voices and from the words I could catch, they were discussing the fishing and the climate here. Olvir didn't seem so frightening now that he was sitting down. Certainly his manner and voice were calm. Yet there was something about him that unsettled me.

I noticed his son sitting quietly beside him, watching

everything with restless, anxious eyes. He saw me looking at him and scowled. I smiled and he looked away.

Bjorn went outside to talk and walk with his guest. The boy, Ulf, wandered out too. I could see him standing by the house gazing at the foals. I called Astrid over to me, as she was the only child of our household, and took her outside to move the pickets. I invited Ulf to come with us, thinking the two children might become friends. Ulf followed, but sullenly. When we got close, the grey foal rushed to butt us, looking for food, and to my surprise, Ulf backed away, clearly terrified.

'He's only being friendly,' I told him. 'Come and stroke him. Look, I'll hold him for you.'

Tentatively the boy came forward and put his hand out to touch the foal's coat. Then he snatched it back.

'What is it?' he asked.

'What is it? It's a foal,' cried Astrid. 'Haven't you ever seen a horse before?'

Ulf shook his head, his eyes still apprehensively on the animal, clearly nervous it was going to make a sudden move.

'It's all hairy,' he said.

My eyes widened in surprise. 'Don't you have any animals where you live?' I asked him, nodding across the bay. He looked at me sideways.

'We had chickens,' he said. 'But they died. And there's fish and whales in the sea.'

We took him round and introduced him to the cattle, the goats, and the pigs. He became more confident each time and was brave enough to pat the goat without prompting. He and Astrid were very suspicious of one another, but I hoped they'd get along. It was lonely for Astrid to be the only child here.

'So what do you eat if you have no animals?' I asked Ulf.

'Fish and whale meat, of course,' he replied. 'We collect birds' eggs in spring. And catch puffins in the summer.'

'And how many of you live over there?'

The boy's face closed up. He looked sad. 'Just me and father,' he said after a pause.

'Was there someone else?' I asked gently.

'There was my mother,' he said, his voice tight. 'She died having a baby, and the baby died soon after. And there was Thorir, he was father's kinsman, but he drowned in a storm.'

'So there are just the two of you now?'

Unthinkingly, I put out my hand in sympathy and touched the boy's shoulder. He shrugged away.

'Yes, and I'm staying with him, whatever he says!' he told me angrily.

Suddenly I understood. The broken pieces of vision and the boy's anger all fitted together and made sense. Olvir was going to ask us to foster, or at least care for, his son.

I looked around for Bjorn. He was walking back towards the house, head bent as he listened to whatever Olvir was saying.

The deal was negotiated over mead and nightmeal. We sampled the unfamiliar whale meat that tasted rather like beef. At first we ate gingerly, unsure of ourselves. But once we realized how good it was, we all feasted, glad of fresh meat once more. During the meal, Bjorn accepted charge of the boy. I could see Ragna colour with anger. Bjorn didn't notice and turned to her, expecting her agreement.

'So, Ragna,' he said, 'we're to foster Ulf.'

Ragna's stony face should have warned him but he gave no sign of it.

'I can't take charge of a boy his age,' she said flatly.

Bjorn's face showed shock for a moment, but then the expression passed as swiftly as clouds passing over a field of corn on a windy day. He smiled.

'Of course, you couldn't be expected to do so,' he agreed at once. He looked at me. 'Thora can have charge of him. You don't mind, do you, Thora?'

I shook my head, dumbly. And it was done. I had a child to care for. Ulf was two winters younger than my own brother and would be quite a responsibility.

Ragna was furious; I knew that without looking at her. Her anger radiated from her in waves. She had missed an opportunity to please Bjorn and I had done so instead. I would be lucky to eat at all the next month.

I was aware of Ulf scowling up at me. I pitied him, but I knew his father was doing the best he could for the boy. I could only imagine how hard it must have been for a man on his own to care for a child that age. He must be aware every time he went out fishing and risked his life on the sea, that if he didn't return, Ulf would starve. With us, he would always have people to care for him and teach him the skills he needed to learn.

'I'd like to do you a favour in return,' said Olvir. 'You

spoke of a bathing pool you wanted to build. I'd like to do that for you.'

Everyone stared at him in astonishment. Bjorn gathered his wits first.

'We'd be very glad of any help, of course,' he said. 'But it's far too great a task for one man.'

'No,' said Olvir at once. 'I work better alone. You have enough to do preparing for winter. I'll begin in the morning.'

I was woken well before dawn by the sound of iron ringing against stone. I sat up, confused. Ulf, who lay between me and Asdis, stirred in his sleep. Tucking the furs more securely around him, I got up to see what was happening.

Outside the house, in the wind and the darkness, I could make out the shape of a massive man, stripped to the waist, and swinging a huge tool. His aura was a furious blur of reds and browns, glowing brightly around him in the night air. I stared at him, sleep still dulling my comprehension.

Bjorn joined me.

'I think our visitor has begun his self-imposed task,' he said softly.

'Oh,' I said, understanding at last. I said nothing more. It felt good to be so near to Bjorn in the darkness without worrying who was watching.

After a while Bjorn spoke again.

'Is he safe, this new neighbour? I confess he makes me nervous.'

'There's something not right about him,' I admitted.

'There's too much red in his aura. It suggests anger, but he doesn't seem an angry person.'

I felt Bjorn's fingertips brush mine in the darkness and my heart leapt into my throat. 'Keep an eye on him. And on his son,' he said softly, and then he moved away from me. I felt a moment's disappointment, but then saw that others were emerging from the house, staring at the spectacle of the man working so furiously. But it wasn't until dawn broke that we could see just how much he had done. A great hole gaped next to the house, where Bjorn had marked out the size of the bathing pool. Huge rocks lay on the ground, tossed aside like a child's toys. It should have taken several men to move them but Olvir had pulled them out alone. There was a tumbled mound of topsoil besides.

When I went to call him for breakfast, I could smell the acrid smell of his sweat as it poured off him. Several broken spades and a shattered pick lay scattered about him.

'Don't call him,' said a boy's voice. I looked round to see Ulf beside me. He was looking up at me anxiously.

'He don't like to be disturbed when he's working. He's likely to clout you. I'll take his food.'

Ulf showed me he already held two loaves of bread in one hand and a large chunk of whale meat in the other. I watched as he approached his father warily, putting the food on the ground near him, but taking care to stay back out of arm's reach. Olvir spotted him and lunged at him with a furious roar. I cried out a warning, but Ulf didn't need it: he'd already darted back out of the way. He kept the food between him and his father. On his way towards his son, Olvir saw the food and fell on it, tearing off great chunks of bread and meat with his teeth. He fed ferociously, eating a meal that would have sated two or three grown men in a few moments. Then he shouted in a hoarse voice for ale. I fetched a jug of ale rather than a horn, not wanting to have to hand it directly to him. The ale was downed in one thirsty draught, the jug cast aside, and Olvir attacked his work with renewed energy. It was frightening to watch.

Asgerd and Aud had followed me out of the house and stood watching as Olvir tore rocks out of the ground with his bare hands. 'He's a berserker,' said Asgerd.

'I see,' I breathed, as the truth suddenly dawned on me. That was what I hadn't been able to make sense of in his aura. The ability to go into battle rage. Or in this case, work rage. To fight or work with the strength of many men for a prolonged period. The Viking armies were famed and feared for their berserkers. No one could stand against them. I'd heard so many tales about berserkers, but never seen one.

This explained the danger I felt around Olvir even when he was quiet. He was unpredictable and unstable. His son knew it.

'Shapeshifter too, I shouldn't wonder,' added Aud, silently mimicking a werewolf's howl. 'Isn't that right, Ulf?'

Ulf turned a blank face to her. 'Don't know what you're on about,' he said, and went indoors to eat.

By late afternoon, Olvir had finished the pool and was already digging out the channel to divert the spring. Bjorn and the other men went out to begin the work of finding clay and splitting stones to line the pool. They kept their distance from Olvir who was gradually digging himself away up the hill. They all kept working after dark, lighting a fire to see by. I kept Ulf busy, showing him how to grind corn and feed the animals. He was sullen, but willing to learn.

By nightmeal, there was only a short stretch of ditch still to be dug. Olvir suddenly threw down his tools and stumbled down the hill towards the house. Everyone backed away from him as he entered the house. His berserker fit had left him, leaving him exhausted and weak. Now he was as pale as a ghost and trembling with the effort of standing upright.

Olvir sat down, dirty and sweat-drenched as he was, and called for food. Ulf brought him the generous portion of roasted whale meat that had been prepared for him. He seemed to be having trouble now even lifting the food to his mouth. Only halfway through his meal, he quivered and collapsed. I started forward, fearing that he had killed himself by working so hard. Ulf reassured me.

'Just sleeping,' he said. 'Just cover him and leave him. He's always like that when his rages have been on him. He'll be all right by tomorrow.'

When the tables had been cleared and everyone was ready to sleep, Olvir still lay snoring on the bench where he had fallen. Everyone picked spaces as far as possible from him. Ragna had an attack of prudishness and sent the young girls and unmarried women up into the loft, including me. This, she told us, was where we would sleep from now on.

It was usual to separate out the young women in a household. It had been ignored up to now as we had been camping out. But having a strange man in the house had clearly reminded Ragna of her obligations. It shouldn't have annoyed me to be up there with the slave girls as much as it did. It was Ragna's smug face when she ordered the ladder removed that angered me most.

CHAPTER TWENTY

Slaughtering Month
Gormánuður

I expected Ulf to make a scene when his father left. Olvir took him aside and had a long talk with him. It was a stern talk and Ulf listened with eyes downcast and a red face. And then Olvir embraced his son with surprising tenderness and led him back to me by the hand.

'Stay with Thora, do as she bids you, and make me proud,' he ordered Ulf. Then he took his leave of the rest of us and climbed into his boat. Ulf looked after him as long as the boat was in sight, bravely holding back his tears. I stood quietly beside him. When we finally went back to the house, Bjorn paused beside us and ruffled the boy's hair.

'This seems hard, Ulf,' he said kindly, 'but it's usual in your situation to be fostered. You'll grow accustomed. And your father will visit often, I'm sure. Not every child is that lucky.' He smiled at us both and moved away.

I thought of Bjorn's own background and knew that he spoke from the heart. I was sure Ulf would settle in well. My only concern was to shield him from Ragna, who clearly resented his presence in her household.

'She needs children of her own,' said Asgerd when I

spoke to her about it. 'But Bjorn won't go near her, so that's not likely. I'll help keep Ulf away from her. I'll tell Astrid to teach him to tend the animals.'

I looked across to where Bjorn was sitting talking with Erik and Thrang, and I wondered what it was that kept him so determined to stay away from his own wife. I could scarcely believe it could have anything to do with me. She was a pretty woman and eager to please him. It was surprising she hadn't won him over yet.

The men finished the pool after Olvir's departure and it worked as well as anyone could have dreamed. There was hot, fresh water waiting for us every time anyone wanted to bathe. We took it in turns; some nights the pool was for the men to wallow in, other nights were for women. The pool was so hot it almost scalded the skin, warming us right through to our bones. I could see it was going to be a wonderful thing in the depths of winter.

All the women except Ragna spent long happy days at the beginning of autumn gathering berries. We roamed far and wide, exploring the empty landscape with its wind-swept, sun-drenched hills. At first we took Ulf with us to keep Astrid company. He ate berries until his stomach gave out on him and I had to treat him with my precious herbs. After that, he stayed with the men and helped them where he could with their work. He gradually began to settle in with us, looking up to some of the men, avoiding others. I still saw the homesickness in his eyes from time to time but his hostility faded gradually.

We returned from berry picking each evening,

browned and weather beaten, our pots, cloths, and aprons full of bilberries, crowberries, and a few late stone bramble berries. We stained our fingers and our tongues dark red as we picked and ate from the low, scrubby bushes and plants. The weather was so fine that despite the cold, we wondered if we had reached the land of the gods. Ragna's resentful presence when we returned each evening reminded us that we hadn't. She was fiercely jealous of the freedom we were taking, out of her control. If she had been able to walk further she would have come with us, robbing our outings of their joy.

Normally many of the berries we picked would be preserved in the skyr, the curds that we made for the winter. Berries protected against winter sickness. But we had no cows giving milk, and so no skyr. Instead we shared the berries out at mealtimes, and I wondered how we would fare through the long dark and cold that was coming.

During our outings, I replaced some of the herbs Ragna had destroyed. I picked the leaves and roots of the stone bramble for stomach disorders and coughs. I selected some bilberry leaves for gastric problems and for night vision. Crowberry leaves and stems might also prove useful, so I collected a few. I never took more than half the plants in any spot, leaving the rest to seed and flourish for the following season. The selfheal plant I only found once more beside another hot spring. I feared my stocks were low as we entered a winter in a strange place, unsure how long it would last or how harsh it would be.

It was good when the last walls were put onto the house and we had proper shelter from the cold nights. It was dark and smoky indoors now, but we were glad of the warmth during the long, cold evenings. Bjorn was still supervising the building of the internal walls, such as the animal stalls.

We hoped the sheep could winter outdoors, though that remained to be seen. Eventually the horses might be able to stay out too, but this winter and probably next winter too, they were too young. All the other animals would be brought indoors once the weather worsened. As I watched Bjorn work, and admired his carpentry skills, my thoughts strayed to Aki. One of these stalls should have been for him, I thought sadly. We had only four foals left now.

'Husband,' I overheard Ragna say one morning, 'you are spending a long time building these stalls, but you haven't yet built our bedroom. When will you do that?'

Asgerd grinned at me and rolled her eyes.

'Gripe, gripe,' she whispered with a grin. 'Will she ever stop?'

Bjorn answered without looking at her or even stopping work. 'In time, Ragna. We sleep well enough with everyone else.'

I saw several people smirking as I left the house for another day of berry picking. The sleeping arrangements were the subjects of jokes and smothered laughter among the women. None of us could avoid knowing that Bjorn slept on the sleeping platforms in the main room with the other men and never went near Ragna.

Ragna didn't encourage other women to like her. She hadn't succeeded in hiding her angry, destructive nature from us for long. We were all wary of her, quick to do her bidding, careful not to cross her. Any of us that did, went short of food for a day. With the men she was more cautious and restrained, hiding her true nature, smiling and flattering them. Bjorn, especially, she strove to please most of the time.

I had to be careful to avoid Bjorn in Ragna's presence. She watched us both like a hawk. It was torture. To share the same house with the man I loved and yet to have to guard my every look, almost my every thought. To plan my journeys to the door to avoid walking too near to him, without openly looking to see where he was. Not that I needed to. I found, in this strange state of things, that I became more acutely aware of Bjorn's presence than ever. In order to avoid him, I needed to know where he was at all times.

'Where is Asgerd?' I asked Aud one sunny morning. We were all gathered for berrying, but I didn't want to go without my friend.

Aud shook her head. 'Ragna told her to stay behind and clean,' she told me.

I bit my lip.

'Go on ahead,' I told the others. 'I'll catch you up.'

I hurried back into the house and into the wing that had been built as a latrine. There was Asgerd, sprinkling sawdust. An empty bucket lay discarded beside her.

'Are you finished?' I asked. 'Can you come with us?'

Asgerd shook her head. 'No, I'm to stay.'

I glanced swiftly over my shoulder to check Ragna was nowhere near.

'Let me take your place,' I said in a low voice. 'She's punishing you for being my friend. It's not fair.'

'No. It'll just cause trouble. Go, Thora,' said Asgerd. She didn't look at me as she spoke. I heard Ragna's dragging footsteps behind me, and turned to look at her.

'Is there a problem?' she asked.

'I would like Asgerd to come with us,' I said boldly. 'To have a day in the fresh air. She's stayed behind several times and the winter is approaching.'

'We could all do with fresh air,' said Ragna in a hard voice. 'But there is work needing to be done. You don't mind leaving me here alone to do it every day.'

Her eyes bored into me. We both knew that none of the household tasks were as important right now as the gathering of food. The house was new and only half finished. The men were still working on it. But Ragna wouldn't see reason. I brushed past her and left, feeling guilty about leaving Asgerd behind. Besides, her company and humour would be sorely missed yet again. And her hands to pick.

The steep walk up the hill to catch up with the others made me short of breath and went some way to calm my anger. But it must still have showed in my face. When she saw me, Aud said: 'You shouldn't fight with her, Thora. It only makes everything worse.'

'If no one stands up to her, she'll become more and more of a a tyrant,' I argued.

'And in what way have you prevented that today?' Aud asked. 'Don't be silly, Thora. She loves a good fight. It doesn't upset her like it does you. Leave be.'

'Surely,' I said, 'if we stand up to Ragna, and show her kindness and fairness at the same time, it'll make a difference in the end?'

The others shook their heads at me. 'You obviously don't know her sort,' remarked Aud.

Asgerd had one day's picking with us and then the fine weather broke. There was a night with a heavy frost, and when we awoke at sunrise, all the ground was white as though it had snowed. Later, a mist rolled in from the sea and we dared not stray from the house in case we got lost. The mist brought an autumn chill with it that made us all shiver if we moved too far from the fire.

'That's it for berries, then,' said Asgerd sadly. 'The frost will have killed them.'

'They were good while they lasted,' I said. 'I'm worried we may go hungry this winter.'

'We'll have no fresh meat, that's for sure,' sighed Asgerd, tucking a stray strand of dark hair behind her ear. 'It's strange, isn't it? It's slaughtering month, but we have no animals to spare to slaughter. No feasts. Just endless gruel and dried meat.' She sniffed at the pot I was stirring for breakfast, and pulled a face.

I grinned. 'By this time next year there'll be sheep to butcher,' I reminded her.

'A year!' groaned Asgerd. 'Unless the men can hunt some game.'

I looked sideways at her. 'I've seen nothing,' I told her. 'All the time we were out. No signs of larger animals. No tracks, no droppings. The only grazing that's been done is by our own animals. I don't think there's anything to hunt.'

'Then they'll have to fish,' said Asgerd decidedly. 'We can't live the winter on what we have. We won't even have any milk or skyr.'

I felt uneasy at the thought of the winter ahead. I looked around for Ragna, and saw her close by.

'Ragna,' I said to her, 'should we check the food stores and decide whether there's enough for winter? We might need to think about rationing the food already.'

'You'd love a good poke around among the stores, wouldn't you, Thora?' said Ragna, nastily. 'As if I'd need the help of a jumped-up, interfering slave girl to check the quantities.'

My offer had been made from concern and a desire to be helpful. Ragna's answer was like a slap.

'I've never been a slave,' I replied indignantly, keeping my voice low with difficulty. 'I'm no slave or servant of yours. I'm a free woman and a healer.'

Ragna hunched an impatient shoulder and limped away towards her husband who was sitting too far away to have heard this exchange.

'Jealous cat,' muttered Asgerd. 'If we do run short of food this winter, I'll personally cook her and serve her to the men.'

This was so outrageous it should have made me laugh. But I only managed a faint smile. I was still smarting.

The men used the day to work on the inside of the house. It was cramped and noisy as they put up partition walls for the animal stalls at the far end. I sat grinding corn with Ulf as an unwilling helper. There was cutting and banging, noise and dust all around us. At last I saw that besides the sleeping platforms they were also constructing a private bedroom. Ragna directed and watched with great satisfaction. She was getting her way at last. I felt sick to the stomach. Suddenly, I had to get out of the house.

'Come on, Asgerd,' I murmured. 'Let's go and check on the animals.'

She took her wrap and followed me, looking only mildly surprised.

We stepped out of the dusty, smoky house into a grey, muffled world. After we had taken just a few steps from the house, the noise of the carpentry faded and the house disappeared into the swirling mist. The air was raw and it was raining. The fine misty rain settled on our hair and eyelashes and gathered into droplets.

Asgerd clutched my arm.

'Thora, we'll get lost,' she said. 'Why do you want to be out in this? It's not safe.'

'I couldn't stand it in there,' I told her. 'Will it be safe enough if we stay within earshot of the house?'

'I suppose so,' admitted Asgerd reluctantly.

We both walked carefully in the direction of the horses. I'd helped picket them yesterday and thought I could remember where they were. However, we wandered too far to the right and would have passed them had Asgerd not heard the sound of their teeth tearing up the grass.

'This way,' she said tugging me towards the sound. A dark shape loomed out of the mist ahead of me. It was the grey foal who had been Aki's companion. He didn't have a name. I ran my hands over his damp coat. In return, he lifted his head and nickered softly.

'Sorry, I've no food for you,' I told him, patting his neck and stroking his mane. The foal lipped my hands and then went back to tearing up mouthfuls of grass. We found the other three foals, also grazing nearby.

'Well, they don't seem the least bit bothered by the mist, do they?' Asgerd said.

'No, they don't. I'm more worried about the sheep. They aren't tethered and could wander off the edge of the cliff.'

'They're stupid enough for that,' agreed Asgerd. 'But all the animals are thriving here. It's a fine country and a wonderful climate. Until today, that is.'

I frowned and looked around us, peering into the mist. 'It's been wonderful up to now,' I agreed. 'But I admit I'm worried about the winter.'

'Why?' asked Asgerd, sounding surprised.

'I think the weather may be harsher than we can well imagine, or than we've ever experienced,' I told her. 'Not to mention exposed. It's the vegetation. Have you noticed how small everything is?'

When Asgerd shook her head, I continued.

'Most of the plants here are the same or similar to the ones at home in Norway. But they are smaller and closer to the ground. Look at the trees. They are tiny. More like bushes.'

Asgerd chuckled. 'Here's a good one for you,' she said. 'How do you find your way if you get lost in an Icelandic forest?'

'How?' I asked, caught off my guard.

'Stand up,' Asgerd joked. She laughed but the sound was muffled by the mist and rain. I smiled, despite my worries. Asgerd's good humour was always infectious.

We dared not search for the other animals in the mist.

We might get lost. It was hard enough to find our way back to the house safely. When we walked in through the door, beaded with moisture, I realized at once we would pay dearly for our stolen hour.

The men had laid down tools and were sitting hungrily eating the bowls of broth that Ragna was ladling for them. Each had received a piece of the flat bread that Asgerd had baked that morning.

'Asgerd,' snapped Ragna. 'Go sweep out the animal stalls.'

'But it's meal time,' I objected.

Ragna looked pleased at my words. Always a bad sign. 'She missed her chores,' she sneered.

'We were checking on the horses,' I explained. But I might as well have saved my breath. Asgerd went off quietly to clean. I turned to follow her, but Ragna called me back. Angrily, I took a place on the bench, where Thrang moved to make room for me. Ragna passed me a bowl with only the smallest scraping of broth and no bread.

I sat and stared at it. I knew I must distance myself from Asgerd. She would suffer from friendship with me and so might Astrid and Erik. I looked over at Erik, sitting quietly on a bench on the other side of the fire. He didn't look at me. Ragna wouldn't hesitate to starve him too. He was still not back to full strength even though his cough had cleared.

I sighed quietly and ate the small amount of food I had been given. I was hungry and it did nothing but whet my appetite. Silently, Thrang pushed half of his own bread towards me. 'Take it,' he whispered, looking down at me.

I glanced at Ragna and her eyes were on us. I shook

my head at Thrang, knowing that if I accepted, he too would go short of food tomorrow.

'You need your strength,' I murmured. How many more people would Ragna punish to get at me? I understood at last what she was doing. She wished to isolate me. Without friends, she thought I would be weaker than her. Well, I had some training that would help me. A healer was used to working alone.

CHAPTER TWENTY-ONE

The fog lasted four days and then a breeze sprang up from the east, blowing it away. The days were bright, but short and cold. The sun remained low in the sky. I knew from Thrang that eventually the daylight would fail altogether. That was something I'd never experienced in our part of Norway. I watched the stunted plants yellow and wither as the light failed and icy winds began to blow from the north. Snow fell on the mountains on the far side of the bay, gleaming white by both sun and moonlight.

Now that winter had arrived, Ragna requested Bjorn to set up her loom. It was assembled in a prime spot at the fireside, for maximum light. Ragna set to work at once. It was a revelation to all those of us who understood the skill. She selected the softest, finest garns from her stores. Her fingers flew over the loom weaving the yarn so fast that the eye could scarcely follow the movement of the shuttle. It wove in and out of the threads, the length of woven cloth growing visibly.

'I've never seen anyone who could work like that,' Asgerd told me. 'Weaving is my skill, but I can't work so fast or so evenly.'

'There must be something . . . no.' I bit back the words I had been about to say.

'Tell,' said Asgerd, pinching my arm playfully.

I leant towards her till my mouth was close to her ear.

'I'm amazed they let her go,' I whispered. 'She must have been worth a fortune to her family. Why marry her to an unknown chieftain?'

Asgerd wrinkled her nose as she stared at Ragna, considering my question.

'They got a good trade,' she whispered back at last. 'A ship, livestock, gold . . .'

I shook my head slightly, still not satisfied. I watched Ragna's usually fierce aura glow with more peaceful colours than usual as she worked. Something about all this bothered me.

'I think they needed to get rid of her for some reason,' I murmured at last. 'Something lies in her past or in her character. Thrang said so straight away, and I think he was right.'

In just two days, Ragna brought a soft woollen tunic and a pair of woollen leggings to the table at nightmeal and showed them to Bjorn.

'These are for you, my husband,' she said, presenting them to him. 'Perhaps you'd like to try them on for size and comfort before we begin the dyeing.'

Bjorn fingered the cloth.

'This is fine cloth,' he said. 'Thank you.'

Ragna's usually closed face lit for a moment at this praise.

'What colour would you like them to be?' she asked him.

'Whatever you choose,' he replied peaceably.

'Then I'll have them dyed red for you. Thora claims to be skilled with plants. She will know which to select.' She turned and smiled her false smile at me. 'Thora, I'll put you in charge of the dyeing.'

I bit back the objection that sprang to my lips.

'Poor you—to be in charge of the dyeing,' whispered Asgerd with a grin.

We both knew it wasn't the actual dyeing that was the problem. I'd already collected the mosses and plants that could produce different colours in the fabric and it was no problem to steep these. It was setting the colours afterwards that every woman dreaded. Collecting the urine from the cattle and soaking the woollens in it. And the daily lifting and airing as the scent of the urine grew more rank.

I rose the next day expecting to begin the work. But the morning was about to take an unexpected turn. I was sitting at breakfast with the early chores done and the grinding of barley begun, when the household scene faded before my eyes. The room went dark and silent. I felt my bowl slip from my hands as they became chill and numb.

A ship. An unknown ship in the waves. Behind it two more ships, heavily laden. Heading in towards our bay. On deck stand many people and animals. They are pleased to be here. They pass the island and head towards us. We will make this our home, someone says.

The vision ended abruptly. My companions faded back

into view. I noticed Asgerd first, staring at me, a look of concern on her face. They were all staring at me. I saw I had spilled my porridge down my tunic and my wooden bowl lay upside down before me. I felt annoyed that I had spilled my food. I was so hungry. And cold. I shivered.

'Ships, Thora?' asked Bjorn. His voice seemed loud in the silence. 'Are they close by?'

'Very close,' I said. 'Three of them.'

As I spoke, I saw the blood leave his face. He was suddenly deathly pale. I could see a painful question burning in his eyes. He wanted to know if these people were Svanson's kin come to take vengeance.

I thought back to my vision. Had it been a war party? No, the people hadn't been dressed in black. I was sure of it. And they had had women and children with them. And lots of animals and cargo.

'Settlers.' I spoke the one word aloud and I could see Bjorn relax visibly. He took a deep breath. He looked ashamed of his fear and jumped to his feet to give orders.

Among all the voices, I heard Thrang saying: 'But that's impossible. Who would travel so late in the year?'

No one answered him. Bjorn was asking me how soon the ships would be here.

'They're in sight,' I told him.

At this, everyone rushed to put on cloaks and we all poured out of the longhouse and followed the path to the shore. Many of the men were sceptical, but not for long. There were the ships, heavily laden and low in the water. They were being rowed towards us. There was an excited murmur. Visitors would provide interest and entertainment.

Someone was tugging on my sleeve. I looked down and saw Ulf. He was looking at me as though I was a ghost.

'How did you know that?' he asked, awed. 'I reckon you must have seed 'em earlier.'

'I haven't been out of the house today,' I told him. 'Sometimes I see things in my head.'

The boy stared at me, confused but intrigued.

'Can you learn me that?' he asked.

I laughed, but gently, so as not to hurt his feelings.

'It's not something you can learn,' I explained. 'I was born with the ability.'

Ulf looked disappointed.

'It's not always a nice skill to have,' I told him.

The ships were close enough now, that we could see the people's faces. They had adjusted their course so they were heading straight towards us. I felt nervous, hoping I had read their intentions correctly. Everyone around me was excited though, at the thought of new company.

One by one, the ships beached on the black shingle. Men jumped out to pull them up out of the water, and our men joined them. There was talk and laughter. I drew a sigh of relief.

A tall, fair-haired man in an imposing cloak stepped forward. He was a very young man—barely more than a boy, I thought. His beard was sparse on his face and his skin was smooth. But he was tall, strong, and carried himself with confidence.

'I am Helgi son of Thorolf,' he announced. 'This is my wife, Bera.' His wife, who had been helped down from the boat now, went to stand at Helgi's side. She was tall and fair and despite her youth, I could see at once that she was heavy with child.

Helgi beckoned another man forward. He was older, proud, with a slightly cruel twist to his mouth. I disliked his aura. It was a permanent purple, oozing arrogance. 'This is my kinsman Arn, son of Styr,' Helgi said.

As Bjorn stepped forward to welcome the newcomers, I saw suspicion flash into Arn's eyes. The suspicious thoughts were reflected in his thought colours. My heart skipped a beat with fear. In place of Ragna, who had not been able to accompany us to the shore, I went and stood beside Bjorn, wanting to support him. Thrang obviously felt the same because he came to stand on the other side of Bjorn. His tall, imposing presence was a great strength.

'I am Bjorn Svanson,' said Bjorn at last. His voice did not betray any anxiety. 'This is Thora Asgrimsdottir and Thrang Einarson, my companions and dear friends. My wife would like to have joined me in bidding you welcome. She is waiting in our home to greet you.'

I disliked the sceptical lift to Arn's brow as Bjorn introduced himself.

'Bjorn Svanson?' he asked, politely incredulous. 'Chieftain in southern Norway?'

My heart beat uncomfortably fast, and my disappointment was bitter indeed. Were we about to be exposed by these unlucky visitors? They had no business sailing so late in the year. We should at least have had the winter in peace.

I felt Bjorn straighten his shoulders beside me. I

admired the nonchalant tone as he replied. 'Is it possible that we've met before?' he asked Arn. 'It's always a pleasure to renew acquaintances.'

It was a bold stroke. For a moment, I could see Arn's confidence was shaken. But as I watched, a slow, insolent smile spread over his face.

'If we had, I doubt I would have remembered you,' he sneered.

There was a collective intake of breath behind me at the stranger's rudeness. None of our people were armed, but men on both sides clenched their fists. Helgi stepped forward swiftly. 'I apologize for my kinsman's rudeness,' he said, putting a firm hand on Arn's shoulder. He tried to sound jovial, but there was a nervous edge to his voice. 'We intend no offence to you.'

'No offence taken. For now,' replied Bjorn after a brief pause. 'But your kinsman will need to mind his manners if he wishes to be invited in friendship.'

It was a tense moment. I awaited the outcome with baited breath. But Arn stepped back, spreading his hands in a deprecating gesture.

'I apologize,' he said.

It sounded less than sincere, but Bjorn took advantage of the truce to invite his visitors to our longhouse for a meal. The free men and women accompanied us to the house with one or two slaves in attendance. The rest stayed on the ships. I followed uneasily, watching Arn. As he climbed the hill to our house, his cloak fell back and I saw he was wearing a sword. I felt a shiver of fear pass through me. I had to warn Bjorn.

'A fine hall,' remarked Helgi as he entered the

longhouse and looked about him. 'Worthy of a great chieftain.'

Bjorn nodded graciously, accepting the compliment, acknowledging that Helgi was trying to make amends for his companion's rudeness. And truly, this was a fine building. I saw it afresh through the strangers' eyes. Lofty and large: the dwelling of a man of consequence.

Ragna came forward, and Bjorn introduced his wife. Arn stared at Bjorn even harder than before. I could see him shaking his head and muttering under his breath. My unease turned to sick anxiety. Either he had known the real Svanson or he didn't believe for one moment that this small, dark-haired man could be the Viking chieftain he had heard of.

I helped Aud and Asgerd prepare a meal for the strangers. We were obliged by the laws of hospitality to feast them as best we could, though I suspected it made heavy inroads into our precious stores. Ragna seemed proud to have us cook and serve what we had, however. She loved to show off her status and consequence in front of visitors.

We prepared the rest of the whale meat, broached a barrel of salted fish, and Ragna got out a whole cheese. Some of our barley grain was hurriedly pounded to make flatbread. I watched this, longing to know how much food still lay in the store. And I wondered how long the visitors would stay. I could see the same thought on Asgerd's face. But Helgi ordered two barrels of mead to be brought up from his ship and everyone else looked delighted. The men fell to drinking from their horns and the talk soon grew merry and boisterous.

In the bustle of setting out the tables I managed to whisper to Bjorn without anyone seeing. I warned him that Arn was armed. Bjorn listened intently. I saw a look of trepidation dart into his eyes and we both glanced at my father's sword where it hung on the wall. I feared Bjorn would need it before this visit was over. And I was painfully aware, from his brief fight with Thrang, that Bjorn was far from expert with a sword.

We sat down to nightmeal early, and everyone ate hungrily.

'So, how do you come to be sailing so late in the year?' asked Thrang between draughts of mead. 'Have you come from Norway?'

'No,' Helgi replied. 'We came to Iceland two summers ago from a Viking settlement in Ireland. We had built a house here, further along the coast and begun a farm. But we had trouble.'

He had everyone's attention now. We watched impatiently as Helgi paused to take a draught of his mead.

'It must have been serious trouble to uproot you so soon,' commented Thrang with a frown.

'It was,' agreed Helgi exchanging a glance with his wife. 'We were a long way from here. In the west fjords. There was good farming land and a fair climate. A great deal of rain, of course. And the winters are harsh here, as you will see yourselves before much longer. But we were troubled by a werewolf.'

There was a sudden, horrified silence in the hall. I felt my own heart lurch with horror.

'It took our sheep, one by one. And then our pigs. One

of our poor slaves even had a child taken,' he said, and a look of sadness crossed his face.

'Did you see it?' asked Bjorn with slight scepticism in his voice.

'Are you calling us liars?' demanded Arn at once, his tone aggressive.

'No,' said Bjorn, his thoughtful gaze resting on Arn. 'It was a friendly enquiry.'

'Arn saw it,' Helgi told him. 'He said it was the size of a bear with shaggy fur, red eyes and foul breath. And it left huge prints.'

I thought Arn looked just a little uncomfortable as this was related. Bjorn's eyebrows rose.

'Are you sure it wasn't a bear, or an ordinary wolf?' asked Grim.

'There aren't any wolves or bears in Iceland,' said Thrang and Arn at the same time. Then they glared at one another.

'We heard it howl on moonlit nights,' said Bera with a shudder. She put her hands protectively on her belly, and edged a little closer to Helgi.

'And we had trouble with hidden people,' Helgi continued. 'The milk turned sour, the stores were pilfered. It became impossible to go on living there. So once the harvest was in, we braved the autumn storms to find a new home.'

'That was an undertaking indeed!' exclaimed Bjorn. 'When I think of the work it has been to build a homestead. And you gave it all up again. The hauntings must have been severe.'

'I've heard tell of trolls, elves, and fairies,' said Ragna.

It was surprising to hear her speak out in front of so many people and a hush fell. 'We had trouble in my home on the Faeroe Islands too from time to time. They can make life impossible.'

Our visitors smiled gratefully at her understanding.

I was less sympathetic. I had never heard of any of the hidden people breaking into a locked food store. It sounded more like human pilferings to me. I kept my thoughts to myself, though I could see, glancing at Bjorn, that he shared the same suspicion.

'You really dismantled the whole house again?' asked Thrang. He sounded awed.

Helgi nodded. 'I wouldn't ask my wife to have our child in such a haunted place. You have no such trouble here?'

We all shook our heads. I guessed a few people were thinking of Olvir, but no one liked to mention him with Ulf sitting among us. Besides, so far Olvir had been a help to us, not a problem. Whatever some of us might think of him. 'And is there land here for the taking?' asked Helgi diffidently.

Even though I had known what was coming, my heart jumped uncomfortably. I liked the look of Helgi and his wife, but I could see at a glance that Arn was trouble.

'There are few settlers here,' said Bjorn. 'Only us, and our good neighbour Olvir, who has his home on the far side of the bay,' said Bjorn cordially. 'I'll show you the extent of my claim tomorrow. I hope you'll decide to settle here and be our neighbours. Meanwhile you're welcome as our guests.'

He smiled as he spoke and looked so lordly that my

heart swelled with pride. It was as though he had been a chieftain welcoming guests to his table all his life. But I wondered if he would regret his generosity as the winter came.

CHAPTER TWENTY-TWO

In the event it took only three days for trouble to break out.

Helgi and Bjorn took Helgi's horses and rode the perimeter of Bjorn's land claim. They discussed which land Helgi should take and where he should build his house. The two men seemed to be swiftly forming a strong friendship. Ragna was wary of Bera but not unfriendly. I dared not approach Bera under Ragna's jealous eye, but I liked the look of her and knew that it would be my task to deliver her baby. Quite soon too, I judged.

I'd noticed the first evening our guests were with us, how heavily Arn drank of the mead. This proved to be a strong habit with him. He called for mead every night and took so much he could barely keep his seat on the bench. The talk and storytelling after nightmeal was rudely interrupted by his raucous shouts and snatches of song. I could see that Helgi was both ashamed of and embarrassed by his kinsman's conduct, but he also seemed to be afraid and didn't rebuke him.

Bjorn was asked to tell the story of how we came to Iceland. He cast an anxious glance at me, which I hoped no one else noticed. Then he began to speak. He told the tale from the point at which we sailed from Norway and this seemed to catch Arn's attention.

'Hey, noble host and chieftain,' he slurred, 'I notice you miss out the bit where you knocked your master on the head and threw him overboard. Or whatever else it was you did. Or can you give me another explanation for why you look more like a boy-loving slave whose hair has grown out a bit than a Viking chief?'

There were gasps of indignation around the hall. Bjorn leapt to his feet at once. He overturned the table in front of him and gave a shout of rage. As well he might. It was an insult beyond any man's pride.

'Say that again if you dare!' he roared. He flung his cloak back from his shoulders and I saw that Arn was not the only one to be wearing a sword at his side.

For a moment everyone was frozen into horrified silence. Then there was a noisy, panicked scramble as we all tried to get out of the way of the two armed men.

'You don't dare to repeat it then?' demanded Bjorn. His voice was steady and confident. He had barely touched the mead.

'Arn, apologize!' cried Helgi urgently.

Arn ignored him, pushed himself away from the bench and got up, swaying a little on his feet. He was a tall, powerful man, probably experienced in sword play. I was terrified for Bjorn.

'I say you are an escaped slave in a girl's tunic. Not even man enough to bed your own wife. Who do you prefer to snuggle up to at night, then, the nice strong sailor man here? Or perhaps the boy?'

A furious murmur passed through our household.

'How dare you insult your host?' roared Thrang. He stepped forward angrily, fists clenched, but Stein held him back. This was Bjorn's fight. Such a slur on Bjorn's manhood could be avenged only by death. He had to fight Arn.

I felt anger mix with my terror. How could this man make such trouble, when we had housed and fed him for three nights? It went against all the rules of hospitality. I was also appalled that he had seen through our deception so easily. Would Helgi take his side? I couldn't read his expression or his aura from where I stood.

Bjorn drew his sword and it flashed in the firelight as he lunged. There were screams from those nearest as they scrambled further back out of reach of the deadly weapons. Arn parried the blow easily and made a thrust of his own. The clash of steel on iron in such a confined space was loud and very frightening. People leapt out of the way. Asgerd pulled Astrid right away, down to the animal stalls, but most were too curious to go so far. Our future depended on the outcome of this fight.

Bjorn attacked ferociously, raining down blow after blow. Arn seemed to hold him at bay effortlessly. I thought the drink had made no difference to his fighting skills. I backed up against the wall, my hands slick with sweat, as far from those lethal blades as possible. It was clear Arn was the more experienced swordsman. Of course he was. He'd probably trained since he could walk. But his drunken state was beginning to tell. He fought from pure instinct. If Arn had been sober, Bjorn would be dead by now.

Arn staggered and had trouble regaining his balance.

His movements slowed. As Bjorn twisted out of his reach, Arn struggled to turn and focus on him again. He was swaying now, the sweat dripping from his brow. Bjorn was still alert and light on his feet. But Arn had such skill. I watched him parry yet another blow from Bjorn with ease, scarcely moving as he twisted the blade harmlessly aside. I heard a cry of fear among the other whimpers and tears around me and realized it was Ragna. She was whispering prayers under her breath, her eyes huge in her face with horror as she watched Bjorn fight.

Bjorn rushed his opponent once more, causing several of the women to scream. He smashed his sword down on Arn's with such force that it bent his opponent's blade. Bjorn had Foe Biter, my father's sword, and its blade was edged with steel. It was worth more than all the treasure in this house. Arn's sword was a home-forged weapon, greatly inferior.

Both men were sweating now, and Arn's breathing was ragged. It was loud in the comparative silence of the longhouse. A flush of anger and exertion had spread over his face and neck. He needed to straighten his sword. He circled Bjorn, judging his moment. Arn lunged, and the blow would have gone through Bjorn if the sword had been straight. A fierce exchange of blows followed, and Bjorn was forced back right into the terrified onlookers on the far side of the hall. He stumbled trying to avoid them. A woman screamed, a high, piercing shriek that went right through me. It was Bera. Arn swiftly bent to straighten his sword beneath his feet. But Bjorn hadn't been distracted. His eyes never wavered from his opponent. With a yell, he lunged at Arn wildly and opened his sword arm from wrist to elbow. The blood welled bright red from the wound.

My instincts told me to run forward and bind the wound. But I held back. He was our enemy and the fight was not yet over.

Bjorn ended it quickly. He kicked Arn's sword away from him as the wounded man stood clutching his arm and held Foe Biter to his throat.

'Yield,' he hissed.

'If you were a man instead of an overgrown slave girl, you'd kill me,' snarled Arn.

Bjorn dropped his sword and punched him in the face. There was a sickening crunch as he blackened the man's eye and split his cheek open.

'Get out of my house and never set foot on my land again,' bellowed Bjorn.

I felt a chill in my stomach. Though I didn't want to watch another death, I knew Bjorn should kill him. He had been insulted beyond endurance. It was the only way to regain his honour. But it was too late. Arn picked himself up and ran from the house, leaving a dark, sticky trail in his wake.

Thrang stepped forward and clapped Bjorn on the shoulder. He obviously didn't feel Bjorn had disgraced himself. I looked once more at Helgi. His kinsman and his host had fought. Whose side would he take? By rights, he should support his kinsman, no matter how in the wrong he'd been.

But Helgi wasn't even looking. Instead he was bent over his wife whose sweat-drenched brow was creased in agony. As I watched, she let out another terrible scream.

Desperately, Helgi looked to Bjorn. It was as though the fight had never happened.

'Do you have a midwife here?' he gasped. 'Someone help her, for the love of Odin!'

All the men in the room took a horrified step back. Still shocked from his fight, Bjorn looked frantically at me. I moved forward, aware that I was confused and shaking in the aftermath of the fight. As I crouched down beside Bera she groaned and gasped for air. Her brow and her hands were clammy, her tunic wet. The waters had broken. The child was on its way.

My long training reasserted itself, and I immediately took charge.

'Help her into the bedroom at once,' I ordered Asgerd and Aud who were standing near. 'She needs some privacy.'

Ragna would be furious with me for commandeering her room, but I would deal with that later.

'Is she your midwife?' I heard Helgi's anxious voice asking as I accompanied Bera to the room. 'But she's just a child herself.'

Over the sound of my own voice giving orders for strips of clean cloth and calling for my medicine chest from the sleeping loft, I heard Bjorn say: 'You can trust Thora completely.'

I felt warmed by his faith in me and that gave me strength after the shock of the fight. The necessity of helping Bera also steadied me. I had assisted at many, many births over the years. At first I had only accompanied Sigrun, and then delivered babies myself. In the last year or so, if there were no problems, I had been left in charge.

Bera clutched my hand and groaned.

'What do I do?' she begged. 'It's my first time, oh . . . ow . . . it hurts . . . '

I reassured her and stayed with her as the night wore on. The pains intensified and Bera shouted herself hoarse. I couldn't detect anything wrong, but the baby was large and didn't come. Bera was growing tired. We prayed together, calling on the goddess Frigg for her support and aid. Between pains, I persuaded Bera to walk.

Suddenly the pains ceased and Bera leant against me, panting with relief.

'You're nearly there,' I told her. Sure enough a great shuddering passed through her body. The baby was on its way. The most dangerous part of the birthing had come.

I felt the importance of delivering this baby safely. Of course, the health of the mother and baby were always vital. But I was also aware this was my first real test among all these new people, in this new land. They all trusted me. Helgi and his wife were depending on me. If I failed, they might turn against me like their kinsman, Arn.

It was a long night. At last, near dawn, Bera gave birth to a healthy baby boy. She was exhausted, but happy to hold her child.

'Ingvar,' she named him, stroking his tiny face with gentle fingers.

Helgi tiptoed in to peep at his new son, and gazed at him, eyes shining with joy. A young warrior, as gentle as a lamb, tamed by the sight of his newborn child.

Both Helgi and Bera embraced me and thanked me. Outside the room, I caught a glimpse of Helgi embracing Bjorn and calling him his brother. I knew that I'd been right. He wouldn't turn on us now.

But when Bjorn stepped outside, he saw at once that one of Helgi's three ships had gone. Helgi discovered that ten of his slaves and a good part of his harvest had been on board. Of Arn there was no sign.

CHAPTER TWENTY-THREE

There came a day when the tired winter sun no longer lifted above the horizon. Then it failed to give any light at all, even at midday. It was truly winter.

Some of the slaves whimpered the first day there was no light and spoke of the great wolf Fenris having swallowed the sun. Ragnarok, the day of judgement, was upon us, they whispered.

'The sun will return,' Helgi's people told them. 'It will be freed again in the spring.'

Bera, who was happily nursing her baby boy, also told me that there was nothing to fear. 'It will be dark for two moons. And in the summer the sun doesn't leave the sky for months,' she told me, a happy glow on her face.

It was a joy to have visitors among us, especially such kind and friendly people. After Arn's departure there had not been one cross word spoken between the two households. Goodwill flourished, diluting Ragna's presence and brightening the darkness of winter. Most days, our men joined Helgi's and all worked on reconstructing Helgi's house further across the bay. They had chosen a spot for it in the last of the light and were now working by moon and firelight. The women worked at the fireside preparing food, spinning and weaving, dyeing, sewing clothes and shoes. It was sociable, with talk and stories going on all day while we worked.

The only anxiety that tempered the pleasure of the guests' company was how our food supplies would hold out. Ragna let no one have so much as a glimpse into the storeroom, so only she could gauge how much we had left. She wouldn't discuss it with me even when I tried to speak to her.

Helgi was supplementing with food from his own stores, but he and Bera were also anxious having lost so much of their own harvest to Arn. They at least had cows giving milk which they gladly shared with us. Once more there was fresh cheese and skyr to vary our diet. It seemed for a week or two that happier times had arrived. But all too soon a shadow was cast over us.

One of Helgi's slaves had been unwell when he arrived. We hadn't noticed at first. He'd dragged himself around for a few days trying to do his share of the work, until Helgi noticed and ordered him to rest. I attended him but didn't think he had anything seriously wrong with him. I was mistaken. One morning, he collapsed at breakfast.

The man's name was Thors and he was in a high fever, his skin hot and dry to the touch. The whites of his eyes were bloodshot and sore. I ordered him laid apart from everyone else at the far end of the living quarters, near the animals. I tended him, giving him plenty of water to drink as well as infusions of angelica to strengthen him, and a tea made of willow bark to lower his fever. He wasn't a quiet patient. The fever had him in its grip. He thrashed around and raved.

'Some people will use any excuse to shirk their share of the work,' muttered Ragna, doling me out an even smaller portion of skyr than usual for breakfast. 'In my father's household, a sick slave was left to fend for himself. Not nursed like a precious child.'

'And in *my* father's household, a slave's life was held in the same respect as a free man's,' I snapped back. Then I wished I had held my tongue. It never did any good to anger Ragna. When I heard her mutter 'slave lover' for my ears only, I ignored her. I comforted myself by thinking that she was married to one. She chose to disbelieve Arn's accusation, but I knew the truth.

Thors reached his crisis in the small hours of the second night. I had stayed up watching him, concerned that he was very seriously ill. The man cried out in fear and pain, babbling of fire and blindness. While his aura glowed with colours around him, I didn't fear greatly for him. He seemed strong. But as those colours began to fade, I redoubled my efforts to cool the fever. I wiped his arms and shoulders with a damp cloth and tried to pour a little willow bark tea into his mouth. It ran uselessly out again. He wouldn't or couldn't swallow. I implored him to wake up and respond to my pleas to drink. I shook him gently and patted his face. He was beyond my aid. Under my horrified gaze, his aura faded to white and he died.

There was nothing I could have done. The gods had claimed him as their own and I had to accept it. It was never easy though, to tend someone and to fail. I sat still beside the body until morning, and then I went to Bjorn and told him what had happened.

Thors was buried on the hillside under a cairn of stones. The men did this while the women burned his clothes. We washed the place where he had lain and I burned aromatic plants to cleanse the air of impurities. We all hoped that was the end of it.

For a few days, it seemed it was. I watched everyone with anxious eyes and saw no sign of the disease. I saw plenty of fear in their faces, as they, too, wondered who would be next. But then Asgerd fell ill. One by one, men and women sickened. I nursed them day and night, more patients than I could manage. Rummaging through my precious stores I selected elder, meadowsweet, and more willow bark, all of which could reduce fever. None of them were plants that I had yet found in Iceland and I had no idea what I was going to do if they ran out. The thought sent chills down my spine.

As soon as Helgi's house was habitable, he fled there to live in the unfinished shell of a building with his wife, baby, and those of his people that had not yet fallen sick. They hoped to save baby Ingvar from infection.

'I'm so sorry to have brought this on you,' I heard him say, clasping Bjorn's hand. 'So very sorry. Tell Thora that once again she has our gratitude. We're deep in her debt and yours.'

While I cared for all the sick, I was especially concerned for my friend, Asgerd. I cast the runes for her over and over, following their guidance. I dosed her with the willow bark and she responded well, calming and sleeping or lying quietly for hours at a time. Ulf also took the disease, but the runes told me he was strong and would recover. I tried to trust their wisdom and still my fears.

I had little time to spare for those who kept well, but I watched Bjorn from a distance when I could, afraid he would sicken too. I forgot to watch Thrang, who collapsed quite suddenly at nightmeal one evening. It took four men to lift him to the overflowing end of the house where the patients lay. I could see at once that he would be difficult. He fended me off angrily one moment and then the next begged me to stop him dying.

Asgerd was the first to pass her crisis and live. I was deeply relieved and watched tenderly over her as she slowly recovered. As soon as she could sit up I sent her back to the main part of the house where Erik could care for her.

I was growing weary. For weeks I'd only slept in snatches. Late one night when I thought the whole house was sleeping, I dozed off, propped up against the wall next to Ulf. I was awoken by a light touch on my sleeve.

'Thora, are you all right?' asked a low voice.

I had only the dim light of an oil lamp to see by, but I knew Bjorn's voice. I turned my head to look at him, watching the flickering light cast moving shadows across his face.

'I'm well enough,' I whispered. 'Only tired.'

'I can't sleep for fear you'll take the disease,' Bjorn whispered.

'I never get ill. And you need your sleep,' I said, keeping my voice expressionless. I wouldn't let him see how much his words moved me.

'So do you. Is there no one who can help you nurse these people so that you can get some rest?'

'No. I've already thought about that. The women I

trust are either already sick, or I don't wish to expose them to the fever. You shouldn't be here either.'

'I'm not afraid,' he replied. 'How are they?' He nodded towards my patients who currently numbered eight. Some lay quietly, others tossed and moaned in their fever.

'Most are very sick,' I told him. 'I've never seen this illness before. I have no name for it. I'm especially worried about Ulf. He's just a child. I don't know how we could explain to his father if he . . . '

In the darkness, Bjorn took my hand in his and held it in a comforting clasp. For a moment, I couldn't breathe. I should pull away, tell him to leave. But the long days and nights of nursing had left me exhausted and weak, and I allowed it. I sat quite still, though my heart was pounding in my chest and my ears were singing.

'And how's Thrang?' asked Bjorn after a few moment's silence. He spoke as though nothing had changed. As though my hand wasn't resting in both his. I tried to do the same.

'He'll recover,' I said. 'He's as strong as a bear.'

We sat without moving. I could hear a storm blowing up outside the house. The wind whistled in the roof and found its way in through even the smallest chinks in the wall, making the flame on the lamp dance. It was bitterly cold. I thought vaguely that I should stuff the gaps. Perhaps when I was less tired.

Someone cried out nearby. It was Kari, one of our men. Drawing my hand from Bjorn, I went to him. He was burning with fever, his eyes staring and bloodshot. As I watched his aura began to fade. I felt sick. I'd watched death many times in my life, but always hated to see young people die. Gently, I laid my hand on his brow and spoke soothingly to him. He couldn't hear me.

'Is he . . . ' Bjorn began to ask. I shook my head at him. 'How do you know?' he whispered.

'His aura,' I murmured. 'It's bleeding all its colours.'

Bjorn looked horrified.

In a few moments it was over. I bent forward and closed the man's eyes. The sense of loss and failure overwhelmed me for a moment. Another life I had been unable to save. Two people had died now and I hadn't been able to help them. I'd let them down.

'I wish . . . ' I began in a whisper. I paused, but I could see Bjorn was waiting for me to continue. 'I wish with all my heart I had Sigrun by to advise me. To reassure me that I've done all I could. If only I wasn't so tired . . . '

Bjorn knelt beside me and put a hand on my shoulder. I pushed him away, but he didn't go.

'It's not your fault, Thora,' he whispered. 'I've never seen your equal. Without your care, many more would have died.'

As he spoke, I felt his arms go around me. Too exhausted to resist, I leant against him. I could smell the clean, fresh-air and wood-smoke scent of his woollen tunic, masking for a moment the smell of sickness that surrounded us. I could feel Bjorn's lips against my hair, his breath on my cheek. Time stopped, and in that frozen space I was comforted. I don't know how long we sat like that in the darkness, but a weak cry from Ulf broke the spell. I pulled away and went to him.

'Thora,' he fretted, 'I'm so thirsty.'

I lifted him and carefully held a goblet of water to his lips. From the corner of my eye, I saw Bjorn kneel beside the dead man and pick up his body in his arms. He carried him away and I heard a wail of distress from the other end of the house. Wearily, I took a cloth, dipped it in some water and began gently wiping Ulf's overheated skin, murmuring soothing words to him.

Thrang recovered and so did Ulf. Aud, the oldest member of our household, was not strong enough to fight the fever and succumbed, bringing the death toll to three. I grieved for her and wept as she was laid in a grave beside the other two.

No one else had fallen ill. As the last of my patients began to pull through, I could sit by the fire for short spells. This was a mixed pleasure as it exposed me to Ragna's mutterings about how useless I was to let three patients die.

After a day or so, I ventured outside to bathe in the hot pool, crunching through the new-fallen snow, relishing the fresh winter wind and the clear black air contrasting with the steamy heat of the water. There was no moon, but the sky was strewn with jewel-bright stars and the snow gleamed white, lighting up the landscape. The bath gave me new courage and energy, refreshing my spirit as well as my body.

The temperature dropped steadily, until we could barely keep warm unless we were right by the fire. The northern winds howled mercilessly, cutting like a knife through even our sturdy wooden walls, finding every tiny chink.

'We need a stone layer outside the timber of the sea-ward wall,' Thrang advised Bjorn. 'That will keep the wind out.'

The following day, Bjorn led several men out into the darkness in a hunt for rocks and stones to pile against the side of the house. The men took it in turns throughout the day to come back inside, thaw their frozen fingers over the fire and drink something hot.

I was standing outside the door breathing the fresh air when they stopped work for the day. The air was so cold it burned as I breathed it. Bjorn and Thrang paused by me as the others went in.

'Can you smell the ice on the wind?' Thrang asked me.

'It smells of the sea. Very clean and cold,' I said, sniffing.

'It's certainly cold,' agreed Bjorn. 'We need many more stones.' His voice sounded strange, as though he had sat too long in the smoke from the fire. 'We'll keep working tomorrow. I'm sure it will help.'

He shivered and pulled his cloak more tightly around himself. As he turned to go inside, he staggered and half fell against me. I caught his arm. I could feel the heat from his skin right through his thick woollen clothing.

'You're ill!' I exclaimed, struggling to keep the panic out of my voice.

'I think . . . I might be,' said Bjorn weakly. Thrang caught his other arm, and between us, we supported him into the house. I was already saying prayers under my breath, begging Eir that it was not the fever. Please, spare him that, I said silently. Surely it had run its course now?

Ragna got to her feet as she saw us, fear flooding her aura.

'What's wrong?' she cried, sounding just as afraid as I had done.

As Erik rushed forward to take Bjorn's weight from me, I was free to touch his brow and his neck. His eyes were pink and his face was flushed. There could be no doubt.

'What were you doing working out in the cold?' I asked him. 'You have the fever.'

I turned to Thrang. 'Take him . . . ' I began.

'No,' shouted Ragna. There was a silence as everyone looked at her.

'Put him in our room,' she said sharply. 'I'll nurse him.'

'Ragna, please,' I began, appalled.

She glared at me through narrowed eyes.

'You've killed three,' she said for everyone to hear. 'Do you think I would trust you with my husband?'

No one moved. 'I said, take him into our room,' she shouted at Thrang and Erik. Both of them looked to me. There was doubt in their faces. But there was nothing I could do. I couldn't countermand Ragna. I sat down help-lessly and felt fear and despair flood me as he was carried into the room he'd never once entered since it was built. Ragna shut the door on me.

CHAPTER TWENTY-FOUR

Bjorn's fever mounted over the following days. Ragna wouldn't even let me glimpse him. She refused to answer my questions or take my advice. Feverishly, I cast the runes, but for once they failed me and I could get no clear answer from them. I suspected it was my own fears clouding their message.

'Reason with her, please,' I begged Thrang and Asgerd. They tried, but to no avail. Ragna locked herself away with Bjorn, emerging only at mealtimes, looking pale and drawn. There was intense anxiety for Bjorn in her features, and I would have pitied her if she hadn't been putting his life at risk. It was clear she cared about him and had no fear of the sickness on her own account.

To make matters worse, two more people fell ill. One was a slave woman of Helgi's, who had stayed behind because her child had been sick, the other was Jon. I had my hands full again.

The following morning, Asgerd came to find me, a look of panic on her face.

'Thora, can you spare a moment? It's urgent.'

My heart stood still.

'Not Bjorn,' I whispered through lips that were suddenly numb.

Asgerd shook her head.

'No, but it's bad. Come.'

I followed her, slightly surprised when she led me into the normally locked store room. Stupidly, I stared around, looking for the sick person.

'Where . . . ?' I asked, looking at Asgerd for an explanation.

'Look around you, Thora,' said Asgerd. 'What do you see?'

'Nothing,' I said, and then it dawned on me and I sat down suddenly, shock taking the strength from my limbs. The store room was practically empty. It was only midwinter and we should have food stacked up in here. There ought to be barrels of skyr, dried and salted meat and fish, grain, cheeses, butter and whatever else had been grown or foraged.

'Two sacks of barley, half a sack of rye.' Asgerd counted the remaining stores on shaking fingers, her voice unsteady. 'One barrel of fish, some dried meat and some salt. There are still two butters and a large piece of cheese. That's it, Thora. For five months. Even if the last of Helgi's people went home tomorrow, which they won't, we are still eighteen adults and two children. This will only last us a month. Perhaps two if we start going very hungry right now.'

It was too much to take in. My head was spinning. I stared helplessly at the meagre supplies.

'What are we going to do, Thora?' asked Asgerd with desperation in her voice. I realized she was looking to me to take a decision. To find a solution. I remembered Thrang's words to me on the Faeroe Islands. 'Starvation isn't pretty,' he'd said. And now, thanks to Ragna's poor housekeeping, we were staring it in the face.

'How can we have eaten so much already?' whispered Asgerd, shaking her head.

'We've been a lot of people,' I said hesitantly, trying to work it out myself. 'Perhaps the stores were not chosen carefully enough . . . '

'Why didn't Ragna tell us?' wailed Asgerd. 'We could have rationed the food long ago.'

'What did she say just now?' I asked her. 'How do you come to have the keys?'

'She handed them to me. Said she didn't have time to run the household and nurse Bjorn. Now she's shut herself in her room.'

'Leaving the problem to us. Well, better now than later. I'll speak to Thrang. He's a practical man.'

Asgerd nodded. I felt as though we were standing on a cliff, slowly being dragged towards the edge. What else could go wrong?

214

CHAPTER TWENTY-FIVE

Thrang walked through the snow to Helgi's house. He brought back the news that everyone there had escaped the sickness so far. Helgi sent some supplies back with him. Not enough, but it was a help.

'Helgi sends thanks for your hospitality,' Thrang told me, snow melting in his hair and beard so that it dripped onto the earth floor. 'And he hopes these gifts will be acceptable.'

'It still won't be enough,' I told him anxiously.

'I'll fish,' Thrang told me. 'I've agreed with Helgi that as soon as this strong wind lets up a little, we'll take some men out. I don't want you to worry, Thora. You have enough to think about.' His voice was kind. 'I'll look after you,' he added, patting me clumsily on the shoulder before turning away to hide his embarrassment at this display of concern.

That burden lifted a little. But I was still full of anxiety about Bjorn. If only I could ask Thrang to resolve that problem for me too. Even though I suspected his solution might be to hurl Ragna out in the snow.

'Please, just let me see him,' I begged Ragna when she emerged to take some food at nightmeal.

'Never,' she hissed at me, her eyes wild. Then she

clutched her cloak closer about her and shivered. 'Don't think you can use your skills to take my husband away from me. It's me he needs. Me he wants. And I have skills enough to care for him myself.'

'But no medicines,' I said. 'Won't you at least take what you need from my stores?'

Ragna put down her bowl of barley porridge almost untouched and shivered again.

'Are you well?' I asked her, suddenly suspicious.

'I'm fine,' snapped Ragna. 'I don't need any of your poisons.' She dragged herself to her feet, leaning heavily on the table, and began limping towards her room. I watched her, suddenly certain that she was about to take the illness herself.

'Ragna,' I called, getting up to follow her, 'are you sure . . . '

I was too late. Halfway to her room, Ragna fainted, collapsing in a heap on the floor. I rushed to her side and could feel the beginnings of the fever burning in her skin. She was stirring almost at once, fighting to be conscious.

'Take her to . . . ' I began to order Grim, who stood ready to lift her.

'No,' begged Ragna, clutching my hand. Her eyes pleaded with me. 'Not there. I want to be with Bjorn.'

As I stared down at her suddenly vulnerable face, I felt the first stirrings of real pity.

'Please,' she begged.

'Very well,' I agreed. I led the way into Ragna's room, where Grim laid Ragna down across the room from Bjorn. That way she could see him, but not disturb him.

Then, and only then, did I turn my attention to Bjorn,

who lay wrapped in furs, his fever dangerously high. I felt a lurch of fear at the sight of him. Had he gone beyond my help? Bjorn stared up at me as I approached him, but it was clear he didn't recognize me with those red, glazed eyes. He looked clean and cared for, but he needed to be cooled. I began to strip his covers away, calling urgently for water.

'The fever needs to be nurtured,' objected Ragna feebly.

'No,' I answered curtly. 'Not after all these days. That's not how I work.'

I bathed Bjorn's face, neck, chest, and arms and trickled willow bark tea into his mouth. He groaned a little, and tried to swallow. And when Ragna, her own fever mounting, drifted into an uneasy sleep, I allowed myself to stroke his hair back from his face. He barely stirred, and cold dread seized me. Bringing his fever down should have made him more alert, more aware, but there was little change. I chafed his hands and spoke to him in a low voice, but he didn't respond.

Ragna was shivering convulsively as her own fever mounted. I laid extra furs on her, helping her to draw the heat she needed. Her icy hand clutched mine again.

'You'll care for me, won't you, Thora?' she muttered fretfully. 'You'll be kind. You won't hurt me?' Her voice shook with delirium.

'Of course I'll look after you,' I told her reassuringly.

Ragna soon lost all sense of where she was as her fever rose. I went from the one to the other, talking to them, soothing and encouraging them. My weariness was forgotten in my longing to see Bjorn improve. I cast the runes for him and prayed at length to Eir. I wiped his brow tenderly, calling softly to him to live.

Gradually, I could feel the fever leaving him. He lay quite still, breathing deeply. I prayed this was a healing sleep, not the prelude to death. I laid my hands on his shoulders and called on Eir to spare him, to give me the strength to cure him. His aura was faint, but as I prayed, it grew stronger, shimmering with the passing of his dreams. I allowed myself to hope.

Ragna, at an earlier stage of the sickness, was restless all night. I tended her when I needed to, always returning to Bjorn, looking for some sign of change. I prayed to Freya to give me a glimpse of the future, but she didn't oblige me.

It was two long, agonizing days before Bjorn opened his eyes.

'Bjorn?' I whispered eagerly. 'Do you know me?'

'Thora?' he croaked, and then coughed. I lifted him carefully to help him drink a little water. His skin was cool, quite free of fever. My relief was intense, bringing tears of gratitude to my eyes.

'How do you feel?' I whispered shakily.

'My head . . . hurts. I've had such dreams. I dreamed you wouldn't nurse me. I kept calling for you, but you didn't come.'

'Hush,' I said quietly, laying a finger on his lips. 'I'm here. You've been very ill. But you're going to get better.'

'Hold my hand,' he whispered. 'So I know you're close by.'

I glanced at Ragna, to make sure she was too unwell to

be watching. I took Bjorn's hand and held it in both mine while he slowly fell asleep again.

In a few days he was mending and Ragna, too, was over the worst. She had not taken the illness as badly as Bjorn. I went to take a little food at breakfast, sure that I should be hungry with the long watching. For some reason, the morning porridge tasted sour and unappetizing. I gave my portion to Ulf and got up to check on my other patients who were almost recovered now. To my surprise I found the floor wasn't quite steady. It felt like the first days aboard the ship. I shivered and sat down again.

'Thora, are you all right?' asked Asdis, staring at me.

I wanted to tell her I'd taken the fever after all, but my voice wouldn't work any more. From a long way away, I heard Asdis calling someone and then Thrang was beside me, catching me before I could fall. He laid me down in a pile of furs. I tried to get up again, but I was so very, very tired. My throat hurt and it was so cold. The house faded around me, reappearing in confused snatches. And in my dreams, I kept seeing Bjorn, walking away from me, hand in hand with Ragna.

CHAPTER TWENTY-SIX

Yule
Ýlir

It was Yule before I was up and about. My illness had
lasted many days. I was the last to take the fever and the
last to recover. I sat quietly by the fire, watching Ragna
and Asgerd take turns at the loom, while Ulf and Asdis
pounded grain. Everyone else came and went. We were a
reduced household now. All Helgi's people had gone and
we'd lost two. It was also a more peaceful household.
Ragna seemed to have been softened by her illness and
was being milder to everyone, even to me.

On the eve of Yule, there was a pounding on the door.
Bjorn went to open it. A flurry of wind blew in making
the fire flicker and smoke. A giant of a man entered with
a huge barrel under each arm.

'Olvir!' cried Bjorn, welcoming this unexpected guest.
He was completely dwarfed by the visitor.

There was a yell of excitement from the other end of
the longhouse. Ulf had been helping muck out the animals, but when he realized his father had come, he ran
the length of the hall, all dirty as he was, and flung his
arms around his father's legs. Olvir laughed, put down his
barrels and picked up his son instead, tossing him into the

air. Ulf shouted for joy. I smiled, pleased to see him so happy.

We had a Yule feast after all. Olvir's barrels contained salted fish and he sent men down to fetch a fresh catch from his boat as well.

'You braved the crossing in the dark?' asked Bjorn.

'It's not so dark,' grinned Olvir. 'There's moonlight and the last fall of snow is still lying.'

After the long spell of sickness, all of us were delighted to feast on fish, and open the last of the ale. With full bellies, we all gathered around the fire for talk, poetry, and story telling. Bjorn told us stories properly for the first time. I listened spellbound to his tales of our gods, heroes, and kings. He also told several tales I'd never heard before of elves and fairies. Bjorn said he had learned them from a foreign traveller, but I guessed these were stories from before his captivity. He was a gifted entertainer.

Olvir amused us with tales of his fishing trips, of whales that swam beside his boat, and of mermaids he'd seen in the distance. Even Thrang was persuaded to speak briefly of his travels to distant lands.

The following morning, Olvir sought me out for advice.

'I have a cut that won't heal,' he said, lifting the sleeve on his right arm to show me a long gash in the skin that had festered. It was angry, swollen, and hot to the touch. I asked him how he had done it, but he said he wasn't sure and shifted uncomfortably at my questions. I guessed he'd been in one of his rages and hadn't felt it at the time. I spread a salve on it.

'This should help, but it will need several applications,'

I told him. 'I'd like to keep an eye on it. Cuts like this can be very serious if they're left. How long are you staying with us?'

'I can stay a few days,' he growled. It was obvious he wasn't displeased to spend some time with his son and with plenty of company around him. I couldn't imagine the loneliness he endured on the far side of the bay. For me, that would be no life at all.

One evening, five of us were invited to Helgi's. Helgi turned up with a horse so that Ragna could ride, and Bjorn, Thrang, Olvir and I walked with them. To my surprise, Ragna made no objection to my accompanying them.

'You can walk with Olvir, Thora,' she said with a smile. 'He doesn't have company very often.' Her face was calculating as she spoke, despite the smile, and there were colours in her aura I didn't quite trust, but I agreed readily enough, seeing no harm in the plan.

The weather had turned surprisingly mild, and heavy rain had washed away all the snow from the low-lying land. It was a dark, wet walk and we all steamed as we sat down at Helgi's fireside.

We were well fed and after nightmeal we were entertained with tales of their settlement in the west fjords. Helgi also gave us gifts as thanks for our hospitality through the autumn and winter. To Bjorn and Ragna, he presented the horse Ragna had ridden here. Both were quite overwhelmed by the generosity of our friends.

I was deeply touched when Helgi presented me with a silver necklace set with stones and a tiny, fluffy black kitten that had been born since their arrival here. We had no cat in our house and I held the tiny creature with delight, as it licked my fingers and miaowed.

'These gifts express our heart-felt thanks for your services as a midwife and a healer,' Helgi explained.

I felt my face flame.

'But one of your people died,' I said in a low voice. 'I failed you.'

Bera looked sad. 'No,' she said. 'Many more might have died without your nursing. You made yourself ill, caring for them. And look, Ingvar is well. He's a treasure.'

She smiled fondly down at the baby in her arms as she spoke. He had grown and thrived since I saw him last, but still had a look of fragility about him. I leaned over and gently touched his cheek. It was so soft.

'May Freya bless you, Ingvar,' I said.

We stayed overnight at Helgafell, as they had named their home, and walked back again the following morning. It felt strange to think in terms of day and night, morning and evening in this perpetual dark. The rain had gone, the stars were bright and the temperature had dropped again. There was a wind blowing that cut through everything. I shivered, despite my warm clothes, and was aware that my illness had weakened me. I'd had no visions since my fever first started and I felt everything less strongly. Even my distress at Bjorn's marriage had faded to a dull ache.

I could make out Bjorn and Helgi in front of me, deep in conversation. Ahead of them, Olvir was leading Ragna's horse and listening as she talked earnestly. I needed all my breath for walking, and kept pace beside Thrang in companionable silence, the little kitten in my arms.

I was exhausted when we reached home, but offered to check Olvir's cut again. Handing the kitten to Astrid, I sat down beside the fire so that I could see properly. The cut was healing nicely now. The heat had gone out of the injury and the swelling had gone down.

'This is good,' I told him, summoning a smile, despite my tiredness. 'It's healed well. It'll look after itself now.'

Olvir rolled his sleeve back down.

'You have great skill,' he said.

'I was well trained,' I told him. 'But any healer could have done as much.'

'You saved people's lives during the sickness,' said Olvir, staring at me. I started to feel uncomfortable. 'You saved my son's life. Ragna told me.'

I remembered Ragna's accusations of letting people die and felt confused. She could not have changed towards me this much, I felt sure.

'You entrusted him to us,' I said to Olvir. 'I felt responsible for him.' I looked around to see if Ulf was nearby but I couldn't see him.

I became aware that nearly everyone was listening to our conversation.

'You'd make a wonderful mother,' said Olvir. 'Will you marry me?'

'You . . . you aren't serious,' I stuttered, rocked completely off balance.

'I am,' he said simply.

I could hear stifled giggles around me now. Everyone

who had any business to be around the fire was sitting listening, as well as many who didn't. I looked around at them, wondering if this was some kind of bet or wager to make me look foolish.

'You're beautiful, talented, and desirable and I want you to be my wife,' Olvir continued.

The giggles around us broke out afresh. Olvir smiled and I edged a little further away from him.

'What's going on?' asked Bjorn. He'd approached us, obviously drawn by the merriment.

'I'm asking Thora to marry me,' explained Olvir. He seemed completely unembarrassed by the situation. Bjorn looked thunderous.

'And what does Thora say?' he demanded.

'She hasn't replied yet,' explained Olvir earnestly.

I cast Bjorn a look of desperation. I had no idea what to say or do. We were all a little frightened of Olvir, scared to do or say anything that might trigger his berserker rage. But that didn't include agreeing to this preposterous proposal.

'You and I need to talk together,' said Bjorn sharply, glaring at Olvir.

The two of them slung on cloaks and went out into the darkness. As the door closed behind them, all the women, and many of the men too, burst into gales of pent-up laughter.

'I've never heard anything so funny!' Asgerd practically wept with laughter. 'Does he really think you'll go and live all by yourself with him on the bare mountainside?'

'And survive on fish?' added Asdis, wiping her eyes.

'He must be nearly thirty years old besides,' chortled Asgerd. 'His teeth are terrible and so's his breath.'

'I think it would be a very suitable marriage.' Ragna spoke from beside the loom. She sounded annoyed. 'What other offer is Thora likely to get? Besides, he loves her and she'll never go hungry over there.'

'He hardly knows her,' exclaimed Asgerd. 'He just thinks she'll make a good mother and cook and she can heal his cuts whenever he's been roaming as a werewolf at night.'

Erik threw back his head and pretended to howl, and everyone except Ragna laughed again. Ragna snorted and turned back to the loom. 'More fool you, Thora, to throw away this chance,' she said.

I felt a coldness steal into my heart. I realized Ragna had probably suggested this marriage to Olvir. That's what they'd been talking about with such animation on the way back from Helgi's. She'd seemed friendlier to me, but she wanted me out of her home just the same. I should have known better than to expect anything like real kindness from her.

'I'm sure lots of men will want to marry Thora,' Asgerd defended me loyally, coming to sit next to me and putting an arm around me. 'So beautiful as you are,' she added more softly to me.

The sudden kindness coming on top of so much unwelcome attention made me want to cry. I could feel tears stinging my eyes. Such weakness, I thought, blinking them back. But I still wasn't strong, and my throat burned with the effort.

Bjorn returned alone from his walk.

'Where's our guest?' demanded Ragna at once. 'What have you said to him?'

'He'll be back in a moment,' said Bjorn briefly. 'Thora, a word with you, please.'

I got to my feet, unsure what Bjorn wanted to say to me. He nodded to me to follow him towards the far end of the house. We walked until we reached the animal stalls. Here it was dimly lit and cold, far from the fire. Just one oil lamp burned in a niche in the wall, so that the animals weren't in complete darkness. The cows' steamy breath misted the air, smelling of hay. Ulf and Grim were grooming the horses, but Bjorn sent them away. I was glad that Ulf hadn't been listening when the others made fun of his father.

This was probably the only place to hold a private conversation in such a full house. I wondered what Bjorn wanted to say. A dreadful doubt seized me that he might want to urge the marriage proposal. I didn't think I could bear that.

'Thora,' Bjorn began. He took a few paces away from me and then back again. He set his hands on my shoulders and looked earnestly at me. 'This proposal. I know I must accept that you'll marry someone. It would be better for you. But . . . I don't advise this.'

His words were hurried, urgent and low. They filled me with relief.

'I'm sure he's a good man,' he added. 'But it would be no kind of life for you, over there. I'd fear for you.' Bjorn paused. He let go of me and turned away, leaning his head and forearms against a partition wall. He was breathing heavily. I stood in silence, struggling to gather my thoughts.

'I wasn't thinking . . . of accepting . . . ' I began hesitantly.

Bjorn let out a sigh of relief and turned back to face me.

'You're quite sure?' he asked. 'Do you want me to tell him?'

I looked at his face, the way his dark curls tumbled to his shoulders and his eyes shone in the faint lamplight and my heart filled with love for him. His face was creased with anxiety and there was no trace of the smile I loved. I wanted to reach up and smooth his frown away. I wanted to reassure him that I cared only for him. But I would never, ever be able to tell him that.

I understood why Ragna wanted me out of her house. I *was* a danger to her. My love for Bjorn was as deep as ever. If anything, it had grown stronger. At this moment, as we stood in the semi-darkness together, I felt that he loved me too. Ragna could come between us, but she couldn't destroy the way we felt. In that moment, I realized that I *should* leave here. But I couldn't marry Olvir.

Bjorn was still waiting for my answer.

'Yes, please tell him,' I managed to say. 'Thank him, but it's definitely no.'

Bjorn gripped my shoulder a moment and then left me.

I stood quite still, listening to the cattle munching, the horses shifting their weight and snorting through their feed trough. It was peaceful here, but I was in turmoil.

Before I could even begin to recover my composure, a large figure approached.

'Thora?' he said. It was Thrang's voice. His presence irritated me. I wanted to be alone to think about what had happened, to reflect on the undercurrents of feelings that I sensed running between Bjorn and me.

'What did you tell him?' Thrang asked.

'I said no,' I answered.

Thrang nodded. He stood still beside me. I felt awkward and made a move to rejoin the others, little as I wished to hear their questions and teasing. Thrang stopped me with a hand on my arm.

'Wait,' he said. Then he said nothing for some time. For so long that I thought I must have misheard him. Then at last he spoke and his voice was even more gruff and hoarse than usual.

'What they were saying, before. This won't be your only proposal,' he said. 'Because I . . . well . . . the thing is . . . I should like you to consider marrying me.'

I was stunned. I stood gaping at Thrang, unable to believe what I was hearing.

'You were destined to sail the seas,' he said, an ardent note creeping into his voice. 'I've seen it. You are completely at home aboard a ship. Marry me and follow your destiny.' As he spoke, Thrang moved closer to me and I backed away until I was up against a door to one of the stalls. A horse put his head over the door and nudged me in the back, pushing me into Thrang's arms. He clutched me as though I were a barrel of mead, crushing me in his embrace.

'Marry me,' he repeated, bending down to try and kiss me.

I struggled to be free, pushing against his chest.

'Please . . . don't,' I cried. Thrang released me and we stood staring at one another. My face was hot with embarrassment. I was badly shaken. If I'd heard these scenes in a story, I would have laughed. But there was nothing funny about being caught in the middle of it myself. It was all so completely unexpected. I'd had no idea either of these men cared for me in that way. Their auras had shown me nothing. Or perhaps I hadn't looked closely enough.

'You . . . you're a good man,' I stammered. Then my voice grew stronger: 'I respect you. I like you. But I couldn't live my life at sea. I belong on land.'

'There's another side to you,' insisted Thrang.

I shook my head mutely. If only he would go away and leave me in peace. I dreaded Bjorn finding me in the middle of this scene so soon after the last. It was humiliating. Perhaps I should have felt flattered at all this attention, but I didn't. There was no pleasure in rejecting men of honour and courage when they laid bare their feelings.

'Please, Thora, consider what I've said,' said Thrang. He turned and left. I sank down on the cold, bare floor and put my head in my hands, dry eyed and miserable. How could it be that two men wanted to marry me, while the man I loved with all my heart was tied to another?

CHAPTER TWENTY-SEVEN

Frozen Snow Month
Þorri

Neither Olvir nor Thrang spoke of their proposals again and, to my huge relief, Olvir soon took his leave. I gradually recovered my equanimity. And there was a new source of interest, which prevented me becoming the subject of too much gossip. We all discovered what Bjorn and Helgi had been discussing so intently at Yule. All our men were to spend some portion of each day training in arms. Helgi had promised to instruct them in sword fighting. Bjorn claimed he wanted the household to be able to protect itself from pirates and raiders. I knew that Bjorn was afraid of vengeance killers pursuing us from Norway when spring came.

How Bjorn had explained to Helgi that he was ignorant of skills that any Viking chieftain would have learned as soon as he could walk, I had no idea. But every afternoon throughout Ram Month and into Thorri Month, after the chores had been done, the men of both households met to fight with swords, wrestle, and learn to wield a battleaxe.

'Tell me, Thora,' said Ragna, sitting down beside me one evening, as we all listened to the sound of iron clashing and men's shouts outside. 'Why would a master want to teach his slaves to fight? It seems a dangerous thing to do.'

Her voice was civil as it usually was when she spoke to me now. But her aura showed no kindness as she looked at me. I knew she hadn't forgiven me for refusing Olvir.

'They will all be free men half a year from now,' I said. 'Bjorn probably feels he owes it to them to be able to defend themselves.' I felt her stiffen in shock beside me.

'Free men? What can you be talking about?' she demanded.

I realized that no one had spoken to her of the bargain Bjorn had offered our people.

'Bjorn offered them their freedom if they gave him a year's labour in the new land,' I explained carefully. Her face was a mask of shock and anger.

'What was he thinking of?' demanded Ragna. 'How can he run a farm with no slaves?'

'Most won't leave,' I reassured her. 'It's not easy to set up a household with no tools, no stock, and no wood for building. But they will have the choice. To leave or to stay and work for a wage.'

Ragna sat rigid by the fireside, clenching and unclenching her fists. She was muttering to herself. I moved away, but heard the word 'madness' repeated again and again.

The men had finished fighting now. Distantly, I could hear them laughing and joking as they stripped and climbed into the hot bathing pool. But when Helgi's men had gone home and Bjorn returned for nightmeal, Ragna took him aside. We could all hear the suppressed rage in her voice and feel the fury in her wild gesticulations. I could also see the rage of her colours as she argued with him. Bjorn stayed calm, arms folded, but around him too, I could make out pulses of anger. I could imagine the kind of things she was saying about slaves and how that would make him feel. But despite his anger, he had a glow of compassion and kindness. It was a constant colour, an inherent part of his personality. He wouldn't give in to Ragna, but neither would he hold this against her. He would stay polite to her, but distant, as always.

A few days later, a messenger arrived from Helgi's just as the men were about to set out. He spoke to Bjorn.

'Bera asks whether Thora could accompany the men when they come to Helgi's today,' he said. 'She's worried about the baby.'

I looked to Ragna for permission, wondering what her reaction would be. But she said yes at once and even smiled. I felt uneasy, wondering what her motive could be. I climbed into the sleeping loft and unlocked my chest, selecting a few items that were likely to be needed and then locked the chest again, tucking the key into a pocket in my tunic.

When I came back down the ladder, I found that Ragna had told Ulf he must stay behind today. His face wore a sulky look, for he loved to learn to fight with the men. To my surprise he stopped me on my way out of the door and hugged me. He wasn't prone to displays of affection. I couldn't help feeling that something strange was going on. But Ulf's aura was mainly resentful, which didn't surprise me. I hugged him back, ruffled his hair and reminded him that Helgi's men would be coming to us the next day.

As I stepped out into the darkness, I saw Bjorn had ordered the horse saddled for me. He insisted on lifting me into the saddle and leading her himself. I was touched by his kindness and glad of his company.

Snow had fallen again in the night and the men waded calf deep into the fresh, powdery fall, creating a path for us to follow. A bitterly cold wind was blowing in from the sea and I was soon shivering, almost wishing I was walking not riding. I buried my hands in the horse's mane and hunched my shoulders against the wind. I concentrated on watching the wind whipping Bjorn's hair back from his face just ahead of me and on the colours glowing around his head and shoulders, bright in the darkness.

When we arrived, I found Bera walking up and down by the fire, a fretful Ingvar in her arms. He was flushed, red-faced and tearful. I asked for water to clean the horse dirt off my hands and then examined him carefully. I could find nothing wrong but I could see him biting angrily onto his fist and then crying out.

'He's teething,' I told Bera with a smile.

Her anxious face relaxed into relief and pride.

'I was so afraid it was the fever,' she confided.

I selected a piece of precious clove from my bag of goods. Another item which would be difficult to replace so far from the trade routes. I resolved to speak to Bjorn about my shortage of remedies at the next possible opportunity. I ground a little clove and mixed it with some fat before rubbing it onto the gum.

'You can do this a few times a day,' I explained.

I spent a happy day with Bera and the baby. We talked and laughed, free of the constraints that dampened my spirits at home. I had a light heart when Bjorn lifted me onto the horse to hurry home through the icy chill of the winter night. We talked a little on the way home, Bjorn recounting some anecdotes of their afternoon's training. The happiness of the day still filled me when I climbed to the sleeping loft to replace my unused remedies in my chest. But when I reached into my pocket for the key, I had a shock which wiped the smile from my face. It wasn't there. My heart skipped a beat. What had I done with it? I thought anxiously of the ride in the snow and wondered whether it could have fallen. But it had never happened before. I thought of the iron key lying lost and rusting in the snow, and I knew that wasn't right. That wasn't what had happened. It was here with me in the loft. I could feel it.

By the feeble light of an oil lamp, I searched the loft, running my fingertips over the boards and feeling into the corners. Then I took my bedding and shook it out piece by piece. As I lifted the last sheepskin, there was a clunk and the key fell onto the boards. Breathing heavily with relief, I sat for a moment, turning it over in my hands and staring at it. How could this be?

As soon as I unlocked the chest, I knew. Someone had been in here. They'd been careful but everything was just a little tumbled and the last of the willow bark had been spilled. I ran my fingers over the contents of the chest feeling fear and dread constrict my breathing. These plants were a source of great power. In the wrong hands they could cause real harm. Some plants that are medicines in tiny doses can be fatal if taken in any quantity.

One particularly deadly poison sprang to mind. A piece of root from the aconite plant, bought at cost from a Russian trader. I couldn't say why my mind jumped to this plant. No one here but me could possibly recognize it or know how to use it. Nonetheless, I felt for the leather pouch in which I stored it.

The pouch was empty.

Trembling, I climbed down the ladder and took a place by the fire. Everyone was gathered around preparing or waiting for our meagre nightmeal, exchanging news and stories. Fearfully, I looked from face to face, questions running endlessly through my mind. Who could have stolen the deadly root? Who would know what it was? How had I come to lose the key in the first place?

One person I could rule out at once. There was no way Ragna could have climbed into the loft. Her leg would not have permitted it. And it was clearly none of the men, for every one of them had accompanied us to Helgi's. I questioned Asdis in a whisper as we crept to bed that night. Of all the young, unmarried slave girls, I trusted her the most. She was a kind, gentle girl, who would never harm anyone.

'Tell me, Asdis,' I asked, 'has anyone been up here looking through my things today?'

'What do you mean? I don't think so,' Asdis answered surprised.

'Did anything unusual happen?' I persisted.

'No, we just worked. Ragna and Asgerd wove,' she said

uncertainly. 'I sewed and Ulf pounded grain. Vigdis, Enys, and Hild swept and cleaned and cooked . . . Until Ragna sent us to bathe, that is.'

'She sent you out to bathe?' I pounced on that at once. 'In the middle of the day?'

'She said it was a good time, with the men from home,' faltered Asdis.

'And was she alone in the house then?' I asked.

'Yes. No! Ulf was with her. What's this about, Thora?' whispered Asdis.

'Nothing I can tell you,' I said biting my lip. I didn't want to frighten her or anyone else. I was more puzzled than ever. What worried me most of all was that someone had known what to take when they hunted through my chest. They had recognized the plant. That meant they would know how to use it as well. But who, besides me, had knowledge of such things? Someone in the house was keeping a dark secret.

It was long before sleep came to me.

I tried to get Bjorn alone to confide in him, but Helgi's men were with us the next morning after chores and he was surrounded by company all through the long, dark day. Helgi even stayed to dine, having brought a contribution to our nightmeal. The little food we had was shared out fairly, and goblets of whey were passed around. I took mine warily since the theft of the aconite. I dipped a finger into the liquid, rubbed a little on my lower lip and waited. I watched everyone around me eating and drinking with fear churning in my stomach, dreading to see any of them succumb to the effects of poison. They ate fast and hungrily, their appetites sharp after a long day. We had had too little food for weeks now.

My lip began to tingle. Just a little at first, but then it turned into a fierce burn and I could feel the skin swelling and heating. I looked down at my goblet in horror. Someone had tried to poison me. Someone wanted to *kill* me.

I looked at Ragna, but she sat quite calmly beside Bjorn, neither her face nor her aura giving any clues to her thoughts. She wasn't looking at me. No one was looking at me.

With difficulty, I restrained myself from leaping to my feet and shouting the truth. We had guests. Accusations of poison could cause a rift between our families. All trust would be gone. I had to find the culprit myself.

As discreetly as possible, my hands shaking, I poured my drink onto the ground. It trickled treacherously across the earth floor in an innocent white stream, wasted food that my body needed for nourishment. One of the dogs, thin and scraggy with lack of meat, rushed to lap it up. Feeling sick, I fended him off with a foot until the laced whey had soaked into the earth.

CHAPTER TWENTY-EIGHT

Góa Month
Góa

At last a time came when it definitely grew light for a short spell. After that, the light returned fast, longer each day. There was rejoicing and happiness. We couldn't hold a feast to celebrate as our food was now almost gone. We were constantly hungry, surviving on what little fish Thrang and the others could catch in the bay. They hadn't had much luck. But the light gave us hope.

In the short daylight spells, outdoor work could resume once more. The forge was completed. Those who weren't fishing cleared snow and began building a dairy by the stream. They also built a summer shelter for the animals.

Several of the men and one woman in our house developed winter sickness. Their gums were swollen and sore and their skin showed a rash. I'd been expecting it. It gave me an excuse to speak to Bjorn.

'We had no skyr to preserve the autumn berries,' I explained to him. 'So this was certain to happen. It was just a matter of time. We need to slaughter a sheep.'

I'd caught Bjorn beside the dairy. The others had gone

indoors and the light had faded completely. I shivered as the cold penetrated my thin leather shoes.

'Slaughter a sheep? Now?' he asked, his brow wrinkling in surprise. 'How will that help? It'll make poor eating. And we have few enough of them as it is.'

'Sheep's brains,' I told him. 'Eating them cures winter sickness. Without berries, it's the only way.'

He nodded, looking almost bemused. 'Very well,' he agreed. 'I'll speak to Ragna and make sure it's done.'

I smiled at him, relieved. No matter how strange or unreasonable my advice sounded, he always trusted me. We stood looking at each other, neither of us wanting to be the first to turn away.

'There's something else,' I said, hesitantly. 'I haven't known how to tell you . . . '

Bjorn looked concerned at once, his expression easy to read on his open face.

'What's wrong, Thora?'

'About a month ago, a root was stolen from my chest of medicines. My key was taken and then put back. I've searched and watched, but I still have no idea who has it.'

'So we have a thief in the house,' said Bjorn. 'Why would they steal from you? What does the root do?'

I hesitated, dreading the disclosure I must make. 'It's a deadly poison,' I admitted.

Bjorn inhaled sharply and his gaze became intent.

'And why would you keep such a thing?' he asked. He sounded pained.

'It can be a medicine in very tiny doses,' I explained. 'It affects the heart.'

'Have you ever used it?' Bjorn asked.

I nodded. 'Once,' I told him. 'That was the reason I traded it. But it isn't something I'd wish to see in the wrong hands.'

Bjorn paused a moment, clearly pondering my words. Then he looked up at me again, brisk and practical.

'Who could have taken it?' he wanted to know.

'The women and Ulf were the only people who were in the house that day. But I'm not aware any of them would know what it is or how to use it.'

'Probably the person who took it doesn't know what it does,' Bjorn said in a comforting voice. 'Perhaps they've thrown it away. We have no other healers in the house.'

'Not that we know of,' I said reluctantly. 'But I'm afraid . . . someone does know. One night, my goblet of whey was poisoned.'

Bjorn's reaction to this was immediate, and startled me. He grasped my wrist, pulling me towards him, taking my shoulder in a painful grip with his other hand.

'Why didn't you tell me at once?' he asked, his voice hoarse. 'I can't have your life put at risk. Who could it be?'

I put one hand soothingly over his. 'I don't know,' I said. 'But should we warn everyone? You can test your food or drink by touching it to your lip and waiting a moment. The poison burns.'

Bjorn released me and paced away from me. He ran his hand through his long, dark curls and frowned.

'No,' he said decisively. 'It will cause panic and distrust. It could destroy everything we've been working so hard for. I can't believe whoever it was will try again. It's been a month, you say?'

I nodded. It was typical of Bjorn to always believe the best of people. To credit them with remorse, compassion and kindness where they had none. He thought everyone as generous and good as himself. It was an endearing character trait, but a frustrating one at times.

'I understand your reasoning,' I told him, 'but the dangers . . . '

' . . . may never come to pass,' he interupted decisively. 'Thank you for telling me this, Thora. We will reveal it only if it becomes necessary. Now go back inside. I will wait awhile.'

I turned from him and began to walk towards the house. He wouldn't want us to walk in together, causing comment.

'And Thora,' called out Bjorn behind me. I turned, looking at the darker patch in the night that I knew was him, his outline picked out by the starlight. 'Stay vigilant,' he said softly.

Before I could reply, there was an earsplitting roar around us. I couldn't tell whether it came from the earth or the sky. I put my hands up to cover my ears, to block out the dreadful sound. I could see Bjorn doing the same. And then the ground shook violently beneath our feet. It was like standing on the deck of a boat. I lost my balance and fell to my hands and knees in the darkness, the ground cold and wet beneath me. Fear flooded me like a hot wave. Then everything went quiet.

'Thora?' cried Bjorn, his voice loud in the sudden silence.

'I'm here. I'm all right,' I replied shakily. 'What happened?'

I could hear more voices now as others rushed out of the house.

'The gods are angry!' cried one voice.

'The giants are coming, making the ground shake,' wailed another.

Then in the distance a red glow lit the dark afternoon sky. It was a long way inland, as though there was a vast fire in the distance.

'Ragnarok!' they all began to shout. 'The day of judgement has come!'

'That's enough foolishness,' Bjorn spoke calmly but forcefully over the babble of frightened voices. 'I'm sure there's a natural explanation.'

He walked towards the house as he spoke. The voices fell silent. I was reassured by his quiet authority, and sensed the others were too. I pushed myself to my feet and followed him on legs that weren't steady.

'Thrang,' Bjorn said, 'you have been in Iceland before. Can you explain this?'

'I've felt the earth tremble in this country,' boomed Thrang's deep voice. 'It isn't unusual. But I've never seen the sky on fire.'

'You should have tended to the sacrifices, husband,' I heard Ragna's voice cry, shrill with fear. 'The gods have had no blood from us since last summer. Now we'll be punished for failing to honour them.'

All the other voices hushed. Ragna had never openly criticized Bjorn before. He took a moment to reply. I waited with baited breath, not knowing what to think.

'I don't believe that,' said Bjorn calmly, at last. His

voice was strong and confident. 'Please, everyone return to the fireside. We will await events.'

We did as we were told but there was a great deal of quiet wailing and urgent, frightened talk. Couples clung to one another for comfort and Asgerd kept her arms around her daughter. Ulf crept close to me.

We were all mortally afraid that night. Again and again we felt the ground shake, though never as violently as the first time. We prayed, talked, and nobody slept much. Bjorn steadfastly refused to sacrifice any animals, though he promised a sheep would be slaughtered the following day to combat hunger and winter sickness.

'The winter sickness will be the least of our worries with the end of the world approaching,' muttered Ragna darkly. 'It is Ragnarok, the day of judgement.'

Her words caused another jolt of fear in my stomach, but I quelled my anxiety. I trusted Bjorn's quiet confidence.

The world didn't end that night. But in the hours of darkness, the red glow persisted. In the short daylight spell, we could see a tall column of smoke rising into the pale sky in the far distance. Helgi came to speak to Bjorn the next morning, but he understood it as little as we did.

'Perhaps there are huge forests burning inland,' Erik suggested.

'In the winter?' scoffed Grim.

'You have a better idea?' demanded Erik.

No one had a better idea.

The days passed and no worse disasters befell us other than a light fall of ash on top of the snow. It seemed to come from the sky, and Bjorn said it confirmed his theory of a forest fire.

The mystery soon faded from our minds, replaced by a problem nearly as serious as Ragnarok itself. Our food finally ran out.

The sheep had been duly slaughtered and the brains shared. They had healed sore gums and skin rashes. Then we had cooked and eaten every scrap of meat, stewing the bones for stock long after they had ceased to have any flavour at all. Now all we had left was a little butter.

Thrang took the ship and several men, including Stein, and rowed across to consult with Olvir. I walked down to the shore and watched them go just before dawn. It was a still morning, and the sea was sluggish with large chunks of ice obstructing the oars and slowing the ship.

'I hope Olvir can help,' murmured Asgerd, standing beside me, watching her husband as the ship disappeared into the semi-darkness.

'He chose to live over there,' I said, 'because the fishing is better on that side of the bay. So perhaps he can direct them to the likely spots. He had caught fresh fish at Yule, remember?'

I spoke more hopefully than I felt. My belly was empty and crying out for food, my limbs heavy. It was impossible to stay warm and my head ached constantly. If Thrang didn't return with a catch, we would have to start eating our animals or our seed. And that would endanger our future.

'I wish we could eat hay, like the animals,' sighed Asgerd.

'We'll soon run out of that too,' I said seriously.

Bjorn was waiting for me below the house, and asked me to accompany him to Helgi's. I agreed and fell into step beside him without returning to the house. Ragna would be furious later, but I didn't have the energy to care.

'I'm praying for the success of the fishing trip,' Bjorn said once we were out of earshot of the house. 'I don't know how we'll survive otherwise.'

'Thrang says there will be seabirds by Harpa month,' I said quietly. 'Clouds of them, nesting so the cliffs are white with them. There'll be eggs.'

My stomach growled as I thought of eggs. Bjorn sighed.

'Two months,' he said. 'Can we last that long?'

'We have to,' I replied. I wanted him to reassure me as he did everyone else. But I realized he was trusting me with his true concerns, certain I wouldn't panic.

'Are you planning to ask Helgi for help?' I asked hesitantly.

'It's unlikely he has any food spare to trade. But I shall ask anyway. I also want to suggest a trip south as soon as the seed is sown. We need to know what that fire was and to see if there is timber and fertile ground inland.'

Helgi had no food to trade. I checked his people over and found no winter sickness. But there was hunger. They had been forced to ration their supplies as we had done. Baby Ingvar was thriving, but his mother had grown thin with the effort of feeding him.

'Next year, once the harvest is in,' said Helgi cheerfully, 'we will have enough food to feast the entire winter away.'

We all smiled, and hoped he was right, though we could scarcely imagine it.

Bjorn and I stayed to share a small bowl of skyr with our friends and then made our way home through the gathering darkness. The wind was keen and the air damp. Bjorn carried two large dried fish on a string. A gift from Helgi. They would stave off the worst hunger pangs, soaked and stewed.

As we approached our farm we could see that Thrang hadn't yet returned with the ship.

'Tomorrow,' said Bjorn optimistically. 'He'll be back tomorrow.'

CHAPTER TWENTY-NINE

Last Month of Winter
Einmanudur

It was three days before the fishermen returned, but we were well rewarded for our long wait. I'd never suffered such hunger, not even when Svanson had been persecuting my family. But Thrang and the other men had filled the fishing net several times over and packed the catch in ice they had taken out of the sea. We all shouted with excitement as we saw what they had brought.

'Olvir knew the best places, all right,' said Thrang jovially. 'It was dangerous work in the dark, and bitterly cold, but this will keep hunger at bay.'

We roasted fresh fish on sticks over the fire, burning our fingers and our mouths in our hurry to eat. Nothing had ever tasted so good.

'This is like feasting in Valhalla,' sighed Thrang once his first hunger was sated. 'An eternal banquet with the fallen heroes and Odin himself presiding.'

'It'll be even better next year,' Bjorn promised. 'Then we'll have meat, grain and all manner of good farm produce.'

'It looks like we picked the wrong year to winter here,

Stein!' said Thrang, good humouredly, nudging his companion. The conversation died.

'You're not leaving us?' asked Ragna sharply.

'Just as soon as I can get a passage,' said Thrang, with a meaningful glance at me. 'Once the ships start sailing again in spring.'

There was a long silence. Thrang was a tower of strength and a hard worker. Stein was a quiet young man, but respected by the other men and always worked well. Everyone would miss them both.

I wondered if Thrang was still hoping that I'd accompany him when he left. I had thought about his proposal but without coming to any decision. I couldn't imagine this long, dark winter ever ending. It seemed to go on for ever, stretching into the future, unchanging. Darkness, cold, and hunger.

'Olvir sends you his love, Thora,' called Erik from the other side of the fire, interrupting my train of thought. 'He says he'll be over to fetch his bride as soon as the spring comes!'

There was a roar of merry laughter. I shook my head slightly and could feel myself blushing.

'If I could eat like this every day, maybe it would be a good bargain,' I said, trying to join the merriment.

I noticed several people weren't laughing. Thrang watched me from under his bushy brows, a heavy frown on his face. Bjorn looked serious and Ragna was looking hopeful.

'I don't think you should marry him and leave us,' said Jon, a gangly lad of about sixteen winters. His face turned fiery red as he spoke. 'We'd all miss you,' he mumbled, looking down at his plate, overcome that he had spoken out of turn.

'Thora, you have another admirer!' roared Vali, slapping Jon on the back and laughing. Jon turned a deeper shade of red. 'Come on, you brave warriors,' Vali called. 'Who else would like to offer for the fair Thora? Hands up!'

I fled the house without looking to see if any hands went up. I knew it was only good-natured teasing, but it was too much for me. My own heart was sore and bruised, and the subject of the jest was too painful. I stood in the darkness, soon shivering with cold, breathing the fresh, salty air.

The door opened again behind me and Asgerd emerged. She was wearing her cloak, mine lay over her arm.

'You'll freeze,' she said gently, wrapping the cloak around me. After a pause, she added: 'They don't mean any harm, you know.'

'I know,' I said, a little breathlessly.

She put an arm around my shoulders and gave me a little shake.

'I'm sorry Erik started it. I'll speak to him later.' She paused and then added: 'The household is unbalanced. More young men than women. And you are so very young and beautiful, you're bound to turn their heads.'

I shook my head, perplexed.

'You must be mistaken,' I told her. 'I'm not beautiful. That's not why . . . '

Asgerd chuckled. 'You can't see yourself, my dear. The

rest of us see it quite plainly. It's not just in your features either, though they are pretty enough. You glow, somehow. With strength and peace.'

'Please . . . ' I held up one hand, trying to fend off her words.

'I know, you don't want to hear it,' said Asgerd. 'But whatever you do, don't throw yourself away on Olvir the Werewolf.'

'I have no intention of doing so,' I told her. 'But please don't call him that. We have no proof he's a werewolf and it might upset Ulf.'

'All right, I won't,' she agreed peaceably. 'Let's talk about something else. Are you going to accept Thrang?'

I turned to her, startled. I couldn't make out her expression in the darkness.

'How did you . . . ?'

'Erik overheard your conversation—quite by mistake,' Asgerd explained. 'I don't think he's the right man for you either. But better by far than Olvir.'

I nodded. I wanted to explain to her what a danger I was here. A barrier to any chance of Bjorn and Ragna finding happiness together. I wanted to tell her I knew I should go. But I couldn't bring myself to think of Thrang as a husband or of leaving Bjorn. The words wouldn't come and I stood in silence, grateful for her company.

We salted some of the fish and dried the rest. Bjorn and Thrang took a barrel of fish across to Helgi as thanks for the dried fish he had given us. I looked at what was left and calculated we had food enough to eat well for four or five days, or meagrely for twice as many. They would need to go out again very soon.

I tended the cuts, bruises, and frost damage the men had sustained fishing. Thrang had a nasty gash in his arm.

'It's not infected,' I told him. 'The salt water probably kept it clean. It should heal well.' I smeared some paste onto the cut as I spoke and then began to bandage his arm.

'Thank you,' said Thrang. He laid one hand over mine. 'Thora, have you . . . thought any more about . . . what I said?'

'I have,' I admitted nervously, withdrawing my hand, dreading this conversation. I had no idea what to say to him, and didn't want to hurt his feelings.

'And what is your answer? Will you have me?' he asked anxiously.

'I haven't been able to make up my mind,' I told him truthfully, hanging my head. 'I'm sorry, I . . . '

Thrang took my hand in his and held it firmly. 'There is nothing for you here,' he said in a low voice.

'I know,' I agreed sadly.

'You have time to decide,' said Thrang, releasing me.

With each day that passed there was more daylight. The day the sun first appeared above the horizon, there was great rejoicing. Soon, on clear days, we could feel its feeble winter rays warming us. The snow began to melt.

Thrang set off on another fishing expedition. His absence gave me a chance to breathe freely and to think about my future without feeling his eyes on me constantly. I was almost certain I would refuse him, but I questioned my decision. I knew I should leave with him, but I didn't want to. I had had no visions since my illness and some days I feared they might have left me for good. I prayed to Freya to send me some guidance for my decision, but she didn't choose to answer.

And as the snow cleared, I hunted for the last of the crowberries, withered and tasteless from their winter under the snow, but edible still. A small handful each over several days and the last traces of winter sickness left us. Next winter, we would preserve berries for the winter in the skyr, and there would be no sore gums. I could feel confident about this. One of our heifers was in calf. Soon she would give birth and there would be milk all summer.

Bjorn and Grim were busy almost every day in the forge. They were using our precious stock of iron to make weapons. This bothered me no end. I didn't want to believe that Svanson's kin would come seeking revenge. I wished I could think we would be left in peace to farm and prosper. We had no reason to believe that our theft and deception had been discovered, but I remembered Arn, and knew he might make mischief for us. He must resent Bjorn bitterly, and feel he owed him a grudge.

The ringing of hammer on anvil continued. The men began to practise with real swords and then with bows and arrows. I glanced at them anxiously every time I left the house, a sick feeling in my stomach. Perhaps we really might need to defend ourselves.

* * *

Our minds were taken off weapons when Thrang returned. The catch this time was smaller, and the boat had been damaged on a treacherous rock. Bjorn joined him to look at how they could repair it while Asgerd, Asdis, Ragna, and I began to cook the breakfast.

'We've eaten well enough with Olvir,' said Erik. 'He's a generous host. Give yourselves the larger portions.'

He put an arm around Asgerd's waist as he spoke, pulling her close for a moment. 'You are getting thin,' I heard him whisper sadly. 'And so is our daughter.'

We sat down thankfully to the meal, looking forward to eating our fill at least once while the fish was fresh and good. Like last time, everyone's spirits soared temporarily. Ragna had brought out one last barrel of mead that had been hidden away and was rationing everyone very carefully so that there would be more for another day.

'Olvir says that if we'll help him in summer, there's a possibility of hunting a minky whale,' Erik said over supper. 'They're the smallest of the whales here, but still too big for one man to hunt alone.'

Bjorn looked interested. 'That would be good. The oil would be excellent for trading.'

'If any trading ships venture as far as this godforsaken bay,' muttered Ragna into her goblet. I was just close enough to catch what she said, though most didn't. Bjorn took no notice of her dark words, but continued to talk and laugh with Thrang and Erik. Absently, I picked up my goblet, tested it against my lip as always and then sipped. It sent fire into my veins, warming me right through.

'Hey, that was my goblet,' said Asgerd laughing. 'I'll have to have yours!' She reached over me to pick up a goblet I hadn't noticed. 'Hands off my wine!'

'I'm sorry,' I said confused.

'No, I'm sure that one was mine,' argued Vali on the other side of me. He grinned and leaned across me to try and snatch the goblet from her hands. Asgerd laughed and slapped his hands away. 'You've had yours!' she cried. 'Don't steal mine to get extra.'

'No, really, it's mine,' he said with a laugh and succeeded in snatching it away. A little of the mead spilled on the table in front of me, but the rest he poured down his throat, smiling at the indignant cries of Asgerd, and wiping his mouth on the back of his hand.

'You didn't even taste it,' scoffed Asgerd. 'What a waste.'

She reached for his cup instead, glancing at him, clearly half expecting to continue the game and claim that was his too.

But he said nothing. I glanced at him, a sudden fear crossing my mind. Vali clutched his throat, a look of surprise and pain on his face.

'It burns,' he gasped.

My heart lurched in horror. Swiftly, I dipped one finger in the spilled liquid and touched it to my lip.

Aconite.

I grabbed his arm as his body lurched forward.

'Help me,' he gasped.

'I will,' I said, laying a hand on his forehead to reassure him, but I knew it was already too late.

All talk had stopped around us, everyone's eyes riveted

on the unfortunate man. He convulsed violently, crashing backwards off the bench. Thrang and Grim rushed to help him, catching his weight and laying him on a sheepskin while he twisted and writhed. His eyes rolled back into his head. His colours were fading so fast I could see it happening.

'Thora, do something,' cried Thrang.

'What's going on?' I heard Ulf's frightened voice in the background.

I didn't speak, holding Vali tightly, keeping my eyes on his terrified, agonized face.

Vali convulsed one more time, shuddered and went quite limp. He was blue around the lips, his eyes unseeing. I didn't need to lay my hand on the side of his neck, feeling for the throb of his blood through his veins, but I did it anyway. There was nothing.

'He's dead,' I said, forcing myself to speak calmly. 'There was nothing I could do.' As I spoke, the first tears ran down my face. Just a few moments ago, Vali had been full of energy and laughter. None of that remained; only the horror of his death. Who had done this dreadful deed? I leaned over him, whispered a prayer to the goddess Eir and gently closed his lids over his eyes.

'What happened?' asked Asgerd, her voice hoarse with shock.

'He's been poisoned,' I said, my voice carrying right across the hall. 'Please, everybody, test your mead before you drink it. Rub a little on your lip. If it burns, it isn't safe.'

I could feel myself beginning to shake now, as the shock of what had happened reached me. 'Someone has killed Vali,' I said aloud. 'Why?' I could feel anger surfacing beside my grief now. 'Who can live among us and commit murder? The sneaking, sly killings of the assassin?'

I couldn't think straight. Had Vali been the intended victim or not? I had no idea.

There were cries of distress at my words. Everyone pushed their goblets from them. Asdis began to sob quietly. Among the men there were raised voices.

Ragna pushed herself to her feet with difficulty and stood, leaning on the table.

'Fine words from you, Thora. How do you know he's been poisoned?' she demanded sharply.

I caught my breath. This was dangerous ground.

'I recognize the symptoms,' I told her, aware that everyone was listening. 'It's aconite. It's deadly poison.'

'Aco what?' asked Grim. He sounded angry.

'Russian aconite,' I explained, controlling the tremble that wanted to make my voice wobble. 'It's a root sometimes used to treat diseases of the heart . . . but deadly in large doses.'

'Who would have that?' Grim's voice was hard. 'I've never even heard of it.' He looked around as he spoke and everywhere I looked heads were shaken.

'Thora would have such a thing.' Ragna's voice again. She sounded triumphant. Was I the only one who noticed? Of course, whether or not she was the poisoner, she'd be glad to see me blamed.

'Thora?' asked Thrang. He was staring at me as though he was seeing me properly for the first time. As though he didn't like what he saw.

'Yes,' I admitted. 'I had this root. It was locked in my chest. But someone got hold of the key and stole the root.'

'So why did you tell no one?' demanded Ragna swiftly.

'I knew,' said Bjorn. 'Thora spoke to me about it.'

'Ha!' A mirthless laugh from Ragna. She sat down without saying anything else. She didn't need to say more. I could feel the heat of half a dozen pairs of suspicious eyes on me. Some were confused, not knowing what or who to believe. Everyone was frightened and that made them less rational.

'Why would I want to kill Vali?' I asked them. 'I nursed him through the fever barely two months ago.'

'Because he made fun of you,' said Ragna. 'About your marriage.'

'Thora wouldn't hurt anyone!' exclaimed young Jon. His youthful face shone pink with indignation on my behalf. 'She nursed us all when we had the fever.'

'No one ever nursed me with such care as Thora did,' put in Asgerd. 'It was my cup that was poisoned. My cup that Vali drank from. It can't have been Thora.'

'Not everyone recovered from the fever,' said Ragna darkly, speaking over Asgerd. 'And what about peppering my father's wound? That was misusing her skills.'

There was a quiet murmur around us. How many people believed Ragna and how many trusted me? It was impossible to guess. How could any of them turn on me after I had cared for them all winter?

'Enough of this,' said Bjorn standing up. 'None of us suspect Thora. She told me of this theft some time ago, and it was on my advice she kept it quiet.'

'Clever of her,' muttered Ragna.

I felt as though I had swallowed ice. I had worked so hard to help every person here and yet they could be turned against me so easily.

'Why didn't you tell us?' demanded Thrang.

'I didn't wish to frighten anyone. I never dreamed we had a killer among us,' answered Bjorn. His face was drawn and serious. 'But it seems we can't trust one another. Thrang, Stein, Erik, and I will now search the house including everyone's possessions. All of you stay here meanwhile, please.'

We all sat, still and shocked, around the fire. I was acutely aware of Vali's body lying untended behind me. While everyone's clothes, weapons, and bedding were shaken and searched, I sat quite still, looking from face to face. Who could be guilty? Surely they would betray themselves? But every face and every aura betrayed shock, distress, and fear. Some of the women were weeping. It was impossible to guess who the murderer was. Not my friend Asgerd. I couldn't believe it. Nor gentle Asdis. And Ragna couldn't have climbed the ladder . . . My mind circled the same people over and over, making no progress.

Bjorn returned to the high table, the search over. They'd found nothing. The root had been well hidden.

CHAPTER THIRTY

Harpa Month

The last month of winter passed by but fear and suspicion cast its dark shadow over the coming of spring. The dread of another poisoning leeched the lustre out of the long, glorious days. Our community grew mistrustful, everyone testing their food and drink and watching one another.

It should have been a joyful time. The sea birds arrived in their thousands and nested in the cliffs. The noise they made reached everywhere. The men climbed the cliffs and collected blue guillemot eggs. Eating the eggs made us strong again, as did the longer days and the warmth that was now in the sun. The grass grew green and the animals all went out to pasture. They went out thin and dull-eyed and within a few days they were filling out and playful once more.

I felt anything but playful. No one said anything openly to me, but I felt I was blamed. Perhaps not for Vali's death itself, but for keeping the theft of the root a secret. Fewer people came to me for cures and one or two of the men avoided me. My brief spell of contentment was over. Even Thrang, once so protective and attentive, was cool with me.

I spent long hours outdoors watching the spring plants grow and combing the sea shore for useful plants. I sometimes found sea rocket drifting along the shore and collected it. Bera had told me to look out for it. It was a fleshy, tasteless vegetable that grew on the shore but it was edible. No one liked it, but we all ate it. It would be months until the harvest was in.

The men ploughed the new ground. It was hard work to break land that had never been farmed. The topsoil was thin and stony. They worked hard, ploughing in the animal manure we had collected through the winter. They sowed a huge barley field and a smaller rye field. Bjorn oversaw everything, working harder than anyone.

'Thora,' he said to me one day as I returned to the house with two moss campion roots we could stew for nightmeal, 'I have a message for you.'

I paused, waiting for him to hand his tools to Grim. He was hot and grimy from a hard day's work. The sun had already tanned his face golden, but he looked thin still, and strained with hunger and worry.

As he came to walk beside me, he smiled and his face lit with warmth and kindness. 'Bera would like to see you when you can spare the time,' he said. 'It's about the baby.'

I nodded. 'I'll go tomorrow,' I promised him.

Ingvar was teething and fretful again. His cheeks were flushed red and his nose was running. I rubbed a little clove oil onto his gums.

Bera hushed him in her arms.

'I've heard the slaves gossiping,' she told me. 'I want you to know that I don't believe for one moment that you're to blame.'

'Some do,' I said in a low voice. Her outspoken confidence had caused a sudden turmoil of gratitude and distress inside me.

'Don't tell me Bjorn suspects you?' demanded Bera at once.

'No,' I agreed quickly. 'He never makes me feel that he does. But the others . . . a few of the men especially. And Ragna of course.'

'They're all ignorant and stupid,' Bera dismissed them swiftly with a wave of her free hand.

'And yet someone knows aconite root when they see it. A most rare plant. Even more rare than this clove oil, which I bought from the same trader. One among us, other than me, understands both healing and poisons.'

Bera leaned forward, her eyes suddenly keen, her attention caught.

'You say there is another healer among you?' she said.

'Almost certainly.'

'Then the poisoner is a woman. It must be.'

'I have heard of male healers in other lands,' I said hesitantly. 'But I know of no one of Norse blood who would share the goddess's secrets with a man. Besides, there were only women in the house when the root was stolen.'

'So there can be no doubt,' said Bera. 'You are not many women in your house. That narrows the field.'

'Asgerd, Asdis, Ragna, Vigdis, and Hild and Enys,' I

listed the women of our house. 'And me,' I added. 'Astrid doesn't count.'

'Do you suspect anyone?'

I shook my head mutely. 'All of them were in the house when the root was taken. But none of them was alone there.'

'So they suspect you?' Bera's voice was scornful.

'A few do perhaps. I think they mainly blame me for not telling them at once about the theft. That could have saved Vali's life. And there's another thing.'

Hesitantly, I recounted the tale of how I came to pepper the chieftain's wound on the Faeroes. I was ashamed to make such a confession. I omitted to mention the hope I had had of wedding Bjorn myself, describing instead the murder of Kai and the robbery of our ship.

'It seemed a trivial action at the time,' I admitted. 'But I broke my vow to the goddess. I abused the knowledge she has shared with me and used it for harm.'

'You can hardly compare such a small incident with murder by poison,' objected Bera.

'It is a principle. Healing is never to be used to harm or for revenge.'

'Well, I can quite see why you were tempted,' said Bera, tossing her head. 'And I'm sure most of the others can too. You're blaming yourself far more than the others are blaming you, if you ask me.' She had a sharp, decisive way of talking that appealed to me. 'You were tricked and held to ransom, one of your men was killed and you had that she-dog foisted onto your household. How can you even speak of trust and vows after that?'

Her description of Ragna made me want to laugh. The

corners of my mouth twitched and I turned my face away hurriedly to hide it. Bera was always so polite to Ragna. I had had no idea she disliked her.

'I think we should have Ragna for the villain,' Bera insisted.

I smiled faintly. But I shook my head too.

'Impossible,' I said. 'She is the one person who couldn't have climbed into the loft.'

As we talked the matter over, I became aware what a comfort it was to have someone to confide in, to know that someone besides Bjorn believed in me.

To my surprise, Bjorn arrived to collect me before nightmeal. He lingered awhile in close conversation with Helgi and then we set off together through the glowing spring evening.

'What were you discussing so earnestly?' I asked him as we walked.

'I want to take a trip south to explore the land,' Bjorn reminded me. 'It'll have to wait until after lamb-fold time. But we need to know something about the country we live in. I want to know what caused the earth to shake like it did. I'd especially like to see how fertile it is inland. Whether we could live there. Whether there are forests for building and firewood. There's too little on the coast.'

I nodded, my mind busy. There were things I lacked here too. Plants I hadn't been able to find on the coast. I needed willow and elder bark to replace what I had used in the winter. In fact, the list of plants I needed was long.

'Might there be room for an extra person on the trip?' I asked diffidently. 'I don't know how many you were planning to take . . . '

'I don't know, Thora,' said Bjorn. He frowned, looking straight ahead as he walked. 'I'd planned to travel just with Helgi. We're going to take the four riding horses we own between us and travel swiftly.'

I felt embarrassed to have asked. I hadn't realized it was just the two of them going. I would slow them down.

'In that case, of course I can't come,' I said, disappointed. 'But I'm running very low on medicines. We'll have to hope a trader calls here at some point.'

'Many of us owe our lives to your nursing,' said Bjorn. 'I understand your need. I'll see what I can do.'

I flushed with pleasure at his praise. 'Thank you,' I said. 'For your faith in me.' I kept my voice steady as I spoke so that Bjorn wouldn't know how much I felt. I glanced up at him, and found he was looking down at me.

'You're very young to have so much responsibility, Thora,' Bjorn said. 'I wish . . . '

But he didn't finish his sentence. A movement out on the bay caught his eye and I didn't find out what he wished.

'A ship!' he exclaimed.

My heart thudded in my chest and I could see the blood had drained from Bjorn's sun-bronzed face. He turned to me, grasping my hands in his.

'What do you see?' he demanded.

Obediently, I closed my eyes and tried to see. But Bjorn's hands holding mine distracted me. All I could feel was his urgency and fear.

'I see nothing,' I said unhappily.

'Let's hope it's only settlers or traders,' muttered Bjorn. 'But now we must put our training to the test. Come!'

Bjorn turned and ran towards the longhouse, leaping over rocks and dips in the path. I followed as best I could. Ahead of me, Bjorn shouted orders as he approached the longhouse. The men scattered, running to arm themselves and to throw on cloaks to hide their weapons.

'The women and children must hide in the passage,' cried Bjorn.

I encouraged the others to obey him, persuading Ulf that he was too young to fight with the men and helping Ragna into the darkness of the secret passage. The way led out onto the open hillside at some distance from the house. Bjorn had copied the idea from Ragna's home on the Faeroes, knowing such a thing might come in useful.

The enclosed dampness of the tunnel reminded me strongly of my time tied up in the dark on the islands and I shuddered as we all huddled together, straining our ears for some sign of what was going on outside.

'How will we know what's happening?' asked Asdis tearfully. She sounded so young and frightened that I put my arm around her.

'It's probably only a trading ship,' I told her in what I hoped was a reassuring voice. 'This is just a precaution.'

'I'll climb up on the roof and look what's happening!' said Ulf.

'No!' I exclaimed, reaching out to stop him, but he twisted away from my hand, pushed past Asgerd who stood between him and the tunnel exit, and disappeared from sight.

'He's very good at looking after himself,' said Asgerd, not bothering to run after him. 'I'm sure they won't catch him.'

It seemed like a very long time later that Ulf called out to us in a loud voice:

'It's only traders! They're all shaking hands and coming up to the house! You can come out now.'

We all breathed a huge sigh of relief and filed back into the house to welcome the visitors.

The ship was owned by an Icelander who was heading back to Norway via the Faeroes to trade. Thrang was already busy bargaining himself and Stein a place on board when the men reached the house. Our household was breaking up.

I also found an opportunity to speak to the trader, and asked him to bring me certain plants I couldn't do without on his way home in the autumn. We agreed prices, he promised to do his best, and I had to be content with that.

Thrang asked me to walk with him later that evening. We went out into the light evening and walked along the coast, away from the beach where the visiting ship lay.

'I'm leaving in the morning,' Thrang said. 'I asked you to leave with me, Thora. Have you come to a decision?'

I hesitated, looking down at the grass as I walked. I knew my mind and I knew my heart, but I still didn't know what to say.

'We could go to Helgi this evening and ask him to marry us,' said Thrang, without waiting for my answer. 'He is a *godi* and could perform that service for us tonight.'

'Thrang,' I said, pausing and looking up at him. 'Are you quite sure that you don't believe I was the one who poisoned Vali?' I had to know.

'I'm certain it wasn't you,' said Thrang. But he hesitated before he spoke and he couldn't look at me. I felt sure he still had doubts.

'You're a good man, Thrang. I like and respect you. But I can't marry you,' I told him a little sadly.

'You don't love me?' Thrang asked, his voice gruff with disappointment.

'I don't love you,' I agreed quietly. 'I'm sorry.'

Thrang turned and grasped my shoulders. 'If it's Bjorn you love, that will cause nothing but trouble,' he said fiercely. 'Put him out of your mind, Thora. For your sake, for Ragna's and his, you need to forget him.'

Now it was I who couldn't meet his eyes. I could feel the heat stealing into my face and I felt ashamed. I shook my head mutely and left Thrang to interpret that as he would.

'I'm very sorry, Thora,' said Thrang. He bent and kissed me on the forehead, then released me and turned and walked back to the longhouse ahead of me. It was done, the decision was made. I had no choice but to make the most of my future in this land instead of on the wide oceans.

CHAPTER THIRTY-ONE

Lamb Fold Time
Stekktið

When the sheep had been shorn and all the women were busy combing and spinning the fleeces, Bjorn announced his proposed trip south with Helgi.

'The crops are sown now,' he explained. 'This is the time of waiting. I'm leaving tomorrow morning. I put the household unreservedly in Ragna's charge.'

Ragna glowed with pleasure at Bjorn's words and her eyes darted to me in a swift triumphant glance. I stayed quite still. Was I to accompany them or not? I didn't relish staying behind in Ragna's charge. The friendliness she had shown me after her illness had been short lived and hadn't outlasted Vali's death.

'The outdoor work, I entrust to the supervision of Erik,' Bjorn continued. 'I know you'll care for everything while I am away as well as I could myself.'

Erik bowed and looked proud to be chosen for such responsibility. It was unusual to entrust such a task to a slave, but now that Thrang had gone, we had no free men besides Bjorn. And Erik, I reflected, would soon be free. He had been our first friend and was Bjorn's most loyal slave and deserved this trust.

There was lively interest in the projected trip and much speculation on what the two men would find in this new, strange land. Everyone talked till late. As we were putting away the tables ready to sleep, Bjorn added almost as an afterthought, 'Oh, Thora accompanies us on this journey. She needs new plants for medicines, which Helgi and I can't find for her.'

My heart gave a great leap at the thought of this adventure. There was a buzz of surprise and everyone looked at me for a moment. I kept my face impassive.

My eye was caught by Ragna. She was less successful than me at masking her emotions and just now, her face was filled with hate and anger. She glared at me out of narrowed eyes, her aura an angry red. I knew our winter truce was completely over.

'That is hardly proper, husband,' she said in a high-pitched voice, a spot of angry red appearing on each cheek. 'I believe I shall have to forbid it.'

The two of them faced each other in silence. This was disputed territory. The house and the women were Ragna's responsibility. But Bjorn was the master here if he chose to exercise his authority. For a few tense moments I feared his easy-going nature would cause him to give in. But today he held her gaze.

'Thora saved many lives last winter, including yours and mine. She goes with us,' Bjorn said firmly. He turned on his heel, went to his sleeping mat amongst the men and rolled himself in furs for the night. Ragna withdrew in silence to her room.

I heard Bjorn moving about before rising time the next morning and crawled to the edge of the sleeping loft. As soon as he saw me, he brought me the ladder. We put on our cloaks and slipped softly out of the house. A few people stirred drowsily but most slept on. We each carried a roll of furs for bedding and Bjorn carried a small package of food.

'Do you think it'll be safe to rely on springs for water, or should I take a waterskin?' he asked.

'Not all the springs here are safe to drink from,' I said hesitantly, thinking of our own hot spring, which tasted foul. 'But don't go back in the house now.' I was afraid something might happen to prevent our trip. I was looking forward to it so much.

Bjorn looked back at the house and then grinned suddenly, his face lighting up like a child let off work for the day.

'We'll borrow one from Bera,' he said.

We collected our one horse from the picket line and tied our bundles on her back. Then, leading her, we set out for Helgafell. Both our dogs ran ahead of us, sniffing the ground eagerly. They sensed this was no ordinary day. I walked beside Bjorn. We didn't speak much. I was too full of excitement for many words. Bjorn whistled cheerfully from time to time, so I guessed that he felt the same way.

At Helgafell we were met by a setback. No one came out to welcome us and there was an unusual hush over the house. When we entered we were met by Bera, her face pale and shocked.

'I was about to send for you,' she said unsteadily. 'There's been an accident . . .'

My thoughts flew to the baby.

'Is Ingvar sick?' I asked anxiously.

'No, thank Freya,' Bera answered, tears gleaming in her eyes. 'It's Helgi. He went out early to move the cattle and one of them stepped on him. His leg is broken.'

I understood her fears at once. A broken leg could lead to lameness or even death. It was a serious matter for the head of the household. Underlying my concern for Helgi was the thought that our trip would have to be cancelled. I felt the disappointment like an ache.

Helgi was lying on his bed, where his men had carried him, his face white under his summer tan. He was gritting his teeth in pain and sweating profusely. The leg had already begun to swell. I felt it carefully, mindful of the pain I was causing him. Helgi didn't make a sound. Bjorn, Bera, and several others crowded into the doorway and watched anxiously.

'I'll need wood for a splint and strips of cloth to bind it,' I said at last. 'It's a clean break.'

I heard Bera gasp with relief and give the orders. Once I had what I needed, I asked Bjorn and Bera to help but sent the others away. Then Bera and Bjorn held Helgi still while I pulled the bone straight. Helgi gave one great cry and then fainted. I was able to bind the leg to the splint with strips of cloth while he was unconcious, sparing him the pain of it. He came round again as I was tying the last knots. I laid a hand on his brow. He was clammy and cold with shock and pain.

'Rest now,' I told him. 'Move as little as possible.' To Bera I added: 'If only I still had willow bark or elder to ease the pain. I used every shred last winter.'

'I'm so sorry,' Helgi said weakly, his voice hoarse with pain. 'Our trip . . . we'll have to postpone it.'

Bjorn looked thoughtful.

'You won't be riding any distance between now and harvest time,' he said. 'We'd have to postpone it until next year. If you will lend me your horses, I think I'll go on with Thora and explore a little. She urgently needs the plants we hope to find. If there were to be another sickness like last year, I don't know how we'd manage. You and I can do a longer trip together next summer.'

I caught my breath. I was aware of both Helgi and Bera looking from me to Bjorn. Despite my training, I could feel a flush creeping over my face and neck. What must they be thinking? This proposal was as astonishing to me as it must be to them.

'Will Ragna allow that?' asked Bera hesitantly.

'I wasn't thinking of asking her,' admitted Bjorn.

There was a painful pause.

I stood scarcely daring to breathe. It hadn't occurred to me that we could go on alone. But now that Bjorn had suggested it, I wanted to go with him more than I had ever wanted anything.

'Very well,' agreed Helgi at last. 'If you think it's right, I have no wish to say anything. But would you not like someone else to accompany you? One of my slaves perhaps? There may be danger and you might need help with cooking and looking after the horses.'

Bjorn looked at me, a questioning lift to his brows. There was a touch of recklessness about him, and it appealed strongly to me. I gave him the tiniest shake of my head.

'We can manage. And we'll go much faster just the two of us,' said Bjorn, turning back to Helgi. 'We'll take great care, I promise.'

I let my breath go in a sigh of relief. I would have Bjorn to myself for several days. I could scarcely contain myself for happiness. While Bjorn borrowed a waterskin and went to fill it and tie it to one of the horses, I lingered with Bera.

'Are you sure about this, Thora?' asked Bera anxiously. 'You ought not to go alone with him.'

I pretended not to understand her.

'We'll go carefully and take no foolish risks,' I promised. 'We'll look after your horses. And I hope to bring Helgi back medicine in a few days.' I spoke calmly but inside I was in turmoil. What was it going be like to be alone with Bjorn for all that time?

'You know that's not what I meant,' said Bera reproachfully. 'I was thinking of your . . . well, of Ragna's fury when she finds out.'

'Is there . . . ' I hesitated. Then I spoke in a rush. 'Is there any need for her to know that Helgi hasn't gone with us?' I asked. 'I don't mean you should lie to her, of course. But you don't need to send a message to her, do you?'

Bera shook her head and sighed. 'I'll try and keep it quiet,' she promised. 'But there is plenty of coming and going among the houses, and it's bound to get out that Helgi is laid up with a broken leg.'

'I suppose so,' I agreed. 'Well, I'll take the consequences later.'

Bera hugged me and whispered: 'I'm always here if you need a friend.'

I thanked her, and wondered whether, like Thrang, Bera had guessed my feelings for Bjorn. If she had, she'd never let me know she suspected.

Bjorn helped me into the saddle and we turned the horses' heads south. We each rode one horse and led a second so that we could swap when they grew weary. The sun hadn't yet risen as we rode away from Helgafell.

'Are you happy with this?' Bjorn asked me as soon as we were out of earshot. 'It's not too late to change your mind.'

'I'd look pretty stupid riding back now,' I said, with a laugh. I was light hearted, almost giddy, at the thought of days alone with Bjorn. I wouldn't have turned back now for a fortune. 'I need medicinal plants,' I said demurely. Now it was Bjorn's turn to chuckle. There had been very little laughter through the long hard winter, and I guessed he felt as excited as I did at the prospect of this escape from Ragna's dark presence. Whether he attached the same importance to the two of us being alone, I couldn't say. He concealed his feelings almost as well as I did, his aura a steady, almost constant blue. Last summer I could have sworn he loved me. Now I had no idea of his feelings. And in any case, none of that mattered. He was married. We could still enjoy each other's company. Away from the house, we could still be friends.

The sun rose in a cloudless blue sky, shining its blessing down upon us, bathing us in warmth. We needed it as we climbed from the coast into high, rough meadowland.

There were bogs here and there, marked by the cotton grass waving its tufty white heads at us. But the bogs became more scarce and the ground stonier as we climbed.

'It doesn't look as though there's a real pass,' Bjorn said at last, breaking our long, contented silence. 'Just a high saddle between the mountains. You could graze animals here in the summer.'

'It's very coarse grass,' I said doubtfully. 'And even fewer varieties of plants than on the coast.'

'The cattle wouldn't mind that. Nor the sheep,' said Bjorn confidently.

'Are you thinking of expanding your farm?' I asked him with a smile.

'Why not?' he replied seriously. 'There will be more settlers arriving soon enough. We must take what we can use now.'

I hesitated. 'What about Svanson's kin?' I asked. 'Do you think they will come looking for us? Do you think anyone in Norway knows it was not the real Svanson who sailed away with the ships?'

'That, my dear Thora, I can't guess,' Bjorn said. 'It's in the hands of the gods.'

He sounded unconcerned.

'And yet you've been training the men to fight,' I pointed out.

'The gods help those who help themselves,' he responded with a grin. 'Now, for the next few days we are only allowed to discuss cheerful subjects.'

And so we talked and laughed as we rode. We admired the landscape, discussed the possibilities this new land offered us. For a few hours I forgot that I owned nothing and had lost everything to Ragna.

As we began to descend the far side of the saddle of land, a breathtaking view unveiled itself before us. The air was clear and we could see a vast tract of rugged land before us, a silver ribbon snaking its way across it, sparkling in the sun.

'It might be challenging to cross that river,' said Bjorn doubtfully.

'I promised Bera we would do nothing rash,' I told him.

'Then we shall have to find a safe crossing place. Do you think human eyes have ever seen this place, Thora? Or are we the very first?'

I caught my breath. That was truly an incredible thought.

Apart from a few birds, the land seemed completely empty. Untouched. The only movement was the wind in the grass and the shadows of the clouds as they chased one another across the landscape. There were few trees, just endless grassy slopes full of flowers. And in the distance, rising starkly black in the bright morning light, more mountains.

I looked at Bjorn.

'Is it what you expected?' I asked him.

'I didn't know what to expect,' he said in a hushed voice. I sensed he was feeling the same awe that had struck me.

As we rode slowly down from the high ground towards the river, the air grew warmer. The land became steadily less rocky and more fertile. There was an abundance of flowers and several times I pulled my horse up to look at a plant or shrub. We zigzagged across rough ground, and the horses wove through small trees and avoided boggy patches.

We could hear the river long before we reached it. The sound of rushing water filled our ears. We paused when we reached the bank and looked down at the churning torrent. It was so clear we could see every stone on the bottom. Brightly-coloured male ducks swam busily in and out of eddies of water looking for food. I reached out and tugged Bjorn's sleeve lightly, drawing his attention to the brown mother duck that was hovering near the bank guarding her fluffy ducklings. Bjorn reached for his bow, but at the sight of my face he let be.

'We're going to have to eat,' he called over the noise of the river.

'Not now,' I told him.

Bjorn called the dogs off. They had been poised at the river's edge ready to retrieve a duck if he shot it, but at his whistle they set off along the bank instead.

As we followed the river upstream the thunder of water grew louder and soon we could see a great cloud of spray rising up into the air.

'A waterfall,' guessed Bjorn.

Sure enough, as we rounded the next corner we came upon a vast fall; a snow-white cascade of water. The sunlight caught the myriad drops of spray and turned them into glittering rainbows. It was a place of power and beauty.

I dismounted and stood on the high river bank, arms upraised, and prayed. I thanked Eir for sending me on this expedition. For showing me such sights. And I prayed that she would lead me to places where healing plants grew.

When I was finished, I turned and saw that Bjorn was looking, not at the waterfall, but at me. He was smiling, but it was a kind smile, not a mocking one.

'Doesn't it make you want to pray to the gods too?' I asked him.

'Your gods are not my gods,' Bjorn reminded me.

'Who or what are your gods?' I asked him curiously.

Bjorn just shook his head.

'I know you want to forget your past and be Bjorn Svanson,' I said. 'I try to support you. But I can't help but be curious. If you don't want to be asked, you shouldn't drop mysterious hints like that.'

Bjorn laughed.

'Let's save a few tales for our evening campfires,' he suggested. 'We may need words if you won't let me hunt.'

We continued upstream but we didn't find a place to cross the river. When the sun was low in the sky, Bjorn shot a duck that flew overhead. One of the dogs brought it triumphantly back in his jaws, and Bjorn decided we had gone far enough for one day.

We made camp beside the river. Bjorn collected twigs and sticks from the scrubby little trees around us and lit a fire. I plucked and cleaned the duck. We spitted it on sticks and I sat down to watch and turn it as it cooked. The dogs found their own meal, probably of ground-nesting birds, and returned smeared in blood and feathers. They edged close to the warmth of the fire, their eyes on the roasting duck, until Bjorn ordered them to lie further off.

A slight awkwardness fell between us. During the day, occupied with riding and seeing new sights, I had felt deeply content to be alone with Bjorn. Now we were sitting quietly, close together in the quiet and muted light of the evening, it felt less comfortable to sit in silence. All topics of conversation that occurred to me were painful. Bjorn must have felt it too, because he remarked: 'Now we miss Helgi to cheer us up with his jokes, don't we?'

'You could tell a story,' I suggested. 'You are so gifted, and yet you so rarely agree to do so.'

Bjorn looked into the fire.

'My stories are all so full of pain,' he said softly. 'The stories of my homeland that I was so cruelly snatched away from are haunted with sad memories. And the stories I learned in captivity, I told to earn my keep. So they remind me of that time. Now that I'm no longer a slave, forced to do any master's will, it's my pleasure to be silent.'

I'd never heard Bjorn speak of himself in this way. He was usually so careful to have no past but that of the man he was impersonating.

'Won't you tell me a tale of your choice, just because I ask you to?' I said. 'As a favour?'

'No, but I'll tell you a tale of your choice,' he replied, and he looked directly at me as he spoke, his eyes dark in the evening light. A puff of smoke blew between us and I looked away, suddenly shy. I prodded the duck with a stick.

'Tell me of your childhood home,' I said. 'I'd like to hear as much as you'll tell me about yourself.'

Bjorn began to speak. He told me he was from Ireland, a land much greener and more fertile than either Norway or Iceland. The winters were light, wet, and mild. It was warm enough to bathe in the sea in summer, he told me. I thought of the sea here and shivered.

Bjorn talked while the duck sizzled and dripped fat into the fire, and I listened. He told me of his capture and his life in slavery. His family had stayed together and that had been their solace. His sister had been his last surviving family member, and she had been killed by Svanson.

His face still darkened with pain and anger as he remembered this. I wanted to reach out and lay my hand on his to soothe him, but I knew it wouldn't be wise. I kept my hands firmly folded in my lap instead.

'You avenged her,' I said softly.

'Slaves are not entitled to vengeance,' Bjorn reminded me. 'What I did was a crime. I committed murder and theft.'

'We are no longer subject to the laws of Norway here,' I said.

Bjorn smiled, banishing the shadow that had darkened his brow. 'No, indeed, and I count my blessings daily. Though I am sorry that we . . . '

His voice trailed off. I suspected what he wanted to say and was afraid to hear it. A part of me longed to know what he felt for me. But it was neither wise nor prudent to encourage him.

'The duck is done,' I announced, breaking the tension that had been created by his unspoken words.

After we had eaten and thrown the scraps and bones to the dogs, we each laid out our sleeping furs on opposite sides of the fire. I felt self-conscious as I did so, wondering if he had the same thoughts as me; that there was nothing and no one to keep us apart tonight, only the promises he had been forced to make to Ragna on the islands all those months ago.

The temperature had dropped rapidly once the sun had gone behind the mountains and it was bitterly cold. We were glad to wrap ourselves in furs. One of the dogs came, flopped down beside me with a sigh and laid his head across my feet.

'You'll be warm enough,' said Bjorn with a laugh.

I lay back with a sigh looking up at the clear, deep blue sky.

'It's almost a year since we slept in the open,' I said.

'Yes,' Bjorn agreed. 'It seems much longer. Do you remember all those nights on the ship?'

I did remember. I remembered the night it was so cold that Bjorn held me in his arms. I had thought it meant we would always be together. But the gods had had something else in store for us. I wondered if Bjorn was remembering that night too, or whether it had meant less to him. When he spoke, it was of something different.

'When Thrang left us, I was afraid you were going to go with him.' Bjorn spoke so softly that I could only just hear him over the crackle of the fire and the roar of the nearby river. 'He asked you, didn't he?'

'He did,' I admitted.

Smoke blew across me, making me cough. I could tell Bjorn was watching me, but I didn't choose to look back.

'And did you consider going?' he asked.

'I considered it.'

'So what made you decide to stay?'

I wished Bjorn wouldn't ask me. What could I say? That I stayed for love of him? That I still felt certain that our futures were inextricably bound up in one another? Neither my pride nor my good sense would let me say either of these things.

'I didn't love him enough,' I said at last. 'And I think, at the end, it was the same for him. I think he was afraid I might be the poisoner.'

'Then he's a great fool,' said Bjorn impatiently. 'How could anyone who knows you believe you capable of such a thing?'

His words were balm to my troubled soul.

We lay silent a while. The brightness faded from the sky, but it wouldn't get any darker tonight. I could feel the temperature dropping further. After a long pause, Bjorn spoke again.

'I have no right to ask this. No right at all. But if you left, Thora, my life would be empty. All the joy of my freedom and my farm would be gone. I hope you'll continue to make my house your home. I hope you'll stay.'

I took a long time to think about how to reply. You have no right to ask that of me, I thought to myself. But I understand that you gave up a great deal to rescue me from those people on the island. In some ways, your bargain was as hard as mine.

'I can promise nothing,' I said at last. 'Except that I will consult you before I take a decision.'

CHAPTER THIRTY-TWO

We eventually found a place where the horses could swim across the river with relatively little danger and we went on inland. We rode for a full day across open, hilly land and came to sights I'll never forget.

We saw a fire mountain. I'd heard tell of such things, but never met anyone who had seen one for themselves.

The whole area around the mountain was blackened and barren. It was a poisonous, stinking wasteland. Even the water ran hot and foul, evaporating into rotten-smelling steam. The very ground was hot and smoking. As we rode closer, for Bjorn's curiosity was strong, we could see deep cracks in the rock oozing dull, red, liquid fire.

'What is it?' I asked Bjorn astonished. We could go no closer, the heat seared our faces and hands. The dogs had stopped following us some time ago and waited anxiously on cooler ground. The horses too were fretting now and tugging at the bits, wanting to be away from this unnatural place.

'I think the rocks themselves have melted,' said Bjorn uncertainly.

'But rocks don't melt,' I objected. 'You can put them in

the hottest part of the fire. They glow, but they never melt.'

'Perhaps this fire is hotter,' said Bjorn.

We turned and rode away. I was relieved, but Bjorn kept turning in the saddle to look back.

We rode on and came across bright blue pools of stinking hot water. They smelt, as our own hot spring did, of rotten eggs. But much, much stronger. I pulled my cloak across my face and breathed through it, trying to escape the stench.

There were cracks in the bare yellow earth where steam came hissing or whistling out in a never-ending stream. And there were pools of black, bubbling mud, like the cooking cauldron of some giant troll. I scanned the vast, empty landscape uneasily; half suspecting some giant or troll might really appear. It was as if we were walking in some story or nightmare country.

'If it were not for the bright blue sky overhead, I would think we had arrived in the underworld,' remarked Bjorn perplexed as we passed another place where steam poured from a hole in the earth.

We rode on and emerged from between two black, barren mountains into quite a different landscape. A vast green area stretched before us, studded with shining lakes and hills. The dogs bounded ahead of us, happy at the change of scene. They ran with their tails held high and their noses down, sniffing this more promising place.

I looked behind us, and then ahead again.

'How is such a contrast possible in such a short distance?' I demanded.

'I'm as puzzled by all this as you,' said Bjorn. 'I'd never

dreamed such places could exist. We've not found our forests, and however green this place is here, I think we are better off on the coast.'

'I shouldn't like to live too close to that fire mountain,' I agreed. 'And without timber, there would be no way of building a house here. Besides, at least on the coast, there is fish to eat when all else fails.'

Bjorn nodded. 'Yes, and passing ships to trade with. But I had in mind to get away from ships and hide a little.'

I hesitated before I replied.

'I think . . . if anyone comes looking for us, they will find us here too,' I said. 'There will be people to tell them where we've gone.'

Bjorn sighed. 'You are right, of course. And there are no forests on the scale I had hoped. I never imagined all that smoke could be caused by a mountain burning.'

'Do you think the mountain caused the earth to shake as well?' I asked, puzzled. 'We've never found out what happened that night.'

'It's possible, Thora. It's as good an explanation as any other.'

'There are trees ahead though.' I pointed into the distance.

I was right. The lake was a warm and sheltered spot and trees grew taller than anything we had yet seen. No trees that would yield building timber, but I found bark I needed and plants we hadn't found elsewhere. I collected busily, picking, cutting and sorting the plants I found, while Bjorn took the dogs and went exploring nearby and hunted more duck.

The lakeside was swarming with midges that got in our eyes and noses, and bothered the horses, so we pitched camp some distance back from the water's edge.

'And I was afraid we'd starve,' Bjorn said cheerfully. 'There's little enough game in this country.'

'Thank Freya for the birds,' I agreed as I began the messy job of preparing nightmeal.

We were merry that night. I was relieved to have found some of the plants I needed and that made me light-hearted. Constraint had disappeared once more and we talked and laughed as we ate and threw scraps to the dogs.

'There's something I want to ask you,' I said, as the fire died to a warm glow. We were sitting side by side on a fallen log by the fire.

'Ask away,' replied Bjorn with a smile.

I threw another piece of wood onto the flames in front of us. It caught and crackled and then I spoke.

'Your real name,' I said. 'Will you tell me what it is?'

Bjorn's face closed again, with the same pain as when I'd asked him to tell stories the night before.

'My real name is so far back in time,' he said. 'Only my parents used it. I had a slave name most of my life and that's not worth remembering. I'm not that person any longer. Ask me something else.'

I felt sad for the life Bjorn had had. It made my compassion for his present unhappy marriage even stronger. I wished with all my heart that things could have been different.

'I don't have another question,' I said, sadly.

'Then I have one for you. When Kari died of the fever,

you said something. It's piqued my curiosity ever since.'

'I did?' I tried to remember what I might have said.

'You knew he was dying. You said his aura was "bleeding colours". You read auras?'

I felt the colour flood my face and stared into the fire. It had been a moment of carelessness, of unguarded emotion. Silently, I nodded.

'Why do you keep that secret?' Bjorn's voice was very soft, as though he knew he was trespassing on dangerous territory.

'Because people think it's prying. They think I can tell what they're thinking. But it's not like that. I use it to read health . . . and moods too. I can tell a lot about a person from their aura, but not really what they're thinking.'

'And is this something anyone can learn?' asked Bjorn.

'Yes . . . I think so. But some people can see more clearly, more easily than others. I've always seen them.'

'So,' Bjorn said, laying a hand on mine. 'Tell me about my aura.'

I started at his touch, my heart beating uncomfortably fast. I had an impulse to return his clasp, but I made myself remain passive, my hand lying still beneath his. I half turned to look at him. The sun had long gone, leaving us in muted light. I could see his aura glowing around his head and shoulders.

'It's blue. It's almost always blue. It means you are balanced, calm. You're a survivor.'

I glanced up at him again and saw that the glow was no longer a simple blue. There were shades of pink mingling with it, feelings of love and affection. I felt breathless suddenly. I had been unsure of his feelings for me, but now I knew beyond all doubt.

'And is that all you see?' asked Bjorn, lifting my hand to his lips and kissing it softly. His closeness, his touch, affected me so strongly that I could hardly breathe. I wanted him to go on, to take me in his arms. Then the wrongness of my own longings hit me. I pulled away from him and got up.

'I'm . . . very tired now. I need to sleep,' I said, and began to unroll my sleeping furs to hide the fact that I wanted to cry.

'Thora,' said Bjorn reproachfully. I didn't respond, and kept my face turned from him. For a few moments, Bjorn continued to look at me, and then, with a sigh, he picked up his own furs and moved to the other side of the fire.

The horses were picketed close to us, tearing up mouthfuls of lush green grass. We didn't speak again as we settled to sleep. The birds were calling to one another with haunting, eerie cries on the lake. The world was at peace. I took a long time to find my inner calm again.

We travelled on some distance beyond the lakes, but the ground rose steeply, becoming steadily more barren and inhospitable. Even the birdlife became sparser.

'I think we should turn homewards,' said Bjorn at last. 'There is nothing for us here. We're very well off on the coast.'

I agreed, but privately I was sorry to be heading back. These days had been precious, as sweet as summer fruit, and I never wanted them to end. I didn't want to return to Ragna and living at a distance from Bjorn, despite being in the same house. But the farm and the harvest called us home. There was a great deal of work to be done.

We agreed it would be safest to retrace our steps. Bjorn was afraid that if we took a different route, we might not be able to find a crossing place on the river.

The journey home passed much more swiftly than the outward trek had done. We no longer stopped to wonder at every new sight. First we continued to talk and laugh, but as we drew closer to home, we both became more silent. I pondered our situation ceaselessly. We loved one another still; I knew that for sure now. Bjorn was as unhappy as I. But I could see no possible solution. Bjorn could not divorce Ragna. That would be dishonourable. She could divorce him, but I knew very well she never would. She valued her position as head of the household. I sometimes suspected too, that she had feelings for Bjorn, even though he avoided her when he could, and never lay with her. She certainly desired his approval. But her perverse nature prompted her to fight Bjorn and she couldn't help punishing him when he displeased her. How differently I would have treated him in her place.

'I don't like the look of that cloud,' Bjorn broke a long silence to say. I jumped, startled to find the object of my musings so close to me. I looked around me and saw we were already facing the last ascent across the mountains to the coast.

I looked up where Bjorn was pointing and saw a heavy black cloud gathering over the mountains and beginning to roll down their rocky sides towards us.

'Perhaps they'll pass,' I said hopefully.

Bjorn looked doubtful. 'We can try to continue,' he said. 'If bad weather comes in, it could last days, and I don't want to be away from the farm much longer.'

He looked worried, so we pushed on up the hill. The horses puffed and sweated and the cloud rolled closer. When it engulfed us, it was as if someone had thrown water on the fire. All the heat and light went out of the day. We were shrouded in whiteness, unable to see our way. We halted and I slid to the ground, stiff after several hours in the saddle.

'What should we do?' I asked.

'I'm not sure,' admitted Bjorn. 'But it won't help to go back. This weather is moving in fast.'

'Let's go on then,' I agreed reluctantly, pulling the reins over my horse's head so I could lead him.

We moved forward very slowly straining our eyes to see a few paces ahead. Bjorn whistled the dogs to us and kept them close to help us find our way. The mist began to soak into my clothes and chill me. Soon it began to rain. A light drizzle at first and then gradually more persistent.

Our progress was painfully slow and we hadn't yet reached the highest point when the horse Bjorn was riding stumbled. It staggered and managed to avoid falling, but Bjorn dismounted at once. Clapping its flank, he spoke soothingly to it. Then he spoke over his shoulder to me.

'It's late and the horses are tired. We're not going to make it home today. Let's find a place to stop.'

'But it's so cold,' I objected. 'How can we spend the night up here?'

Bjorn handed me his reins, and disappeared into the fog with the dogs. I could hear him calling to them and whistling from time to time, but the sounds were muffled by the fog. It was eerie and frightening to be left alone. I didn't like it. I was relieved when I heard Bjorn heading back. When one of the dogs appeared out of the mist and thrust his cold, wet nose into my hand, I greeted him with relief.

'There's shelter of sorts this way,' I heard Bjorn say. He loomed suddenly dark out of the whiteness and took his horses' reins out of my hands. 'Follow me.'

Slowly we made our way through the fog. The grass was wet and squelchy underfoot. I couldn't imagine sleeping on it.

Bjorn led me up a steep slope to a rocky outcrop. There was a big rock between us and the wind direction and a small hollow we could camp in. It was freezing cold and a far cry from the homely, comfortable camps we had made so far. But I was tired and the rain was falling harder now, so I didn't complain. We picketed the horses where there was grass and then threw our furs down in the hollow hard up against the rock. Sitting on them we turned one skin fur down, and held it over us. Bjorn fetched some sticks that had been tied to his spare horse and used them to prop the skin up to make a low, rough shelter, sloped so that the rain water could run off. We sat huddled side by side as the rain grew heavier and heavier, thudding onto the skin and cascading off the edge. My cloak was soaked through and my hair was dripping. I started to shiver, and Bjorn noticed at once.

'Get that wet cloak off and wrap yourself in furs,' he told me. I did as he said, shuddering with cold as I peeled the wet outer layer off myself.

'No chance of getting a fire lit in this,' I said.

'No, not even if we'd thought to bring any wood,' agreed Bjorn. 'I hadn't planned on spending another night out.'

I prayed silently to Eir and to Thor to send us better weather in the morning. I was afraid to be lost in the fog and the rain on the mountainside like this.

'It can rain for days,' I said anxiously. 'What do we do then?'

'We'll worry about that if it happens,' said Bjorn cheerfully. 'Meanwhile, why don't you pray to those gods you have so much faith in. Get them to sort the weather out.'

'I already have,' I said. 'And I will again.'

'Well then,' said Bjorn and I suspected he was laughing at me.

I got out the last of the ptarmigan Bjorn had caught yesterday. I'd wrapped the leftovers in leaves and it made for a greasy, messy meal. It wasn't enough either. The dogs whined hungrily as we ate and fell on the few scraps we threw them, fighting each other for a bone or a bit of fat. Bjorn and I drank from the waterskin Bera had lent us, while the dogs found themselves a puddle to lap from. There were plenty of those.

When we'd finished our meal, the rain was still falling as heavily as ever.

'Now what?' I asked. I was cold, damp and still hungry.

'There's nothing for it but to try and get some sleep,' sighed Bjorn.

'But it's so cold,' I objected.

He grinned at me. 'It could have rained like this for the whole of our journey,' he said. 'Have you never camped out in the rain and the cold?'

'Only on the ship.'

'Precisely,' said Bjorn. His smile and his light-hearted tone faded. 'I kept you warm on board the ship,' he said seriously. 'I won't let you freeze now.'

My heart thumped in sudden trepidation. Bjorn was unwrapping the furs from around me and himself, making a nest of them. 'Lie down,' he said. I lay with my back to him, slightly curled, half afraid, but anticipating the closeness with a deep and guilty pleasure. Bjorn covered me in a heap of furs and tucked them around me, and then crawled underneath with me, one arm around my waist pulling me close to his chest. I could feel his warmth immediately. His thighs were pressed into the back of my legs and his breath was warm in my hair.

'There,' he said. 'Do you think you'll be warm enough to sleep now?'

I was very far from sleepy. His presence had lit a fire in me. I had to use all my self control to stop myself from turning around and pressing myself against him.

'Yes . . . I'm . . . warmer now,' I stammered, fighting but failing to keep my voice steady.

'Good,' whispered Bjorn, and his hand found mine under the covers and took it in a comforting hold. His hand was trembling.

The night seemed far too precious to waste. I wanted to lie awake and enjoy our closeness. But I was very tired, from the long day in the saddle. The rise and fall of Bjorn's breathing against my back was soothing. As I warmed through, my eyes began to close. Sleep took me and the night passed.

Towards morning, as I was lying halfway between sleeping and waking, aware of Bjorn's arm around me, a vision came to me in a dream. A ship was sailing into our bay. All the men on board were dressed in black. The ship was a shallow-draughted warship with shields placed on its sides and a fearsome dragon carved at its prow. It sailed right up onto the beach and at once the men leapt ashore carrying their weapons. Death stalked the shore. I saw one giant of a man attacking Bjorn. I tried to cry out, to warn him, but as is the way in dreams, I had no voice. Helplessly, I watched as the giant rained blows on Bjorn, until he fell to his knees. His opponent raised his sword high for the death blow. Once more, I tried to scream and this time I succeeded, waking myself up.

I was shaking and crying. Bjorn was beside me, propped up on one elbow, trying to soothe me.

'Thora,' he said, 'are you awake now? What's the matter?'

'They are coming,' I gasped. I turned and flung my free arm around him, burying my face in his tunic, breathing in the damp wool scent.

Bjorn was gently stroking my hair.

'It was only a dream, Thora,' he said calmly.

'I don't have "only dreams",' I said, torn by sadness

and fear. 'It was a glimpse of the future. He was real. He was going to kill you. He will kill you.'

I looked up and met his eyes as I spoke.

'If I am going to die,' said Bjorn, 'then I have nothing left to lose.' And instead of radiating fear, his aura glowed with love and desire. He stroked my hair back away from my face, leaned forward and kissed me on the forehead. I clung tightly to him as he brushed his lips across my temple to my eye. He kissed away the tears of shock and sorrow that I had shed. I was too weak to object. Too terrified by what I'd just seen. Before I knew what was happening, we were kissing in earnest, his mouth warm against mine. I forgot the cold and the fog and even the vision. Only Bjorn existed beside me. They were hungry, desperate kisses, after a winter of pent-up passion and hardship. I never wanted them to end.

Eventually I felt a sharp nudge against my shoulder. One of the dogs had pushed me. Bjorn and I fell apart, breathing fast. I could feel my heart pounding in my chest and I wanted nothing more than to burrow back into Bjorn's embrace and stay there. But he was sitting up now, running his hand through his hair. When he spoke, his voice was not quite steady.

'I love you, Thora,' Bjorn said. 'Nothing can change that. Not my pretence of a marriage, and certainly not the prospect of death.'

I pushed myself up onto my knees on the damp furs and met his eyes. Before I could reply, before I'd formulated my thoughts, he spoke again: 'How soon will they come?'

I was thrown by the change of subject. I'd wanted to tell him about my love for him, my hopes and fears. Perhaps, I reflected, it was better not to say too much. I struggled to bring my vision clearly to mind again.

'I . . . can't tell,' I told Bjorn. 'It was noon, bright with sunlight. It feels close. A few days. Weeks perhaps.' As I spoke, I noticed it was no longer raining, though the fog still hung in the air.

'We must go,' said Bjorn. He stretched out a hand and stroked my cheek. 'I want to defend our home.'

As I began to roll the bedding together with trembling fingers, a wind blew up from the south. It was milder than yesterday's bitter sea breeze. By the time we had loaded the horses and were ready to start, the fog was clearing. I could see a bright blue sky above it. We spoke little as we rode homewards. This was the end of the trip. By this evening we would be back in the longhouse with everyone else.

The images from my vision still hung heavily on me. I couldn't keep myself from speculating when the attack might take place. I couldn't bear to lose Bjorn. I didn't know how to find the courage to face such a certainty. I imagined the emptiness of a world without him. We would perhaps all be killed, or taken as slaves. And the house that we had all worked so hard on would probably be looted and burned. It was a terrifying prospect, and made me feel ill with grief.

As we reached the top of the last slope, the view of the whole bay burst on us, sparkling in the summer sunlight. We could see both Helgafell and our own farm as specks in the distance. The land had been transformed in a few short months from wilderness into two neat, working farms. I had a sense of satisfaction looking down at them, but also trepidation. I saw the fragility of what we had achieved. Was everything going to be destroyed?

'Time for one last rest,' called Bjorn, turning in his saddle to look at me.

I nodded my agreement and slid from my horse. My limbs felt stiff and awkward. Vaguely, I wondered why and decided I'd been tensing them in fear as I rode.

I sat on a low rock, holding the horses. The dogs flopped at my feet, tongues lolling. Bjorn came over to me with the water skin, and I drank gratefully. Bjorn drank after me, and then put his hand over mine, startling me from my reverie.

'Are you angry with me?' he asked.

'No,' I replied. 'How could I be?'

'You're very silent,' he said.

'I'm afraid. I've never been so afraid of the future,' I confessed.

Bjorn let go of my hand, knelt beside me and drew me into his arms. I didn't object. It would probably be the last time we would ever be alone together.

'I'm not afraid,' said Bjorn. 'It's strange. I should be, I know. Your predictions are reliable. But I believe destiny can be changed.'

I tried to feel comforted, but failed, because to me destiny was unchangeable. And the presence of the enemy ship was strong. It was still a long way off, but I could sense it drawing inexorably closer.

'We must go home,' said Bjorn. 'I have to protect my people. I have to protect you.' His voice was both strong and calm. And when he bent his head and kissed me tenderly, I kissed him back. I put all the love I felt for him into that one, last kiss, because soon he might be feasting with the dead warriors in Valhalla, the sacred hall of Odin himself.

'You asked me not to leave,' I reminded him softly, stroking his cheek. 'Well, I won't. I won't go away from here. Your friendship and regard mean more to me than the love of any other man. I'll stay as long as you need me. I promise. But I fear they will reach us soon.'

Bjorn's arms tightened around me.

'Then let's hope we're ready for them.'

CHAPTER THIRTY-THREE

Sun Month
Sólmánuður

Ragna's resentment at our stolen days knew no bounds. The house was a hotbed of strife and anger for weeks. I felt guilty, knowing she was justified. I also feared her. I took no food or drink from her hands, eating only from the communal pot. When thirsty, I drank directly from the spring. There was no proof that Ragna was the thief and poisoner, in fact all the evidence suggested she could not be. But I had no doubt of her hatred of me and would take no risks. It was a comfort to me that everyone in the household grew tired of her tantrums and unreasonable behaviour. Even those of the men whom she had previously won over with flattery and honeyed words, grew wary of her. Asgerd openly supported me against her. And Bjorn's goodwill towards me was constant. Just a smile or a look from him made the day more bearable.

Sun month passed in long, outdoor days working the land and caring for the stock. I made running the dairy my own particular concern. I milked the one cow that had calved and made the skyr each day. I kept my distance from Bjorn in Ragna's presence. I never even looked in his direction if I could help it. I spent time at

Helgafell with Bera, when I could get away. Helgi's leg was healing well and he would soon be up and about.

There was an added incentive to absent myself from the farm. One of the youngest slaves, Jon, began to hang about me, blushing and paying me compliments. He had just entered that impressionable age, and for lack of suitable young women to fall in love with, had fixed on me. Most of the household laughed openly or behind his back. Bjorn was clearly irritated by Jon's behaviour. But it was Ragna that concerned me. She watched us both out of narrowed eyes, and her aura glowed with resentment. She wanted to be the woman all the men adored. I feared for Jon, and discouraged him as strongly as possible. It was hard to be unkind to him though. He was young and vulnerable; one sharp comment would demolish him.

One morning, Jon insisted on sitting beside me at breakfast and offering me some of his food.

'You don't eat enough, Thora,' he whispered shyly. 'You need to keep up your strength. I'm always happy to share my food with you.'

Jon dropped a piece of flatbread into my bowl, looking longingly at me all the while. I gave it back.

'Jon, do you have no sense?' I asked him despairingly. 'Don't you see you are angering Ragna?'

'I don't care about Ragna, I only care about you,' sighed Jon.

I turned away, determined, for his own sake, to ignore him for the rest of the meal, but my eye was caught by Ragna. She wasn't looking at me. Instead her eyes were fixed on Jon. And instead of the usual baleful stare, she had fixed a look of intent expectation on him. I watched her, trying to make sense of it. I saw excitement flare in her aura in bright green and turned swiftly back to Jon. He was in the act of raising his goblet to his lips.

'Don't!' I shouted, and dashed it from his hand.

It hit the table and then bounced onto the floor, spilling its contents in an arc.

'What the—?' asked Jon.

I could hear other exclamations of surprise around me. One of the dogs rushed to the spill and, before I could prevent him, had lapped up a good amount of the whey. I rushed forward to kick him out of the way, but it was too late. The world slowed and sounds blurred. I was half aware of Jon's shocked face as he stared at me. I could see Ragna was angry and Bjorn horrified. I looked back at the dog. He whined and stumbled. His eyes clouded in pain. I caught him and held him, unable to either speak or look away. In just a few moments, the animal convulsed and died.

I knelt on the ground, holding the body, numb with shock and rage. I could hear the voices around me growing in volume. I had no idea if anyone was blaming me this time. Asgerd knelt beside me, putting her arm around my shoulders.

'Thora,' she said. 'Oh, by the gods, Thora, who is doing this?' She reached out with her free hand and touched the poor dog's head.

Jon knelt on my other side, raising shocked eyes to mine.

'You saved my life,' he whispered. He was as pale as a cloud, trembling with fear. Bjorn had come over and was standing in front of me, looking deeply concerned. But his face began to fade from my sight. Something else was intruding on my mind. A completely different picture, that shut off the people around me.

A warship gliding through the water with the sun behind it. It's coming from the east, about to turn into our bay. Fourteen men sit at the oars ready to row. Two men stand at the stern, one holding the tiller. Two more are standing in the prow. All of them wear black and have leather helmets on. The ship is hung with shields and they wear swords or knives at their sides. Vengeance is in their hearts and their minds. Except for one. It seems to me I know him but I can't see his face.

The vision faded and the inside of the longhouse came back into focus. It was noisy with arguments and accusations and I doubted anyone but the three closest to me had heard my words. As soon as I had myself in hand once more, I spoke again, my voice hoarse with fear.

'They are here!'

A sudden silence fell.

'Men in black. They are close now. Very close.'

In a single stride, Bjorn was by my side. He grasped my arm and pulled me to my feet, away from Asgerd and Jon. The dead dog was left unheeded on the earth floor.

'How close?' Bjorn demanded. 'How many men?' He must have been able to see I was still dazed, because he gave me a little shake.

'Eighteen men,' I whispered, terrified. 'They're about to reach the bay.'

I heard a gasp of horror from the men. We were outnumbered.

Bjorn was already dragging me to the door and pulling me outside.

'Run, Thora,' he ordered me. 'Run to Helgi. Ask him if he will send me help. Beg him. And then STAY THERE, do you hear me?'

I nodded blindly. I wanted to tell him to take care, but the words were futile and wouldn't come. He would do what he had to do and the gods would see to the rest. His face was set and determined.

I threw myself into his arms, giving him a desperate hug, aware it might be the last time I saw him alive. Then, with one more look at his face, I turned and ran. I could hear others emerging from the house now and Bjorn shouting orders to them. 'Asgerd, Asdis, Hild, take the two children, get in the ship and sail it across the bay to Olvir. Ask if he will come to our aid. Ragna, take the other women into the tunnel.'

And then I was too far away to hear any more. I was still weak and sick from my vision and my legs shook under me, but I forced myself to keep running.

Helgi was out when I stumbled into the house at Helgafell.

'Out?' I gasped, dazed. 'Is his leg . . . so much better?'

'Yes, he's moving about quite freely now,' said Bera. She turned and ordered a man to go and fetch Helgi. Then she drew me towards the fire.

'Sit down and tell me what's wrong,' she urged. 'You look as pale as a corpse even though you've been running.'

I collapsed beside her as my breathing gradually slowed.

Helgi limped in and hurried forward as I looked up.

I realized I hadn't planned what to say to them. So much of the story was bound up in secrecy.

'Has there been an accident?' Helgi asked anxiously.

'No, but we're in grave danger. Terrible, mortal danger. I've come to beg for your help. If you . . . we would be for ever in your debt.'

As I looked into Helgi's face, I understood why Bjorn had sent me and no other to speak to him. I'd birthed their first child and healed their ills. Helgi would refuse me nothing. There was no doubt in his face or in his aura, only compassion and eagerness.

Haltingly at first, and then with increasing speed, I poured out our whole tale. It was essential to tell our friends the truth about who we really were. If I lied to them now, they would never trust us again. Bera looked amazed, but Helgi's face stayed impassive until I reached the part about the ship arriving in the bay. Before I had finished speaking, Helgi was buckling on his sword. Then he leant forward and grasped both my hands.

'Some of this Bjorn had already confided in me,' he said. 'You're our friends. We'll stand by you.' Then he embraced his wife and was gone, hurrying out of the house, his limp barely noticeable in his haste. I could hear him calling for his men, giving orders. Bjorn would not be facing the assassins alone with a handful of slaves.

I could see Bera looked frightened. I felt guilty at once. I had brought this on these good people.

'Did you have time to send for Olvir?' she asked. 'I'm almost certain he would relish a battle.'

'Bjorn sent the ship across,' I nodded. 'If nothing else,

the women and children who were in it will be out of harm's way.'

Bera bowed her head and began muttering under her breath, invoking the blessings of the gods on her husband. I joined her in prayer, calling on Thor, the god of battle, to pity our plight and to give our men strength. As I prayed, Freya began to show me images once more. The ship was drawing closer. They were passing the island in the bay where the puffins nested. I could see the birds flapping wildly to get airborne or diving to escape from the boat. I couldn't see the faces of the men on the ship, they wouldn't resolve into features. But there was that familiar presence again. The man I half recognized. Who could it be?

'It's Thrang!'

The words burst from me, before I fully knew they were coming.

'What is?' Bera's startled gaze was fixed on me. I opened my eyes and jumped to my feet.

'He's on the ship. He's coming here with the killers.'

'How do you know?' asked Bera confused.

'Freya showed him to me. I saw him.'

Bera looked frightened.

'Surely he couldn't have betrayed you?' she asked. 'He couldn't be leading them here?'

'I don't know. I can't understand it. I have to get back and warn Bjorn,' I cried in great agitation.

'No!' Bera clutched my arm. 'You'll be running straight into danger. Stay here! There's nothing you can do!'

But I pulled free and ran out of the house. The bay was spread out before me, and there, in the distance, was the

306

ship. Even this far away from it, I could sense the thirst for revenge that had driven the men that sailed it across the sea.

The sail was idle, for barely a breath of wind was stirring. The men were pulling on the oars and the ship slid across the still water. So small and insignificant it looked at this distance. But it was an illusion. Our very own Ragnarok, our day of reckoning, had arrived.

Helgi and his men were walking in a line, heading for our farm. I could pick out their sober colours in the bright green summer landscape. I picked up the skirt of my tunic and ran like the wind after them. I'd never run so fast in my life. I ran until my heart was pounding in my chest and I couldn't breathe. Then I slowed to a walk. The ship was drawing closer all the time, crossing the bay swiftly and silently. They were relying on the element of surprise. Well, I had spoiled that for them at least.

I could no longer see Helgi and his men. They must have walked fast. In fact I couldn't see anyone at all at the farm. It all looked deserted. I felt sick with fear. What if we lost this fight? Even if we could win, how many men would we lose?

Thrang's face rose again in my mind and quickened my pace. He had lived and worked with us all last winter. What was he doing on board that ship?

I was closer now, stumbling across the meadow where the cattle grazed, jumping the cowpats. Then I was weaving my way through the small trees where the pigs rooted. My tunic snagged on a branch, but I tore it free and kept going. I could scarcely breathe.

As I ran down the last slope towards the longhouse, a

dark shape rose up in front of me, startling me. Before I could make a sound I was grabbed from behind and a hand was clamped firmly over my mouth. I was dragged down into the wet grass and a voice muttered in my ear.

'Get *down*, Thora! You'll spoil everything running about like this.' It was Grim's voice. I pulled his hand from my mouth.

'I have to find Bjorn,' I whispered desperately. 'Thrang is aboard that ship.'

A muffled oath from Erik who lay beside Grim.

'Whose side is he on?' demanded Grim. 'Has he been paid to lead them to us? How will we know whether to fight him or welcome him?'

'I can't be sure; I don't know,' I replied breathlessly.

'You can't go to Bjorn now. You'll be seen. The ship is almost in.'

Faintly, in the distance, we heard the crunch of gravel as the shallow-draughted warship beached.

'Here they come,' said Erik, wiping his sweaty hand on his tunic and taking a firmer grip on his sword. I could see he was shaking with fear.

'May Thor protect you, my friends,' I whispered to them both.

I'd barely finished speaking when we heard scrunching footsteps as men jumped off the ship. Then there was silence. In only a few moments more, we saw the men. We had a clear view of them here, as they moved silently up from the shore, swords and battleaxes in hand. They looked more like sneaking assassins than righteous warriors. They gave no warning cry, no challenge. One man carried a burning torch and the sight of it sent a shiver of terror down my back. They were planning to burn the house.

I had a broken view of them through the trees as they fanned out approaching the house. I counted them. There were sixteen. Where were the last two?

I saw Bjorn rise silently out of the undergrowth behind the last man as he passed. He cut the man's throat before he realized he had been attacked. He fell without a cry. His companions noticed nothing and continued walking. My heart was hammering but I lay absolutely still. I was too close for safety.

Bjorn had ducked down again. The next thing I saw was a rain of arrows falling upon the attackers. One man fell, another clutched his arm with a loud cry. The rest of the arrows fell harmlessly to the ground. There was a collective roar of rage as the men realized they were being ambushed. The leader spoke at last.

'Where is the false chieftain? Come out and fight! Don't skulk among the bushes like the escaped slave you really are! Face us, if you dare. We'll teach you to steal my kinsman's name!'

If he expected to provoke Bjorn into showing himself, he was disappointed. The only reply the man got was another shower of arrows. One more enemy fell, clutching his leg. There were still thirteen uninjured men and two more somewhere. Where was Thrang? He wasn't here. As I scanned the faces of the enemy, I saw a face I knew. It was Arn. He was the informer, not Thrang. He'd brought these men here. Well, he had made his suspicion of Bjorn clear. But I hadn't imagined he would have travelled all the way to Norway to incite Svanson's kin to vengeance.

I felt my stomach twist with anger against Arn. All this destruction had been wantonly brought about by him. Our lives were hanging in the balance because of one man's vindictive nature. No doubt he had been richly rewarded for his information.

A movement drew my attention from Arn. The man with the burning torch ran forward and made for the house. A companion ran on either side of him, shields raised to protect him.

'Stay down now, Thora,' breathed Grim in my ear. 'This is going to be dangerous.'

As he spoke, I heard the cry of a seabird. It was a signal. Our men and Helgi's rose suddenly out of their hiding places and rushed at the attackers. I stayed where I was, pressed to the ground, hoping not to be seen. A woman had no place in a fight. There was confusion all around me. The clash of iron on steel was horrific. There were shouts and screams and the ground shook with stamping feet as men ran and fought.

Without giving myself away, I twisted to try and see if the men with the torch had reached the house. Helgi and two of his men were fighting a desperate battle with them. As I watched, the torch man leaned back and flung his deadly weapon up onto the roof of the longhouse. It lay there smouldering for a moment. I felt my stomach lurch with dread at the sight of it. That was our home. If it burned, there was no way of replacing it.

With a shout, Bjorn ran towards the house. Dropping his sword, he leapt up, catching hold of the eaves, and swung himself onto the roof. He clambered swiftly across it and grasped the burning brand, stamping on the smouldering rushes where it had fallen.

The leader of the men in black stepped forward and addressed him.

'A stupid mistake,' he sneered triumphantly. 'Now you have no weapon.'

'Wrong,' shouted Bjorn, and jumped down, lashing out at the man with the torch he now held. The man jumped back.

Two men blundered into my line of vision, locked in combat, a sword against a battleaxe. I could no longer see Bjorn. I saw Helgi defeat his opponent near the house, striking him down. The man screamed, then lay still. I put my hand over my mouth, sickened. Battle was ugly.

I searched frantically for Bjorn. Somehow he had his sword back, but he was fighting for his life against a giant of a man. With a shock, I recognized the scene from my vision. This was the man I'd seen kill Bjorn.

My body froze in horror. I wanted to move, to help somehow, but I lay rigid and helpless on the ground. Bjorn's time was very near now. He was fighting hard. Although he wasn't an experienced swordsman, he had my father's sword. That gave him an advantage over any opponent. Even so, I saw him beaten back by the ferocity of the attack.

I could see nothing but Bjorn and his opponent. My ears told me the battle still raged all around us, but I had eyes only for this one fight. Bjorn parried a fierce strike and stumbled back, falling to his knees. He was up again in a flash, but his opponent used the moment of weakness to press close. The huge man was raining blows down on Bjorn, driving him back towards the house, practically pinning him against the doorway. Any moment now, Bjorn would fail to deflect one of the blows and he would be struck. Sure enough, a second later, the sword caught his arm, ripping open his sleeve. Bjorn fell back, his face contorted with pain. I saw blood spread swiftly down his sleeve, dripping onto the ground.

With a cry of triumph, his opponent rushed him, swinging his sword furiously. Bjorn thrust at him, missed, and fell to his knees. The huge man lifted his sword. Time slowed. I recognized everything from my terrible vision. Somehow, I dragged myself to my feet, crying out.

'No! No!' I screamed.

The sword was held aloft for a moment. Bjorn's opponent was enjoying savouring his advantage.

'You killed my cousin, you filthy slave!' he yelled.

The man was staring down into Bjorn's fearless eyes. Then, with a cry, he began to swing his sword down to deliver the final blow.

I started to run towards them, heedless of the battle raging around me. But someone else was closer and quicker than I was. Ragna threw herself through the doorway, flinging herself between Bjorn and the sword.

'Don't kill him!' I heard her cry out.

For a split second, I thought the giant man would stop. Then I realized the sword had a momentum of its own now. It sliced down, cutting into Ragna with a sickening, tearing noise. Her blood flowed dark and red into the ground.

Before the killer could lift his sword to strike at Bjorn

again, another man dressed in black appeared out of nowhere and rushed at him, sword raised. A large man, with familiar bushy hair. He ran the killer through with his sword, pushing the blade home. The enemy fell and died, his face frozen in a mask of fury and pain.

His assailant reached down a bloody hand and pulled Bjorn to his feet. It wasn't until he turned that I saw it was Thrang. Thrang with his hair dyed black and his beard cut short. Where had he appeared from? Thank Thor that at least he was on our side after all.

There was a mighty battle cry behind me, enough to strike terror into the bravest heart. Everyone turned to see Olvir running towards us. He had a huge axe in his hands and his full battle rage was upon him. Olvir wielded his axe furiously, slicing one man's head right off and severing another sword arm at the shoulder joint.

The tide had turned. The assassins, their plan in shreds and their force decimated, turned and fled back to their ship. But there was no stopping Olvir now. He chased after them, bringing them down, one by one. I saw Arn fall, the battleaxe in his back, and I turned away, weak with relief but sickened beyond bearing. The smell of blood and the screams of the wounded filled my senses.

As I turned back towards Bjorn, he knelt and raised Ragna in his arms. She was the colour of whey and limp in his arms. Her wounds were horrific. I moved towards her to see if there was anything I could do to help. She reached up a hand to touch Bjorn's cheek. Then she saw me. 'Save me,' she begged. 'I don't want to die.'

'I'll do everything I can for you,' I promised her,

dropping to my knees in the blood and the churned up earth beside her. 'Don't be frightened.'

I reached out to examine the wound, but before I could do more than pull a flap of her torn tunic aside, she gave a choking sound, and died.

Bjorn looked grey and shocked under the grime of battle. He looked up and met my gaze, and there was pain and horror in his face. I reached out and closed Ragna's eyes. Bjorn knelt there, helpless and lost, still holding her.

The sound of battle was fading around us. The only noise left was the groans of the injured. The men's work was done. Mine was just beginning.

CHAPTER THIRTY-FOUR

It was the first time I'd seen a battle and as I tended the dead and wounded, I prayed I might never see another.

Of the eighteen men that had attacked us, only Thrang and one other was left alive. Thrang was unhurt but the other man had wounds I barely knew how to bind. I did my best, packing the wounds with moss and bandaging them. I gave him a sleeping draught and hoped it would help.

Olvir didn't stop fighting until he had slain every assassin. Even then he couldn't snap out of his battle rage and it took four of our men to convince him not to kill Thrang. He didn't begin to calm down until Thrang had changed out of his black clothes and no longer looked like an enemy.

'What are you doing here with these men?' I asked Thrang. 'When I saw you, I thought you'd betrayed us.' Grim and Helgi stood nearby, listening intently, clearly wondering the same thing.

'Not I,' said Thrang, shaking his head. 'I wouldn't betray my friends. I stayed behind on the ship at first, afraid someone might make that mistake. But when I saw Bjorn hard-pressed, I had to help. I'll explain everything later. For now, there's work to be done.'

Four of our men were injured, including Bjorn who had a deep cut in his arm. And Jon, poor Jon, who had barely been old enough to have stubble on his chin, lay dead among the trees. I wept when they brought his body to me and laid him out beside Ragna. The shock and horror of the battle caught up with me in a rush. I'd saved him from poisoning just a few hours before, and for what? Here he lay, dead with a sword thrust through his heart. I hoped he had at least died quickly and prayed that he was already with Odin in Valhalla. At least death in battle was honourable, I tried to console myself. Jon had won himself a place among the heroes.

I cleaned and bound a gash in Grim's leg. Erik had a broken right arm from a blow with the flat of someone's sword. It hurt him a great deal when I set it.

'You were lucky,' I told him, as he lay sweating and shaking after I had bound it to a splint. 'If the sword had struck you sharp side down, you would have lost your hand.'

One of Helgi's men had a gash in his shoulder. I cleaned and bandaged that. Then at last Bjorn allowed me to see to his wound. He was still kneeling beside Ragna's body, staring at her as though he couldn't believe his eyes. I was reluctant to intrude on his grief, wanting to give him the time he needed to come to terms with what had happened. It would not be easy for him to live with the thought that the wife he hadn't loved had died trying to save his life.

The blood was still seeping from Bjorn's wound, however, and I had to kneel beside him and lay bare the arm to tend it. He barely responded. His injury had bled profusely and was deep, but it would heal. I sighed with relief, packed it with moss and tied a bandage tightly around it to stop it bleeding.

'It will heal,' I told Bjorn.

He looked at me, dazed, still in shock.

'I should be dead,' he murmured hoarsely. 'She saved me.'

'She did,' I agreed. I didn't feel I had taken in Ragna's death yet, nor the manner of it. It seemed completely unreal.

'I misjudged her,' Bjorn groaned. 'I was too hard on her. It seems she had goodness in her that I'd not guessed at. And courage.'

Thrang came up to us, and stooped to grip Bjorn's shoulder.

'She saved your life, my friend,' he said. 'But stay your tears for her a while until you've heard my tale.'

We buried Ragna and Jon on the hillside beside those we had lost in the winter. The assassins we buried at some distance, in a different place. It was hard work, and everyone was exhausted from digging and shedding tears. I grieved for the strangers as well as our own dead, a sense of guilt strong in me. These men had had their lives cut short because of the murder of Svanson and the theft Bjorn and I had committed.

When we all returned to the house, we found Asgerd had taken charge and had cooked a stew with dried fish. She served everyone a bowlful. I sat on one side of Bjorn, while Thrang sat on the other. It felt strange to be openly sitting at Bjorn's side. I had an uncomfortable feeling that

I shouldn't. Ragna would be angry. Then I remembered her lifeless body and felt sick.

I hadn't imagined I'd be able to eat, but I discovered I was ravenously hungry. When everyone had eaten, and been given a bowl of whey to drink, Thrang began to speak.

'I sailed as far as the Faeroes with the trading ship,' he began. 'We stopped over at a summer market there for a few days. People had travelled from all over the islands and further afield to attend it. While we were there, I heard two tales that interested me very much indeed.

'The first was the boastings of a man from one of the northern islands. He was spending freely and had taken a great deal more drink than was good for him. He told the tale to any who would listen of how his father the chieftain had captured some travellers from Norway and tricked them very neatly indeed.'

Thrang paused and his mouth tightened. The whole house was silent, everyone's attention fully engaged. We all recognized our own tale in this.

'This man's sister was trained as a healer,' said Thrang.

I caught my breath. Before he even told the story, everything began to fall into place in my mind. I had known we had a healer living secretly among us. Thrang glanced at me and nodded slightly, acknowledging that I had probably guessed correctly.

'She was a pretty girl to all appearances,' continued Thrang. 'But underneath, she was bad tempered and vengeful. She misused her skills to punish anyone who crossed her, and that was just about everyone, sooner or later. Some died mysteriously. She should have been put to death for her crimes. The chieftain, her father, protected her, but she was forbidden to practise.

'Now comes the part we know,' Thrang said. 'This man boasted that the chieftain had tricked the Norwegian lord into marrying this unwanted daughter and taking her off his hands. That was you, Bjorn,' he said with a serious look. 'They were rid of her and not only that, he was full of how they had robbed us into the bargain. A ship, food, treasure. The girl's name,' Thrang said, pausing for effect, 'of course, was Ragna. Her own brother was happy to blacken her name.'

He stopped talking and we all sat in silence, taking in what he had said.

'I wondered how you came to be married to such a woman,' remarked Helgi. 'She didn't seem a bride any man would have chosen. There were no qualities one might look for in a wife.'

'An understatement, my friend,' said Bjorn. His voice sounded thick with emotion. I could hear the shock and remorse he had been feeling since Ragna's death was now tempered with disgust.

'I *pitied* her,' he added. 'I thought if we treated her with kindness, she would soften, in time.'

'So it was Ragna who had the poison, I suppose,' said Asgerd, speaking up for the first time. 'I couldn't believe it was Thora.'

I felt tears prick my eyes at her words. Asgerd hadn't suspected me. She was a true friend. Others had, though. Ragna had confused them.

Bjorn got up and beckoned Thrang to follow him. Together they went into what had been Ragna's room. We could hear the sound of them going through her things. At last I heard a grunt of satisfaction from Thrang. When they emerged, Thrang held something in his hand which he brought over and presented to me.

'Is this it?' he asked.

I took the fragment of root from him, looked at it and nodded. I slipped it in my pocket and wiped my hand carefully on my tunic.

'But you searched before,' said Asdis. 'Why didn't you find it then?'

'We didn't look thoroughly enough. If you know who the thief is, things are much easier to find,' Thrang replied, sitting back down. 'It was stuffed in a crack in the bottom of the wall under her sleeping place.'

'I couldn't think who else it could be,' I said tentatively. 'The trouble was, whoever stole the aconite climbed up to the sleeping loft to take it. And I couldn't think how Ragna had managed that.'

There was a frightened sob next to me after I had spoken. I looked down to see that Ulf had slid onto the bench beside me. He looked up beseechingly, his tear-filled eyes wide and frightened.

'I did it,' he said, with a hiccup of fright. 'I climbed up and got the things out of your chest. I didn't want to. I *like* you, Thora. But she said I had to or I'd be sorry. She said she'd poison my father.'

Olvir leapt to his feet, looking both horrified and furious.

'A son of mine is turned sneak and thief?' he bellowed. He took a step towards us, but I put an arm around Ulf protectively.

'Ragna was good at making people do what she wanted,' I said, defending Ulf. 'We were all afraid of her. He's just a child. He shouldn't be punished.'

Ulf slipped a cold hand into mine.

'I'm really sorry, Thora,' he said. 'I'm sorry I stole your key too.'

I remembered the hug he had given me the morning of the theft. Everything made sense at last. In the midst of my shock and surprise, I resolved to keep a closer eye on Ulf in future.

'If it was Ragna,' I heard Asdis's gentle voice say, 'then why didn't she try and poison Thora? She hated her.'

Bjorn sent me a swift look, and I felt the colour rise in my cheeks a little.

'She did,' I said. My voice was calm, even though the memory filled me with horror. 'I think perhaps both Vali's dose and the dog's were intended for me. And she had poisoned my goblet once before. But I knew the root had been stolen and was on my guard. I began to realize that someone in the house had knowledge of plants and poisons. But I couldn't work out who.'

I shivered at the memory of the deaths we had all witnessed. Under the table, Bjorn took my hand in a comforting clasp.

'And the second tale, Thrang?' asked Helgi after a pause.

'Ah yes.' Thrang smiled a little grimly. 'The second tale was less of a surprise. I heard tell of a man by the name of Arn, leading a group of warriors to Iceland to track down a slave who had murdered his master and stolen his goods.'

'A simplified version of the tale,' murmured Bjorn. There was some scattered laughter and he grinned reluctantly. He'd never been comfortable with our theft, though he had defended his stolen goods fiercely enough today. I felt some discomfort, hearing Bjorn openly spoken about as a slave, but no one seemed surprised. They had probably guessed the truth long ago. It no longer mattered. He had saved us all from a life with Svanson, and we owed him our loyalty.

'It seems that Arn was a distant kinsman of Svanson's,' Thrang continued. 'He knew enough about him to know, when he met you, that you could not be he. But don't fear. When I sail next, I shall spread the tale of how the men came here and discovered their mistake. You offered them fine hospitality, of course. And then sadly, they were shipwrecked on their way home. I hope that will keep you safe.'

Bjorn released my hand to get up and embrace Thrang.

'Thank you, my friend,' he said.

Helgi, too, rose from his seat and came up to us, offering Bjorn his hand.

'I owe you heartfelt thanks for your help,' said Bjorn.

'No, indeed,' replied Helgi, clearly troubled. 'I feel I'm in part responsible for this attack,' he said. 'Arn was my kinsman. I'm not proud of the part he has played. You've been a true and generous friend to me. A man of honour. I'm proud to call you my neighbour and my friend.'

The two men shook hands and then embraced.

'Thank you, Helgi,' Bjorn said, much moved. 'You can always call on me in time of need.'

Bjorn turned to Thrang.

'I'm grateful to you for bringing us this news. You've made many things clear that were tormenting us. But tell me. How did you come to be aboard that ship?'

'I had to warn you, to help you if I could,' said Thrang, glancing at me as he spoke. 'I left Stein in the house of an acquaintance. I dyed my hair black, shaved my beard short and offered myself as a mercenary, for a large fee. They took me at once. Arn didn't look closely enough to recognize me.'

'And you were able to help. I'm thankful,' Bjorn told him. 'And at last I'm in a position to reward you for your friendship and all you have done for us. The ship the men came in is yours.'

Thrang grinned. 'I hoped you'd say that,' he admitted. 'I'll need to trade it for another, of course—somewhere far away, where it won't be recognized. But it will help me set up as a trader rather than a hired captain, and I'm deeply grateful.'

He turned to look at me. 'I also wanted to apologize to you, Thora, for doubting you,' he said more quietly. 'I had hoped to ask again for your hand in marriage. But I imagine that will be useless now.' He looked significantly at Bjorn as he spoke. I blushed uncomfortably. I had no idea what the future held for me now. It was much too soon to be thinking about it.

'Thora is not thinking of marriage at the present time,' Bjorn said firmly. He turned to the household.

'I hope that none of you will think the worse of me now you've heard this story,' he said, with a slight smile. 'I'm sure there wasn't much you hadn't guessed. I hope you all feel I've been a better master than Svanson. And I'd be grateful to you for your secrecy on this subject so that we can live here unmolested.

'As you know, I don't believe in slavery. I promised you all your freedom if you worked for me for a year. The year will soon be over, and as thanks for your loyalty and support today, I'd like to declare you all free men and women from this moment.'

There was an excited cheer and a babble of voices. I could see Erik and Asgerd hugging each other and their daughter with tears in their eyes. The others were shaking hands and congratulating one another. I smiled at Bjorn, glad he had chosen to do this today. He looked pleased, but behind the smile, I could see he was still deeply troubled. There had been so many shocks for him today. They were going to take a long time to accept.

Someone was tugging at my shoulder. It was Asgerd and I turned to receive her embrace.

'I hope you'll be happy too, now, Thora,' she whispered. We both looked at Bjorn, who was sitting very still, a troubled crease in his brow.

'I couldn't bring myself to be a husband to her,' he said suddenly, sensing us both watching him. 'But I believed there was good in her.'

'I think she loved you,' Asgerd told him. 'But in a cruel and destructive way. She wanted control and she couldn't bear others to be happy. I don't know why,' she added in response to Bjorn's pained look. 'But she went out of her way to cause mischief. She did most of it behind your back, Bjorn, and Thora was the greatest sufferer.'

With those words, Asgerd kissed me on the cheek, and went back to Erik. I sensed Bjorn looking at me and met his eyes. They were still troubled.

'I don't know what to think, Thora,' he said sadly. 'I'll need some time. Do you see our future?'

I shook my head. 'Not at this moment,' I told him.

'I hope that whatever is in store for us, that we'll face it together,' Bjorn told me. He took both of my hands in his. 'Do you agree?'

'With all my heart,' I said, returning his clasp. A sense of relief flooded me. I didn't mind how long Bjorn needed to spend recovering from what had happened these last months. As long as we had a future to look forward to. That was all that mattered.

I remembered our stolen kisses on the mountainside. At the time, it had seemed that would be all that we could ever share. Now suddenly a new life, a new chance had opened up for us. I would never take a single moment of it for granted.

Marie-Louise Jensen (née Chalcraft) was born in Henley-on-Thames of an English father and a Danish mother. Her early years were plagued by teachers telling her to get her head out of a book and learn useless things like maths. Marie-Louise studied Scandinavian and German with literature at the UEA and has lived in both Denmark and Germany. After teaching English at a German university for four years, Marie-Louise returned to England to care for her children full time. She completed an MA in Writing for Young People at the Bath Spa University in 2005.

Her first novel, *Between Two Seas*, was shortlisted for the Waterstone's Children's Book Prize (2008), the Glen Dimplex New Writers Awards (2008), the Hampshire Book Award (2009), and the Branford Boase Award (2009). Her second novel, *The Lady in the Tower*, was shortlisted for the Waterstone's Children's Book Prize (2009).

Marie-Louise lives in Bath and home educates her two sons.